CITY OF BONE AND BRONZE

CITY OF BONE AND BRONZE

ALL THAT IS HOLY BOOK 2

JEREMY KNOP

Podium

For Ashley

All rights reserved. No part of this publication may be reproduced, stored in a retrieval system, or transmitted in any form or by any means electronic, mechanical, photocopying, recording, or otherwise without prior written permission from Podium Publishing.

This is a work of fiction. Names, characters, places, and incidents are either products of the author's imagination or used fictitiously. Any resemblance to actual events, locales, or persons, living, dead, or undead, is entirely coincidental.

Copyright © 2024 by Jeremy Knop

Cover design by Jon Tonello

ISBN: 978-1-0394-5852-9

Published in 2024 by Podium Publishing
www.podiumaudio.com

Podium

CITY OF BONE AND BRONZE

CHAPTER 1

The city of Noyo was a city of iniquity and suffering. A city built upon a mountain of bones. An untold number of human corpses had been laid as the foundation for the great city. Though they hadn't been shackled in chains, these men and women were bound all the same. The supremacy of Azka and other Low Gods of his ilk was the bedrock of this woebegone world.

Sitting on a massive velvet cushion in the open hall of Azka's palace, Kunza gazed out over the cityscape below. Past the smooth columns painted warm, autumnal shades of red and orange, domed roofs of copper and bronze spread out from the base of the pyramid. In the shadows of sharp-angled, cyclopean buildings were wide roads of stone running like rivers beneath gorges of sun-bleached limestone and sandstone. Even from the palace's vantage, the buildings of the inner quarter were colossal and grating to his eyes. Farther in the distance, near the walls, was a tangle of smaller dwellings. Squalid huts and hovels inhabited by those humans lucky enough to have been given residence behind the towering white walls. Had he still possessed the eyes he was born with, he may have wept. But the eyes that Talara had given him—eternally smoldering with the dim reddish glow of dying coals—allowed no tears.

Soft footsteps echoed from the polished stone floor at the far end of the empty hall. Kunza stood as Azka's Chosen filed in through the high-arched doorway leading from the front portico, their massive leonine bodies moving with a languid grace. The eight colossal, bronze-winged lions took their places on cushions spread around the long brazier recessed in the center of the hall, casting a few dismissive glances toward the man in his vulture-feather cape and crow-feather headdress. His skin was freshly ashen to further accentuate the pale gray tones that Talara's blessing had bestowed upon the skin of him and his people.

The eldest of Azka's Chosen, Tialta, settled its hulking frame on its cushion and set its cold, predatory eyes upon Kunza's. "Keep those foul eyes off me, ka-man."

"Don't call me ka-man." Kunza's gaze remained steady and unyielding. The embers embedded in gnarled, scarred sockets flickered. "Your Sovereign, Azka, has already accepted my station and I expect you to respect it as well. I am Talara's emissary and you will treat me as such."

Piata, the Chosen that had come to Kalaro to announce Kutali's death a year before, spoke. "You're a man. And we will treat you like one."

Kunza sat down on his cushion, brushing his cape aside as he lowered himself. Their provocations were nothing. Being a man was not the insult they thought it to be. It was a blessing. To be human was a gift from the High Gods, for men would inherit the earth. Talara had told him so. The reign of Low Gods upon the earth was at an end. Their hubris would weigh them down and they would drown when the Gray came to finally swallow them. That is what his goddess had shown him. She had shown him what was to come, just as she had shown Azka on the day Kunza arrived in Noyo as Talara's emissary.

"Do not get too comfortable, Kunza," Tialta said. "You're here only by Azka's generosity. If you fail to uphold your end of this arrangement, it won't matter what you call yourself. I will rip you to pieces where you sit."

Kunza repositioned himself on the cushion, letting himself sink into it. "Do you doubt my goddess?"

"I doubt *you*," Tialta said. "You may have fooled Azka—through bewitching or guile, I do not know—but you haven't fooled me. You're nothing to Talara. You're a man with delusions of divinity. You're a fraud imbued with dark magics."

Kunza smiled. "Believe what you will but rest assured I will uphold our arrangement."

Azka's Chosen grumbled and whined, but they would do little more. They were bound to their Sovereign's wishes, and Azka followed Talara's word.

The Chosen turned their attention away from Kunza and spoke as if he were not there. Kunza turned his attention back to the cityscape below but listened. Each of the Chosen spoke of the strife in their own dominion. As viceroys of Azka's kingdom, it was not often that all of them were together in one place. They spoke of famine and starvation. Human laborers dying in droves. The output of copper and gold mines in the east was dwindling. The farms of Azka's northern domain were faring particularly poorly. Herds of cattle lay rotting in the plains. But most concerning was the influx of refugees from the Gray-stricken Far North. Desperate humans and godlings and even full-blooded gods were migrating south. One of Azka's northern villages had been raided by a rogue godling a month before. Nearly half of the village's people had been slaughtered. The village's ka-man had been gutted and decapitated. His skull stripped clean of flesh and brain and used as the godling's cup.

The world warped beneath the strain of the Gray, beginning to crack and crumble. Becoming malleable as it had when the Serpent died. A world to be reshaped in Talara's name.

With no introduction, Azka's children came from the opposite end of the hall, where it connected to the central palace, and all the Chosen abruptly ended their conversation. Kunza and the Chosen rose as the godlings took their places before Azka's high throne. They were magnificent creatures, more than twice the size of the Chosen, and their leonine bodies covered in lustrous fur that shimmered resplendently in the shaded hall. Their front legs ended in massive, dexterous paws, and the back legs were vaguely avian with splayed paws and exposed talons. Their wings, folded on their backs, were bright gold, and each feather was as sharp as a blade. Manes of silken bronze feathers adorned their necks and framed their lion heads.

Down the bridge of their noses were intricate designs that radiated a golden glow. These designs ran up over the top of their head and down their neck to their shoulders, a pastiche of sharp, tapering lines intersecting one another in perfect symmetry.

The godlings sat on their raised cushions of purple silk, leaving one empty between them where their brother, Kutali, once sat. The hall was silent. Below, the city's din was distant like a storm rumbling far on the horizon. Thousands of voices became a deep, incessant murmur, human and inhuman workers laboring outside the city's northern wall. The sharp strike of hammer upon chisel. The creaking and groaning of cart and sled. The moans of men and women, lesser giants, and cyclopean slaves as they toiled at the site of Kutali's mausoleum. Yet in the palace, the commotion in Noyo was much like the slight breeze that drifted intermittently through the columns of the hall: a barely perceptible sensation in the stifling stillness of the godlings' presence.

Kunza watched the godlings as they sat frozen on their tier of the dais. Their gaze skimmed around the hall, sweeping aloofly along the assembled counselors, out over the city, and then back to the hall. Golden eyes, detached and dispassionate.

To be a god was to be at the precipice of eternity. *What must a moment such as this be to a being that lives for centuries? What must it be like to be near-immortal?* Kunza's gaze fell to the empty cushion. Not even gods were totally divorced from death. Sooner or later, Talara would inherit all, mortal and divine.

Nearly a quarter of an hour passed in that oppressive stillness. Then through the tall doorway leading to the inner palace came Azka. Everyone in the hall prostrated themselves as he mounted the raised dais on legs like tree trunks. His slumped back was only a man's-height from grazing the ceiling's severe vaulted arches. Azka looked similar to his children, but his features were more exaggerated and more haggard. His once-lustrous coat was dull and thinning. The thick lines of light covering his head, neck, shoulders, and back were faded a sickly yellow. His mane sagged with a somber weariness. The bronze feathers that ran from around his neck down his back were thin and patchy. The skin around his eyes was bald and drooped with age. The finest medicinal powders and salves covered sores that dotted his legs.

With a long, gravelly sigh, the god seemed to deflate a bit in the softness of his dais. "Let us begin, then," he said, rheumy, clouded eyes settling on his children who sat before him.

The oldest of Azka's godlings, Ketabi, sat up, eyes falling upon Kunza. A slight jolt ran up Kunza's spine under the godling's gaze. "Kunza of Kalaro," Ketabi said, syllables rolling together in a low purr. "By Azka's decree, for a year you have been allowed in his palace at your own discretion to gaze upon wonders no mere mortal man has ever seen. In his endless generosity, you were given one year to bring forth the fruits of your supposed relationship with the High Goddess, Talara. You swore at the feet of Azka, Sovereign of the Eastern Wind, that you would bring with you a means of weathering the Gray. So where is it?"

Kunza prostrated himself once more and then rose from his cushion to stand by the brazier. He looked along the rows of Chosen looming over him and then to the godlings and Azka at the end of the hall. He cleared his throat and let his voice loose, loud and slightly raw. "I assure you, Ketabi, I have not been idle. In Talara's name, I bring to you, Azka, a glimpse at the breadth of Talara's power and influence in this mortal realm."

The Chosen nearest him shifted irritably. Kunza's aura was heavy around him, bolstering his words and strengthening his conviction. His goddess was with him. He could feel her cool touch in his chest. "The Gray is a grim pestilence seeking to blot out the brilliant light of your divinity. It seeks to strangle this light. But where there is light, there is shadow." The hard leather soles of his sandals clapped against the marble as he strode forward.

"Get on with it," Tialta said.

"As mighty as you are, even gods cannot weather the Gray alone. There cannot be light without shadow. And that is what Talara offers you, Azka." His aura swirled and surged as he spoke, riled up by his words. He raised his hands before the godlings as if offering himself to them. "I offer to you," he said, "the Shadows."

His arms dropped and with them, six of his apostles dropped from their perches in the vaulted arches above. They slid along the columns they had perched upon and landed, each of them, at the edge of the hall. All of them tall and lanky. Dressed in flowing tunics the color of sandstone, their faces covered entirely save for slits exposing ash-pale skin surrounding clouded white eyes. Only now did the faint, lingering stench of death come from their patchwork bodies. The hall erupted into chaos, but his Shadows knelt before the Chosen and the gods unflinchingly.

"What is this?" Ketabi shouted, looming over Kunza, lips curled and magnificently gruesome teeth bared. "You dare smuggle assassins into Azka's sacred hall?"

"Assassins? Oh no, my godling, my Shadows are not assassins. Unless, of course, you choose them to be." Kunza looked and bowed to Azka, still sitting placidly on his dais. "My Shadows are yours to command."

"And why should we want them?" Ketabi asked. "What use would Azka have of human sneakthieves?"

Kunza smiled a thin, cold smile. "Humans. . . they were originally but now they are so much more. You could not sense them, no?" His Shadows stayed kneeling, heads bent in supplication. They would not move until he told them to move. Unerringly. "That is because they are beyond life and death. They do not eat. They do not sleep. And, most importantly, the Gray does not touch them." Kunza looked at Azka once more and the god's eyes met his. "In the plaza below, you will see one hundred of my Shadows, ready to obey your every command. Given time, Talara could give you an army of these Shadows. But she can also give you something much more. Despite your power, gods are all too mortal. But through Talara, that does not have to be so."

The Chosen turned their attention below to the plaza, where his Shadows stood in a line on either side. But Azka kept Kunza's gaze. In the god's impassive, beleaguered eyes of amber and gold, Kunza saw promise. A promise of a better future. And Azka was the first step toward that promised world.

"Follow my goddess and we shall build a paradise in the midst of this damnable Gray."

CHAPTER 2

The northern reaches of the Night Jungle were sparse and quiet. Towering trees choked with vines and moss stood like the pillars of some long-forgotten temple. Half bare, the drooping branches held wilted, browning leaves. Any color left in the jungle was quickly bleeding away. Dead leaves and rotting detritus crunched beneath Odessa's soft-soled step. The high-pitched, undulating whine of cicadas was distant and muted by the pervasive stillness leaching deep into the jungle like a deafening pall upon the land.

A twinge of pain ran up Odessa's arm. Beneath the wrapping of rune-covered hemp fabric, beneath the scarred flesh, a restless aching in the marrow of her bones radiated from her right arm to her shoulder. She hadn't been able to sleep at all the night before for the incessant ache and occasional sharp jolt of pain. Now as she crept through waist-high ferns and beneath curtains of wilting palm fronds, lack of sleep and anemia were beginning to take their toll. Lightheadedness dulled her senses. Her feet were leaden; she could barely lift them enough to keep from shuffling through the undergrowth like a pig rooting for tubers. Despite her concentration, her heavy feet made enough noise to announce her presence to any quarry she hoped to find unawares.

Her chills had returned, as had the gnawing hunger that food could not sate. A hunger deep within herself that threatened to swallow her whole if she did nothing to relieve it. That hunger urged her forward through the jungle, bow in hand.

Yakun had taught her many things. How to control the flames of stolen godsblood and how to mask her unholy presence with runes. But for the hunger, there was only one recourse: to feed it.

In the year that she had lived in Yakun's grove, so much had changed. She had grown strong. Her arms and legs were corded with thick muscle. The gentle curves of her youthful face had become sharp, severe angles. She had become a woman through and through. Any vestiges of youth that had remained in her were dead. She felt as if she had been reduced to nothing but sharp edges and ever-worsening hunger.

No matter how much she hunted or how many monkeys and rodents she killed, the hunger was never truly sated. It could be lessened. The hunger pangs could be dulled. But the hollowness within her continued to yawn wider.

She was padding down an old, overgrown game trail when she heard the murmuring. Barely perceptible above her own footsteps through the dry leaves and the whistle of her labored breathing.

She stopped, frozen with a breath held trapped in her lungs. For the last year, the only voices she had heard other than her own were those of Yakun and Poko, although she heard Poko's more often than any other. But her searching ears heard the murmurings of a stranger's tongue. It was much too faint to make out the words but there was no mistaking the sound of a strange voice in the jungle.

No one came this far into the jungle east of Noyo. There was little to hunt, as Odessa knew all too well. There was no good reason for someone to journey this far into the dying part of the jungle.

Immediately, she thought of the hunters she had killed. The more time passed, the more guilt had found its way into her heart. Doubt played tricks with her mind the more she ruminated over the blurred events, which grew more vague and indistinct with time. *Maybe Noyo's come to get me. Come to bring the cursed girl to justice.*

To the north, the babbling continued. A stream of noise like an incessant hum ringing in her ears, just loud enough to command her attention.

She knew she should return to the grove and tell Yakun, but the constancy of the murmuring struck her as odd. Before she could fully collect her thoughts, her feet were moving and she was slinking through the undergrowth toward the gibbering voice. Curiosity bid her forward while the hunger inside her gaped wider.

The nearer she got, the clearer the voice became. A foreign voice, husky and warbling. Odessa kept an arrow nocked as she approached. As the voice grew louder, her fear of being discovered by Noyo troops was displaced by a nagging uneasiness. She came upon a small, shallow stream. Babbling along with the stream's gentle music, the voice was clearer now. A few paces from the stream's banks, she followed its winding course downstream toward the voice.

"Withering. Withering. Everything withering," the voice said, syllables rising and falling like waves lapping upon dry, cracked earth. "Land's poison. Water's poison. It's everywhere and it's nowhere and there isn't naught to do about it. Nah, naught to do at all."

Through the tangle of vines and stunted rushes, Odessa could make out a figure downstream. A hunched-over form standing in the stream, talking to itself. She slowed and hunkered down behind a dead kapok tree.

A splash as the stooping figure moved a few paces upstream. Odessa could see through a curtain of vines a long, shaggy-haired neck and a pair of gangly arms hanging in the water. Straggly hair hung from its thin frame, what was once white now a grimy yellowed brown. The arms parted the blanket of water hyacinth and sword plants that choked the stream's surface.

The neck bent toward the water's surface and the babbling paused, replaced by a wet slurping. "Good water," the figure said, wetness dripping from the hair along its neck. "Clean water. Nothing like in Toth, no. Drank puddle water brown as dirt, I did. Poison water. Stomach twisted and turned for days. But kept me alive, it did. Aliver than the rest, I am."

Odessa crept out from behind the kapok, bow loose in her grip as she peered through the vines. She had never seen a creature such as this. Hunched as it was, it stood at least a head taller than she on two bony legs like those of a llama or a goat. Long hanks of thin, scraggly hair hung from its body, obscuring its emaciated figure. Its head was turned away from her now as it dug water hyacinth bulbs from the streambed, but she could still make out two curled horns. It reminded her of the Bruka, but different. More bestial. Yet it spoke so clearly. She reaffirmed her grip on the bow all the same.

"Must gather my strength," the half-starved creature said, chewing on a spongy hyacinth bulb. "That's how I stay alive, yes. Don't linger long. Rest and run. Rest and run." Odessa caught sight of the creature's head as it turned. It was mostly bald save for a scraggly beard of filthy brown that hung dripping from its chin. Its face was nearly human, but the proportions were slightly askew. The nose flatter. The eyes farther apart. And the skin was dark and leathery like a bat's wing. Waxy leaves hung from its lips as it chewed. Vacuous eyes drifted along the stream's banks. Odessa shrunk away from the wide, bloodshot eyes. Eyes filled with nothing but fear and desperation.

The creature was silent. Only the stream's gentle babbling remained. Odessa froze behind the curtain of vines, bowstring taut in her fingers.

"Who's there?" the creature said, voice shaky and pitiful like a scared old man on the verge of tears. She could almost feel its panicked gaze through the vines. A few moments passed in silence, the both of them frozen.

I should kill it. I need to kill it, she told herself. Hunger pangs dug deep into her side. Her heart pounded and her blood ran hot. Her thumb and forefinger throbbed where the arrow sat pinched between them. Her arm itched to draw the bowstring back and let the arrow fly. The hollowness in her chest yearned for blood. But the creature's face was so pitifully human. The fear in its watery, gunk-rimmed eyes. She thought of the wide, panicked eyes of the hunter as he wheezed his last breath through a crushed trachea.

Her fingers loosened and she let the bowstring relax.

"Hello?" she called out, peeking out from behind the vines. She held her bow low behind a waist-high cycad, the arrow still nocked. "I'm not going to hurt you."

The creature only stared back at her, bony body half-crouched and poised for escape.

Odessa's fingers itched and ached but despite their protests, she unnocked the arrow and set it and the bow down against the large drooping leaves of the cycad. She raised her hands so the creature could see them, empty and harmless. "I'm not going to do anything." A slow, careful step forward, parting the vines hanging from the kapok's branches. The creature's muscles twitched at her approach but it did not run. It only stared, wide eyes darting. "Are you well?"

Another step and she was through the curtain of vines and on the gentle slope of the stream bank. Mud sucked at her sandaled feet. She kept her open hands raised at her shoulders.

The creature took a hurried step back. Water splashed around its bony shins.

"Wait!" Odessa said, making the creature flinch with the suddenness of her shout. The creature's body was tense and ready to run in an instant. She took a half-step back. "I'm not going to hurt you, I promise. I just want to help. You're not well."

"Weller than most," the creature murmured. "Weller than most, I am." From the stream's edge, Odessa could see its nose, choked with dried snot. Beneath its filthy, matted hair was raw skin with oozing lesions.

"Are you sick?" Odessa took a half-step forward.

"No. Not sick." The creature looked at her with an animal's frightened wariness. "Poisoned. But I get better. Slowly I get better."

"Poison?" Odessa asked.

"Yes, yes, poison," the creature said. "Poison in the air. A great cloud of it rolling over the land. Killed all but me, it did. I live when others died."

The curiosity that had drawn her from the cover of the vine-draped kapok tree came to a head. Yakun would want to know about this. News from outside the grove was hard to come by, carried only by the rare guest that came in need of healing or spellcraft. Information was vital. If the information was true, that was. The wide-eyed creature babbling to itself in the godsforsaken jungle certainly had a crazed, half-mad look about it. "You said Toth, didn't you?" Odessa's sense of geography was vague and muddled, but she knew the city, a floating city built over a bay on the far northern reaches of the Slateseer Sea. "You're from Toth?" she asked. "That's awfully far away, no?"

"Yes, Toth. Far. Very far. I've run for days and days, trying to run from the poison. Rolling over the land. But the wind carries it toward the rising sun. So I run here. Far, far away from where Toth used to be."

"Used to be?" Odessa took a step forward, hands dropping a bit. "What do you mean 'used to be'?"

"Toth is no more. Toth is gone. All gone. Dragged into the sea. I watched it happen from the hills. Saw it with my own eyes."

"How can it be gone? Toth is supposed to be a massive city on islands and stilts. It couldn't just be dragged into the sea like that."

"But it was." The creature fixed its gaze upon her, its wariness seemingly abated. "First came a wave. A huge wave over that wall. Then the wave grew like a mountain coming out of the water. The wall came crashing down and then came the tentacles. Bursting out of the water. Thick as tree trunks. They smashed through boats and buildings and wrapped around the trees that held the buildings up, and soon the whole city was dragged into the water."

"Isn't the bay and city and everything the Stone Queen's? How did she allow something like that to happen?"

"The Stone Queen is dead. Poison killed her most of the way. Poison had been coming from over the sea for days before the city fell. Gray fog blown in from the bay. It had only just reached our hills when the city fell. On that day, Togatha was already so weak she could barely put up a fight."

Uneasiness crept up the nape of Odessa's neck. Whatever could kill Togatha, the Stone Queen of Toth, was a monster of inconceivable strength. *It must be another god. A god from a faraway land or something.* But the thing that had sent a shiver down her spine had been the creature's mention of gray clouds. *That has to be the Gray itself. Maybe that thing is what is causing the Gray in the first place. Because it has to come from somewhere.* Odessa traced the sharp angle of a rune drawn on her bandage with waxy paint. *Yakun will definitely want to hear of this.*

"If what you say is true, how did you survive?"

"I ran. I ran and ran until I had left it all behind. I left my family and my home and I'll run still farther, I will," the creature said, starting downstream. "You should do the same. When the wind shifts, it may already be too late to run."

Odessa tried to quash the childish fear beginning to tickle her twisting guts and set the hair on the back of her neck on end. *It's mad with shock and fright.* But still, its words had stuck a sliver of uneasiness in her mind. A thorny sliver set to fester in her mind and let take hold the necrotic rot of dread and despair.

The creature splashed farther downstream, bony legs parting the clumps of water hyacinth. The skin on the back of its legs and its tailbone was bare and mottled with open sores and patches of dry, cracked skin. "I ran and I ran," it mumbled. "I run and I run."

Odessa watched as it stumbled away, the flow of the stream pushing at the back of its legs. It ambled toward the southern bank. Her mouth opened to call out, but she realized she didn't know what to say. She didn't know what she wanted. She thought she wanted to help the poor creature. To feed it what little she had in her belt pouch and tend its wounds. But in the back of her mind, some nagging need droned so deeply she could feel its unyielding compulsion reverberating in her bones. The fingers of her bandaged hand played along the fletching of the arrows in her hip quiver. Her bow stood leaning against the kapok a few paces away. An itch in the back of her mind brought with it images of an arrow stuck halfway in the creature's back. The overwhelming buzz filled her mind. White hot urgency lanced through her arm in spasms of agony. Her blood ran hot. Her throat, suddenly parched, tightened and it took all her focus to stay where she was.

Her bandaged hand moved to the knife sheathed on her belt. Her fingers wrapped around the handle until her knuckles ached.

The creature scrambled up the bank and ducked beneath a crooked tree to disappear into the jungle.

Odessa didn't move for a long while. She only breathed, slow and deliberate, as the stream babbled along beside her. She closed her eyes, forcing the throbbing pain building up behind them to subside. The droning quieted eventually but her throat remained dry and constricted. The emptiness in her chest widened like an open wound. She felt sick to her stomach.

With concentrated effort, she slid the half-drawn knife back into the sheath and released the handle from her iron grip. A sigh escaped her lips, one of both relief and disappointment.

CHAPTER 3

Muted daylight dimmed to gray-blue twilight as Odessa returned, empty-handed and hungry, to the grove's hidden entrance. She moved slowly, slouching as her exhausted body resisted the impulse to collapse at every step.

Before she came to the cleft in the mountainside, she had made a long detour, walking the radius of a semicircle surrounding the entrance, veering off often to inspect a carving in a tree's bark or check the integrity of a sculpture of twisted twigs hanging from a branch. Today, the charms and wards were all still intact. But it was increasingly common to find the lapis lazuli eye of a nazar hanging from a branch had cracked or the barkcloth charm folded in a shallowly buried earthen jar had fallen to pieces as if eaten by moths. The barrier that confounded outsiders, mortal and divine alike, was weakening. Odessa thought that was how she had been able to enter the grove before she was even aware of the barrier and its mind-bending illusions. She had inadvertently found a hole in the barrier. But Yakun thought otherwise. He always seemed to err on the side of the fantastical. But since that day, anytime she tried to enter the grove without one of Yakun's waystones, she was assailed by headaches and bewildered by a path that never ended, continuing in a perpetual loop until she gave up and waited for Poko or Yakun to guide her back. Poko, being a fairy, was immune to the barrier's confounding effects.

Parting the curtain of moss, she entered the cleft. Her left hand grazed the cool stone, wetting her fingers with condensation. Beneath her feet, the creek was barely a trickle amid the mud and stone. Her near-daily excursions and the tromping of her feet had churned up the creek bed, turning the creek into little more than a muddy track running beneath the mountain. Farther into the pass, where the creek was deeper and more defined, she took off her sandals and let the cold water and icy mud soothe her raw, blistered feet. The cool, dry air outside the grove left her skin cracked and peeling.

On the other side of the pass, the grove was the same as it had been the first time she stumbled through that cleft in the mountain. Untouched by season or blight, the mossy forest was green and lush. The rich, earthy scent of wet moss filled her lungs and almost dulled the bone-deep hunger grating upon her ribs. Thick fog had settled at the base of the slight hill, and it swirled around her as she made her way up through the ravine.

Fingers looped through the leather straps at the back of her sandals, she held them over her shoulder and let them slap against her back as she walked. Her bow, unstrung after a fruitless day of hunting, she carried in her bandaged hand. Her arm ached and itched, and the scarred skin felt pulled too tight across her flesh.

I'll have to go out farther tomorrow, she thought. *All the animals are thinking like that goat thing. They're all moving south.* Uneasiness lingered in the back of her mind since her encounter with the creature. Some unresolved tension remained in her muscles.

That droning urge she had felt as the creature left was not unfamiliar. Again she was forced to think about the men she had killed. At the time she had been certain those men had meant to do her harm, but now she was not so sure. She was not sure of anything anymore.

Fatigue burned in her legs as she climbed the slight rise. When she reached the tree line, she collapsed against a moss-covered ficus, arrows rattling in their quiver as she slid down the trunk to sit on the wet leaf litter at the base of the tree. She tossed her sandals into the grass in front of her and set the bow down beside her. The back of her head rested against the soft layer of moss upon the ficus's rough bark. Fatigue throbbed in her muscles and thrummed in her joints, hot and acidic. Finally at rest, she could feel her tense, overwrought body relax, melting into the placid calm of the grove. She breathed deeply, looking out over the clearing. At the steep mountainous cliffs enclosing the grove. At the sliver of forest on the other side of the clearing. A grassy mound rose in front of the forest, like any other hillock save for the thread of smoke rising from the top of the mound and the timber wall poking out from beneath a thick layer of sod. The face of the mound that overlooked the grove was a wall of thick logs hidden beneath an overhanging roof of sod. Clusters of pale pink orchids, the same orchids that ran rampant in the grove, obscured the bottom half of the wall, leaving only one space open in the center. The faded red door amid the orchids was ajar.

Yakun said that sod houses needed to breathe. They needed fresh air. Odessa thought that was just an excuse so he did not have to repair the corroded outside latch.

Taking the peaceful stillness of the grove, her worry and doubt and hunger eased with the throbbing of her tired limbs and drowsiness soon overtook her. It was difficult to resist the allure of rest and slumber. Her body was weak and lethargic. Her mind was muddled, her thoughts beset by all manner of melancholy and malaise. Deep sleep was her only respite. Sleep deep enough that even dreams could not reach her.

Her eyes had been closed for no more than a few minutes when a voice disturbed the tranquil repose she had allowed herself.

"Aren't you supposed to be out getting dinner?" Poko asked.

Odessa cracked an eye open to find Poko standing on her foot with their arms crossed. "It's getting dark."

"And yet I see no dinner," Poko said. "How curious."

"You shouldn't be eating meat anyway." Odessa jerked her foot and the fairy bounded to the ground, landing gracefully. Slowly, she rose, using a hand on the tree to steady herself. "It's not right."

"But it's so good!" Poko said. "It's worth a little indigestion."

A huff as Odessa bent to pick up her bow. Bereft of the momentum of constant movement, the more subtle of her aches and pains had caught up to her. When she straightened, she rubbed the small of her back and winced. "There's something wrong with you."

Poko giggled. Both Odessa and Poko knew the fairy wouldn't touch meat unless they were starving. And in the grove, they weren't eating like gods, but they weren't starving either.

Odessa picked her sandals up from the ground with a twinge, and the two of them made their way up the path to the sod house, Poko easily keeping pace with Odessa's shuffle.

"How are you today?" Poko asked.

"The same as yesterday," Odessa said. "Awful."

"We have to do something." Genuine concern made Poko's voice thin and almost pleading. "What Yakun's doing isn't making it any better."

"But it's stable," Odessa said. "You heard him. This is the best he can do right now."

Poko slowed. "This isn't stable though. Just this last month you've barely been able to eat anything."

Odessa stopped, breathing much too hard for the short distance they had walked. "I just need to kill something." She needed blood to stay alive. She needed to take life and breathe in its dying breath to keep the godsblood from burning through her mortal flesh. Life taken edified the spirit and kept the godsblood at bay. "I haven't gotten anything big in a few months. If I can get one good kill, I'll be fine for a while."

"You haven't gotten anything, big or small, for the last four days though," Poko said, stopping beside her.

"I'll be fine," Odessa said. "I've just hunted the same stretch of jungle too much. I need to go where the game is." She began walking again. *I need to go south.* The uneasiness the creature's words had instilled in her was stoked again, simmering in the back of her mind.

"If you say so," Poko said. Poko's short strides soon overtook her slow pace and as she followed the fairy bounding up the path to the house, her hunger swelled, a dreadful cold filling her chest like cold fog filling a valley. She squeezed her bandaged arm as it throbbed. Beneath the bandage, she could feel it growing feverishly hot. Her nails dug through the fabric and into her arm as she walked. She focused on the pain, using it to ground herself. Sometimes pain was the only mooring she had to keep herself from being swept away in that intoxicating swell of bloodlust.

You're not going to hurt Poko, she told herself. The small, wicked part of herself that wanted nothing more than to kill without abandon. *You're not going to hurt anyone, you godsdamned lunatic.* To harbor the hunger, pain was her atonement.

Poko disappeared inside the dimness within the doorway, and the pressure in her chest eased. By the time she had passed the orchids, drooping and wilted but still holding on to the last of their color, the throbbing in her arm was nothing more than a dull ache. She released her bandaged arm before she reached the doorway.

The house beneath the mound was cool and dark. On the opposite wall, shrouded in dim shadows, the fireplace was as she had left it, empty with the bare stone inside swept free of the ash and coals of the previous night. She closed the door behind her and leaned her bow against the wall.

Poko perched on a low table before the fireplace, slender legs swinging loosely. "He didn't start the fire."

"I see that," Odessa said. She unfastened her belt and slid the quiver free to lean it beside the bow. "I'm sure he's busy with something important."

"Like curing you?"

Odessa turned and held the fairy with a stern stare. "He's doing all he can." She cinched the belt tight around her waist again. "And you know as well as I do he didn't have to take us in. He could have just as easily kicked us out and left us to die in the jungle."

"I know," Poko said begrudgingly.

Odessa and Poko had this discussion often, and it always ended with Poko's halfhearted acquiescence. Gratitude was not a virtue that fairies held in high esteem, it seemed to Odessa. Poko did not seem to understand that a man could only do so much. No matter how much Odessa chided Poko, they did not seem to grasp the extent of all that Yakun had already done for them.

Odessa walked across the cramped front room, ducking beneath herbs hanging by a spiderweb of rope from the low wood ceiling and skirting around a large cauldron in need of a thorough scouring. What was left of the firewood she had brought inside the day before still lay in a picked-over pile against the wall between a half-empty clay water ewer and a stack of barkcloth strips. No more had been added atop the few pieces of hard, knotted branches. Bending with a stifled groan, she picked up the wood and took the light armload to the fireplace. With a pinch of dry, crumbling hoof fungus from a box beside the fireplace, she started a fire just as night sank into the grove.

It was almost pitch dark in the house when she finally coaxed a flame from the smoking tinder. When the fire took the kindling and grew steady, her body relaxed and she sank onto the cool packed earth, sprawling out before the fireplace. Since her time in the jungle, she could not abide the dark. She could feel it on her skin, a chill raising the hairs on the back of her neck. In the dark, every sound made her flinch. In the jungle, she had become an animal focused solely on survival. A year after the fact, she was nothing more than a girl scared of the dark.

Sometimes through the crack and snap of the fire, she swore she could hear Talara's rasping whisper on the wind whistling through the grove. At night, in the distance, spirits screamed with the voices of her loved ones. No malevolent spirits could make their way into the grove, but still she could hear the screams of her father, mother, Ayana, and Kimi. When night fell they echoed in her mind, barely audible and always doggedly at the periphery of her thoughts.

"When do you think he'll be back?" Poko asked.

Odessa opened her eyes, not realizing she had closed them. The fire's warm light splashed on the fairy's silver-tinged skin and made their gossamer tunic glow like dewy spidersilk in dawn's golden light. Firelight flickered in their black eyes. Looking into those eyes, a sudden swell of guilt overcame her as she thought of what her hunger had urged her to do mere minutes ago. "Soon," she said, her voice a bit choked.

"I guess he's not making dinner tonight, huh?"

Odessa sighed. "I guess not." She lay on the floor a moment longer, letting her limbs melt in relaxation, before willing herself up into a sitting position. Her body protested with a myriad of aches and twinges of pain.

She poured the rest of the water from the clay ewer into a small cauldron hanging from a hook set in the back of the fireplace. It was not much water, but it would do for a thick stew. The spring they drew from was only a short walk down the hill at the sloping base of the ravine, but in the dark, the path to the spring stretched and twisted. Tough grasses and woody brush would grasp at her ankles, reaching out to ensnare her and pull her into the depths of that pitch black where the goddess waited, needle-lined maw gaping to swallow her whole.

"When was the last time the old man made dinner like he promised?" Poko asked from their perch.

Odessa was rifling through a cluster of short clay pots, prying open lids and peeking inside, trying to remember where she had put the salted mutton. "I don't know," she said, replacing a pot lid and removing another. "It doesn't matter. I don't mind." She was too tired to rise to Poko's prodding. She wondered if all fairies had a penchant for gossip and instigation.

Poko said no more on the subject, only sat and watched her with a knowing look as she reached into a pot and took out the cloth-wrapped bundle of salted meat. She tried to ignore their stare. The arch in their tiny eyebrow that suggested they knew she was hiding something.

"I really don't mind," Odessa said, a bit too defensively. "I used to cook all the time before." She did not say whom she had cooked for before. Even the indirect mention of her family hurt.

The fairy kept staring, head tilted and lips pursed like a disapproving parent. That condescending stare pricked at Odessa's back as she turned away and began unwrapping the meat on the cluttered table pressed against the wall. With a trembling hand, she took the knife from the tabletop and began roughly slicing the tough strips of cured mutton.

"You know what I think?" Poko said.

"I can guess but I'm sure you'll tell me anyway."

"I think you don't know how to give yourself a break. You don't know how to relax."

Odessa shook her head, her braids bouncing slightly. *Relax? How could I possibly relax?* She continued cutting meat. The knife was dull and tore the meat more than it sliced it.

"You don't have to do everything, you know? You got to be more like me. Just rest and repose, Dessa. That's what you need to do."

The knife paused its cutting. Odessa turned, a slight smirk on her lips. "If I was more like *you*," she pointed the knife at the fairy, "we'd be dead in a few days. Starved to death. How's that for rest and repose?"

"But imagine how good you'd feel for those few days. Not a care in the world!"

Odessa opened her mouth and then paused. She sighed and shook her head again. "You're infuriating."

"You don't mean that."

"Oh, I definitely do." A thin, tired smile brushed the corners of her mouth. Poko knew just how to dance on the verge of irritation but she had grown so accustomed to it she almost welcomed it now.

Where would I be without this annoying little bug? she wondered. Without Poko, smiles and laughter seldom came without force or a somber air about them. Without Poko, she would have drowned in her despair many months ago. In the days before Yakun had figured out the most efficient way to sate her hunger, her sickness had left her bedridden and in constant pain. Poko had stayed by her side. Every time she came close to crumbling, Poko was there. Through all the night terrors and sleeplessness. Without Poko, crying for her mother and father and sisters would have broken her entirely.

CHAPTER 4

The stew had only just begun simmering when there came a knock at the door. "I'm coming in," Yakun's voice came from the cracked-open door. Odessa had a tendency to get a little jumpy at night and after the second time she'd answered the door with her knife, Yakun had started announcing himself. "Oh, that smells wonderful," he said as he entered. He took off his faded blue cloak and hung it on a peg beside the door so it draped over her bow. "What are we having, my dear?"

Odessa inwardly grimaced every time he called her that, but she tried not to show it. She stoked the fire beneath the simmering pot with a cast iron poker. "Biltong stew," she said, pushing a half-charred branch in the middle of the coals. The little firewood they had inside was now mostly burned, greedily consumed by the low flames running along glowing red fissures in crumbling charcoal.

"What were you doing out so late?" Poko asked, sprawled out on their cushioned tabletop in front of the fire.

Yakun eased into his high-backed chair facing the fire, relief washing over his wrinkled face. The firelight upon his pale skin cast dark shadows in the wrinkles around his eyes and mouth. Streaks of white in the gray of his shoulder-length hair and his bushy beard flickered in the firelight. "I left this morning to bolster the wards but, as always, complications abound." A tattooed hand touched slightly with arthritis absentmindedly combed knots from his beard. "There aren't enough hours in the day."

"What complications?" Odessa asked, rising from the fireplace with a noticeable wince.

Yakun reached into a pouch on the belt of his tunic and drew his pipe and a small oilcloth bag of tobacco. "Raff came back." He packed a pinch of tobacco into the pipe's bowl with a thumb.

"What did he say?" Odessa asked. Yakun's crow had been gone for nearly a month, relaying messages to Yakun's associates out east.

"My friends in Asha-Kalir will not help. Khymanir's grasp on the city has tightened even more. The city prepares for war and they cannot afford to take any risks." He set the pipe in his lap and tucked his bag of tobacco back into his belt pouch. His eyes met hers. His gaze was soft and kind. "All is not entirely lost. I sent Raff back with a reply. I may be able to convince them yet."

The news should have hit Odessa in the chest like a punch, but she was oddly calm. Numb to the disappointment. Yakun's friends in Asha-Kalir were the only people he knew who had a chance of removing or neutralizing the godsblood. Khymanir had given a small portion of his freemen a rudimentary understanding of his magics so that they may facilitate his work. The magics of Khymanir and Asha-Kalir were those of flesh and blood and bone. It was the magic of body and soul. If they could not help her, there was most likely no mortal alive who could. She understood all of this yet the disappointment was slow to sink in. After a year of being forsaken by all that was holy in the world, she still had some deluded hope that somehow she would be cured. That somehow it would all work out and she could go home.

"Can't they just tell us how to do the magic then? If they tell you what to do, you can do it, can't you?"

Yakun snorted softly and shook his head. "They've spent their entire lives refining their craft. When it comes to their magic, I may as well be a drooling idiot." He picked up his pipe and stuck the stem between his teeth. "Hand me a firebrand, would you, my dear?"

Beginning to feel sick, she picked a small, half-burned twig from the edge of the fire and carried it to Yakun. He took it, pinching it between two fingers and cupping it with his hands, and held it above the bowl of his pipe.

A few puffs and the smell of burning tobacco wafted into the air. Odessa took the twig from him as he pulled the pipe from his lips and blew a plume of smoke into the air. "Finding a cure could take months or even years. And that is if they could devote all of their time to it, which I am sure Khymanir would not abide. For now, all we can do is wait and hope that they at least start to think about it."

"You're right," Odessa said, tossing the smoldering twig back into the fire. The stew bubbled inside the cauldron, its scent mingling with the woody, slightly sweet smell of tobacco.

Poko sat up. "Why can't we just go to them and make them help? Why all the back and forth with birds?"

"Do you know how far Asha-Kalir is from here? How many spans of desert one has to cross to get there? And what kind of gods and monsters call those places home?"

Poko shrugged. "It's bad all over. It might be a bit of a hike but we can manage it."

"An old man, a Forsaken girl, and a wingless fairy would not get far. Let me assure you of that." Smoke rolled from his lips as he spoke. "We probably wouldn't make it through the Severed Gorge."

"Azka must have caravans going back and forth all the time though, right?" Odessa asked a bit timidly.

Yakun took a long, dragged-out puff from his pipe and let the smoke out in a loose cloud that obscured his face as it wafted to the ceiling in swirling ribbons. "Putting yourself within Azka's reach would not be wise. I can obscure the signal smoke that pours forth from that godsblood in your veins but the scent of it will still linger on your skin. You're safe at a distance but if Azka or his Chosen, or any blasted god for that matter, gets close enough to catch your scent, they will find you. The grove is the only place where you can be truly safe." Another puff from his pipe. "For now, that is."

"I know," Odessa said, sitting down beside the fire again, watching the flames flicker beneath the cauldron.

Poko frowned but said no more on the subject. Yakun puffed on his pipe, filling the room with redolent tobacco smoke. "How fared you in your hunt?" he asked Odessa.

"I didn't see much of anything," she said. She stirred the stew, her encounter with the creature in the stream caught in her throat like a fish bone. The lingering urge stayed her words. How close she had come to putting an arrow through the poor creature's back. Shame constricted around her throat. She kept stirring, round and round. "I did see one thing."

Yakun said nothing, but Odessa could feel his eyes on her back, waiting expectantly. She swallowed. "It was a goat-man thing. It told me Toth got pulled into the sea. And whatever did it brought tainted air with it, and the wind carries it east."

"A goat-man thing?" Yakun asked. Odessa turned to glance at his expression, to see if he believed the creature's story. He chewed at the stem of his pipe, his gaze distant. "Your father once said some creature from the ocean tore Keshekki from his cliffside palace and left in its wake clouds of noxious gas. It was I who helped clear his lungs of it. Spores of some kind." He puffed, the tobacco packed in the bowl glowing orange for a moment. "I wonder . . ."

"You believe it?" she asked.

"I'm not sure," he said, eyes still distant in the realm of thought. "But it is interesting." He was quiet a moment longer, lost in thought.

Odessa licked her lips and swallowed hard, wanting to tell Yakun about her worsening urges, but she couldn't. Yakun had been kind enough to let her and Poko into his home and attempt to rid her of her godsblood but if he knew what wicked thoughts intruded in her mind, there was no guarantee that his kindness would extend far enough to protect her. If Yakun or Poko knew how deep her hunger truly ran, would they continue to stay by her side? A lump formed around the words stuck in her throat.

Yakun was chewing on the stem of his pipe, lost in a labyrinth of thought, when the stew finished simmering. He did not stir from his distant rumination even as Odessa lit the oil lamp sitting on the table beside his chair. Only when Odessa held a steaming bowl in front of his face did his eyes focus and he returned to the dimly lit room and the pleasant scent of stew.

After a moment's surprise, he quickly set his pipe on the table and took the wooden bowl in both hands. "Thank you," he said. "It looks delicious."

A tired smile touched the corners of Odessa's lips as she sat cross-legged in front of the fire.

"Are you cooking tomorrow then?" Poko asked, chewing on a small, steaming hunk of potato Odessa had given them.

Yakun's spoon stopped short before his open mouth. "What?" He looked from Poko to Odessa, who kept her eyes on the bowl in her lap. "Was I supposed to cook tonight?"

"It's fine," Odessa said, shaking her head. "I don't mind cooking."

"No, it's not fine," Yakun said. "I will cook tomorrow. I won't forget again, no matter what complications arise. Even if the gods strike me down right now with lightning and flame, I will still make dinner tomorrow."

Odessa's thin smile grew a bit, even showing a bit of teeth. Yakun's little blasphemies somehow made the gods of this world and the world above seem distant and small. It was comforting in a strange, vague way. Each of his small blasphemies refuted divine omnipotence. To her, it felt like proof that even Talara and the other High Gods could not reach her.

"I really am sorry," Yakun said before blowing on the stew in his spoon. "You're already exerting yourself too much and I force you to make dinner." He shook his head as if ashamed of himself before he slurped a spoonful of stew. "Oh, that's good," he said and then paused, his spoon held midway between mouth and bowl. He licked his lips and let out a breath like he was still smoking his pipe. "It's got a bit of heat, doesn't it?"

"It shouldn't," Odessa said. Yakun had little tolerance for spice, and she had become accustomed to using chili peppers sparingly. "I only used a few peppers and they were still pretty green." She ate a spoonful of the thick, creamy stew. She could taste only salted meat and tomato. "It's not hot at all."

"I will never understand how you people can handle that spiciness. I'll bet you the gods gave humanity those peppers as a punishment. Why else would food hurt so much?" Yakun blustered but he continued to eat nonetheless, occasionally stopping to catch his breath and complain.

After two more of Yakun's rants about chili peppers, Poko convinced Odessa to give them a sip from her spoon. Odessa had not eaten much of her small portion—nausea had begun to bubble up her esophagus and she had none of the willpower to refuse the fairy's request.

Poko took the spoon's neck to steady it in her trembling hand and drank like a man draining a ladle of cold water on a hot day. When they had their fill they released the spoon and tilted their head. Lips smacking, their brows furrowed.

"Old man's right. It's got a little heat." Poko wiped their mouth with the back of their hand. "We're going to have to get your taster cured too if you think that isn't spicy."

"Ah, vindicated at last," Yakun said, his half-empty bowl sitting in his lap.

"It wasn't nearly as bad as you made it out to be, though. The way you were talking I expected to be chewing on hot coals or something."

Odessa took another taste and, swirling it in her mouth, detected a hint of heat in the now-lukewarm stew, but it was subtle. Nothing to complain about at all.

Another spoonful, despite her stomach's queasy misgivings. She closed her eyes, blocking out Poko and Yakun bickering about the cuisine of fairies and humanity. Saltiness and tomatoes. The faint flavor of meat and potatoes. And a subtle warmth of chili pepper. She frowned. *I'm losing my sense of taste.*

The godsblood was eating away more of her each day. She would have to feed the hunger. Soon.

CHAPTER 5

Exhaustion sucked at Odessa's limbs like quicksand and threatened to drag her to the floor. She forced herself to stay upright, her back and neck beginning to ache. Spurs of bright, sharp pain shot from her shoulder and along her collarbone. She set her jaw and breathed heavily through the pulsing pain. It was always worst at night.

Poko snored gently in the front room and Odessa wished she could join them in slumber. Instead, she stood on cool slate tile, covering her nakedness with the same cloth that she had used to wipe stale sweat and grime from her body a moment earlier. At first, it had been hard to undress for Yakun's examinations but eventually, it had become routine.

In the candlelight, Yakun carefully unwrapped the bandage from her outstretched arm, rolling it around his hand as he unwound it from around her bicep.

"How did you feel today?" he asked. "How was your fatigue?"

"It was about the same as yesterday," she said. "Had to take a lot of breaks to catch my breath. Lightheadedness comes and goes." Yakun was unraveling her bandage from the middle of her forearm. A dry fissure cut through gnarled skin a dark shade of burnt umber. Dried blood from the day before stained the skin around the fissures and clefts in her skin.

Yakun nodded, his unraveling moving farther down her forearm. "Tomorrow, you slaughter one of the goats. That should give you enough strength to carry on."

"I can't. I've had to kill too many of them already. There aren't that many left in the grove."

"You can't go on like this."

"I won't have to," she said. "I'll get something tomorrow. All the game has run south, the goat-thing said. I haven't been going far enough to the south."

Yakun began unthreading the linen from between her fingers and around her hand. "Yes, the goat-thing." In the candlelight, his icy eyes glinted as he worked. "You should have killed it."

A tremor jerked her hand back. "But it could talk. It could reason," she said. "It wouldn't be right. You can't kill things that think."

"Sometimes you don't have a choice." The last loops of linen were coming off her fingers. "It's natural. Whether beast, man, or divine, everything dies eventually. There is no difference between a beast that thinks and a beast that doesn't." He finished unwrapping her hand. We're all flesh and blood and bone."

He set the roll of dirty linen on a table cluttered with jars and stacks of parchment. When he turned back to her, his eyes held an earnest sympathy. "You've been forsaken by the gods. You don't have the luxury of such soft, simple moralities." He shook his head. "I hate to say it, but it's true. To survive in a god's world you must be cunning. You must see the world as it truly is. A world of predator and prey. A world that is nothing more than a mountain of corpses you must climb over if you don't want to be buried among them." He took a jar of oil from the table.

"I'm sorry," she said, looking down at the tiles beneath her feet. An arcing line of bronze was set in the tiles just in front of her toes and ran around her in a circle. A bronze ring that would take magic like an iron takes heat. The dormant energy in the circle on her skin was charged with an electricity that always made the hairs on her arms stand up. Energy that could quickly turn the circle into a prison if she let the fire in her veins overtake her. As if the precaution of the circle was not enough, Yakun felt the need to again impress upon her what she was. Like she could ever forget. Like she could ever delude herself into believing she was or would ever be normal.

Yakun stopped in front of her, his feet just outside the circle. "It is not your fault," he said. "I know what it is like. I was born god-fearing and decent. I thought blind subservience was the only way a man could live. But it is not." He set the jar on a small chest beside the flickering candle and a low wooden wash basin. "It takes time, unburdening yourself of the holy poison called dogma, but eventually you will learn how us Forsaken few live. Now hold your arm out and let me have a look."

She did as she was told, letting him poke and prod between her fingers and up her wrist. Sometimes he took the candle and held it close to her arm to inspect the fissures and cracks. Drops of hard wax marked the floor and he continued adding more.

"Looks to still be the same color as before," he said, lifting her arm by the wrist and examining her hand. "Maybe a bit darker near your fingertips compared to last week." The dark lines running beneath her skin were growing thicker and merging together from her elbow to her fingertips. Her fingers were nearly black with the vascular mass of lines.

He let go of her wrist and she let her arm drop. The candle was back on the chest, dripping tallow. He put a foot over the circle's edge and she held her breath. *It'll be over quick,* she told herself.

His cold hand sent a shiver rippling through her. His fingers worked up her arm, brushing against the fissures and cracks and squeezing the flesh around them. Kneading her hard, gnarled skin. Slowly and methodically moving up. Tracing the web of dark lines.

His fingers worked her skin more gently as he came to her shoulder. They followed the dark lines below her collarbone, rubbing where the lines faded into the bronze of her skin. "I don't think they've spread much," he said, his fingers lingering for a moment.

When he had thoroughly massaged her dully throbbing arm, he took a washcloth from the basin and wrang the water from it. She flinched when the wet cloth touched her shoulder. Cold water ran down her arm as Yakun worked his way down, scrubbing away the old oil and dried blood.

Jaw clenched and eyes shut tight, she tried to find the oasis within herself as Yakun had taught her. To find the place where she was most at peace. Her breath whistled through her nose in short bursts. Her chest was tight and suffocating. All she found was fire and blood. Kalaro, bathed in the light of the plaza's massive fire. The hands of people she had once called family and friends tearing away her clothes. Scrubbing her skin until it hurt. Until she was clean enough to not sully the afterlife.

In the fire, there were screams and cries, barely human in their harshness. The scrubbing was rougher. The hands of Kalaro were rubbing ash on her raw skin, packing it into her bleeding wounds.

"You're doing well." Yakun's voice came through the fire and smoke, a tether for her to hold onto. "You're almost done."

Odessa breathed deep, focusing on the cold tile beneath her feet and the circle's energy pulsating against her skin. But she could still hear the screaming. Taste smoke choking her throat. She wanted to open her eyes but irrational fear sealed them shut. As if when she opened them she would find herself back in Kalaro, about to climb the steps to her demise. *The past is dead,* she repeated in her mind as Yakun had instructed. *The past is dead and I am alive. The past is dead and I am alive.*

Amidst the screams, one voice rose above the rest. The ka-man's voice broke through the screeching bedlam. "You cannot hide, Odessa. I will have you bow before me and you will be my instrument of cleansing. My vessel and my scourge." The ka-man's voice stretched, becoming rough and raspy as he spoke. "There is no hiding from me. There is no life outside what I afford you. You will find no salvation out there. Only pain and horror." The ka-man gave way to Talara, her disembodied whisper booming in her mind. Echoing in her skull, a chorus of righteous indignation and condemnation. "You are mine and when you are strong enough, I will have you totally and immutably."

A chill ran through Odessa's body. She tried to pull free from the hands that held her in front of the fire, but they held firm, ghostly fingers digging into her flesh.

"If you continue to eschew your destiny I will bring you to heel," Talara said, the words loud and abrasive. The towering fire sputtered and belched sparks in its last guttering gasps. Behind the dying fire, obscured in a churning, impenetrable darkness, was Talara. Odessa could feel the goddess's presence like a dense pressure bearing down on her every molecule. Permeating her very being with grave-cold dread.

"My mercy comes at a price," Talara said. "Cease your hiding and become what I require you to be. Or I will have you brought to me in pieces."

The fire flared in one last explosion of incandescence, and Odessa fell back whirling.

She landed on the tile, a sharp burst of pain in her tailbone. Her arm throbbed, waves of stinging heat pulsing beneath her skin. Blood wet her right arm and dripped onto the floor. Her eyes whirled blindly. Fiery afterimages swirled in her vision. She tried to rub the afterimages from her eyes, but as she reached for her face a great weight fell upon her. Her arm jerked down and was pinned against her chest. She crumpled to the floor, a pressure so great it crushed the air from her lungs and kept her from moving even a twitch.

She could barely hear Yakun's voice over the thrumming crush of energy crashing upon her. "Weight of the world, become shackle and chain. Weight of the world, become shackle and chain." A low, crooning chant looping again and again, each repetition bolstered the swell of energy. She gasped and tried to suck in a breath, but the unrelenting force would not allow her. When Aséshassa had used the same kind of magic on his brother atop the Mount of Ascension, Ogé's strength and iron will nullified it. But Odessa was no god. The magic of man, a facsimile of true divine magic, was too much for her to bear.

Her vision darkened, the tile in front of her eyes blurry and dim. Yakun's voice faded, and even the rush of energy sounded distant.

Without warning, the crush of force was gone. She gasped in a shallow breath and coughed, rolling onto her belly and propping herself up on a shaky arm.

"Odessa?" Yakun asked, his voice strained.

Odessa's forehead dropped to rest on the tile. Her back heaved as she alternated between gasping, coughing, and retching. Her throat was raw and her thoughts muddled as they flooded back into her mind, where smothering blackness had begun to take hold.

"Odessa!" Yakun shouted. "Are you there?"

A confused groan was all she could muster in reply.

"What's going on?" Poko's voice called from behind the door of Yakun's sanctum.

"Odessa!" Yakun said. His hands, fingers splayed and tattooed palms exposed, were poised for another incantation. "Are you there? Have you lost your godsdamned mind or not?"

The muscles in her neck twitched and trembled as she lifted her lolling head from the floor. Yakun stood a few paces outside of the circle. In the candlelight, she could see how the color had drained from his pale face. His mouth was a hard line and his brows were knit above narrowed eyes, sharp and wary. The fingertips of his right hand were bright red, a stark contrast to the faded blue runes on his pale skin.

Odessa tried to speak but for a moment her tongue could only form a sputtering of garbled syllables. Her heart still pounded from the nightmare she had found herself slipping into. Her thoughts moved much too quickly to get a hold of. "What happened?" she murmured, rolling to sit on her knees and clutching the fallen cloth to her chest again. "Why are you looking at me like that?"

Yakun looked at her a moment longer and then, with a sigh, let his hands drop. The tension in the energy around her lessened and she could breathe easier. His body slouched and he sat slumped on the chest. The hardness in his face softened, but there was still something in his eyes, some sharpness that had not dulled with the rest of his demeanor.

"Your arm, Odessa," he said flatly with a slight edge of reproach. "It burst into flame. If I hadn't jerked away fast enough my hand would be nothing but a charred stump right now." He held up his reddened hand, layers of skin peeled away from his fingertips. Blisters were already beginning to form along the outer edge of his little finger.

"No," she whispered. "There's no way. I can control it now." To her dismay, her arm was hot and the skin at the edges of the furrows and clefts was red and wet with thin streams of blood. The bone-deep throbbing left in the wake of the flames was unmistakable. In the circle in front of Yakun lay the burned remains of the cloth he had used to wash her arm. Her eyes misted. "I can control it, I swear. I don't know what happened."

Yakun dipped his scorched fingers into the basin of water, showing neither pain nor relief. His eyes remained on her, inscrutably attentive. "Is there something wrong?" he asked, the question sounding more like an accusation. "Are you angry at me, perhaps?"

"Of course not," she said quickly. Anger had been the gateway to controlling the flames. It was easy to coax them from her arm with rage and hate. They could emerge unbidden if her anger was strong enough. But she had gotten past that. She could restrain it now. "I don't know what happened. I closed my eyes and tried to find my oasis, but it didn't work. I was back home on that night again and I heard . . ." She cradled her throbbing arm in her lap, blinking away childish tears. "I heard the ka-man and Talara and there was fire and next thing I know, I'm on the floor."

Yakun leaned forward, pulling his hand from the water and letting it drip onto the floor. Poko's shouts from the other room continued but Yakun ignored them as if they were not there. "You heard Talara?"

Odessa's stomach dropped. She had never told Yakun that Talara had spoken to her through the mouth of Obi's corpse—she'd feared he would refuse her. She had told him everything but had skirted around the goddess's explicit involvement. It had always been mitigated by the ka-man and Obi, but now she had come dangerously close to exposing the High Goddess's vested interest in her. If Yakun knew that Talara wanted her personally, he would abandon her. She knew it. And he would have a good reason. Making an enemy of a High God was suicide. Guilt squeezed her throat but she couldn't tell him the truth. "It had to be Talara," she said, trying her best to feign a bit of uncertainty. As if the voice she had heard was not the voice that often graced her nightmares. "I'm sure of it."

"What did she say?"

"She . . ." Odessa started. "She said that I was damned. And that I would never see my family ever again." She wanted to tell him the truth, but she couldn't bring herself to do it. "She said that no matter what I did, there is going to be no salvation for me and that there is no avoiding my fate." Skirting the truth made her deception all the more painful. But once she had forced the words out they began to tumble into place, weaving a thread of lies that wound around her throat and compounded the suffocating grip of guilt. "But my nightmares never made the fire come before. Why would they do it this time?"

Yakun ran his fingers through his beard and his eyes became distant for a moment. "Shit," he whispered. "Shit, shit, shit." He rose and looked at her. "Your flames came out because that was no normal nightmare. It had to be some malignant spirit or something such as that." He began to pace around the room, rifling through cluttered tabletops and overladen shelves. "The wards must be much weaker than I thought."

Odessa's blood ran cold. If that wasn't a nightmare, then it wasn't a spirit either. That had been no trick of the mind. No trauma unearthed by a maligned spirit. Talara had found her. Arm unbound and wards faltering, Talara's gaze had fallen upon her again.

CHAPTER 6

From the ramparts of Noyo's great walls, Kunza watched the construction of Kutali's tomb. Far past the hovels that clung to the outside of Noyo's walls, the sprawling worksite was a hive of bustling activity. The foundation of the godling's mausoleum was laid, massive slabs of limestone sunk into hard clay. Now teams of humans, lesser giants, and cyclopean slaves dragged huge blocks of sandstone up earthen ramps to build the tiers upon which the tomb would tower. Kunza had seen the tomb's plans. A huge complex of fluted columns and statues to sit atop a tiered pyramid with magnificent staircases rising along each side. It would take a decade to build. Huge, intricate statues of Kutali, his siblings, and their Chosen were to surround the tomb and line the staircases. A mosaic would span the entire floor, elaborate reliefs would grace the outer walls of the tomb, and an ossuary of gold and bronze and marble would be built within it all. An ossuary fit for Kutali, son of Azka. The amount of artistry Azka had requested made for an incomparable undertaking.

The sound of chisel against stone was clear on the ramparts. The collective groan as teams hauled the blocks up the ramps, one after the other. All of it marked by the occasional crack of a whip. Each team was led by a supervisor brandishing a whip and club. These supervisors were all lesser giants, but of a different clan than the rest so they had no reservations about meting out punishment to their own kind.

Kunza had seen the aftermath of one such punishment when he had first taken a tour of the worksite. A lash from a giant's whip would cut deep into the meat of a man and even break bone.

"Astonishing, is it not?" a low, guttural voice said from behind him. "There are more than five thousand in the quarries alone."

The giant came to stand beside Kunza and looked out over the northern plains. An expanse of yellow and brown stretched out to the horizon beneath a smoky gray sky. "A monumental undertaking, to be sure."

The giant's accent was thick and gruff, each syllable like stones grinding against one another. The giant's hands on the crenulated wall were massive, the color of slate. His thick fingers, each nearly the width of Kunza's wrist, were adorned with bands of gold, silver, and jade. The giant leaned forward, looking out over the construction. The wall's embrasures came up to Kunza's chest but to the giant, the rounded merlons came up to only his navel.

"What can I do for you, Grand Mason Ur-Mak?" Kunza asked. Behind them, two of the Grand Mason's personal guards stood glittering in bronze scale mail. They were always with Ur-Mak, watching from behind the spectacled visor of their helmet, brutally spiked maces in hand.

"Nothing," Ur-Mak said. "I just wanted to admire my work. Much the same as you, I see. You come here often." The giant's head turned toward Kunza, appraising him with small, dark eyes. The giant's face was a slab of rough skin and sharp angles. He looked into Kunza's smoldering eyes steadily, not shying away from them.

"It is quite the undertaking," Kunza said. "You are doing the memory of our lost Kutali a great honor."

"I only wish to pay homage to our Sovereign and his line." Ur-Mak smiled, flashing his sharp, almost canine, teeth. A few of his lower teeth had been replaced with gold replicas. "I heard you gave Sovereign Azka quite the gift the other day."

"Yes." Kunza shifted, searching the giant's face for the reason for this conversation. "As proof of my devotion to our High Goddess, I gave to our Sovereign a few of Talara's soldiers."

"You are truly Talara's Chosen then?"

"I am her emissary, yes."

"For a High God to bless a human. It is remarkable," Ur-Mak said. "And these soldiers, they were human as well?"

"Yes," Kunza said reluctantly. "For the most part."

"Were they truly inside the hall with Azka and his Chosen without being detected?"

Kunza frowned. "That's quite the rumor."

A toothy smirk split Ur-Mak's face. "Rumors about Talara's Chosen human abound."

"I don't care for gossip."

"But that's the thing about rumors. Whether you care for them or not, they remain. And rumors can kill as well as a blade can."

Kunza glanced along the parapet. Far down the wall, a few of Azka's freemen stood guard. "I suppose that is true," he said flatly. "But to the might of a god, both of those are as deadly as a wet fart."

The giant grinned wider. "Very true. But as a fellow upstart in Noyo, I give you this advice." Ur-Mak leaned down, his smile fading fast, and whispered in a tone as hushed as massive lungs could allow, "Tread carefully. You are stepping beyond your stead and it does not go unnoticed."

Surprise momentarily softened the tense wariness in Kunza's body. "Thank you for the advice, Grand Mason," he said, unsure. "I have not made many friends in Noyo, that is for sure."

"This city is no place for friendship, I've learned." Ur-Mak straightened, his smile returned with a wistful quality about it as his focus shifted to the construction. "When the Stone Queen sent me here, there was little love for me and my kin. But we have risen high in Noyo. And in a short time, you have risen to a very precarious height yourself. I only wish to spare you that fall."

"I appreciate your concern," Kunza said, polite but with a slight edge of wariness.

Ur-Mak's attention was wholly fixed on the construction below. "It will be a work of art like no other," he said quietly, the words a low rumbling. "Peerless in the entire world."

Another whip cracked in the distance.

"You will be leaving for Kalaro again soon, yes?" Ur-Mak asked.

Kunza nodded. "Tomorrow. At dawn." He wished the giant would leave. He could not himself leave first; it would be improper. Kunza was afforded certain allowances due to Talara's esteem, but he was still human.

"Whenever I can step away from the work here I would like to see the Stairs of Ascension for myself. Hewn by the High Gods' corporeal hand. It must be quite the sight."

Kunza thought of making the climb when he'd still been a weathered kaman. How blind he had been, too blind to see the wonders the High Gods had left in their wake. "It truly is a sight to behold."

"And you yourself have been busy building, haven't you?"

Kunza was thankful he did not have his old eyes. They would have surely betrayed his placid composure. "The goddess has been kind to Kalaro. I would not compare our work to that of the High Gods, but we do our best to accommodate our expansion."

"Talara must truly love your people. Everywhere you look, cities and towns, they grow hollow and wither away." The giant's smile widened again. "If your works ever require assistance, I am sure I can spare a mason or two. My masons can work magic with stone, I promise. You will not be disappointed."

"Thank you, Grand Mason," Kunza said blandly. "You are too kind."

"Kindness has never been a virtue my kin have in excess. But I feel you and I share a common goal."

Kunza's scarred brow furrowed as much as the tight, gnarled skin would allow. "And what would that goal be?"

The freemen in their quilted armor were walking toward them now but Ur-Mak paid them no mind. "We both serve our gods wholeheartedly."

And what gods would they be exactly? Kunza's unblinking eyes gave little indication of his suspicion. The freemen hurried past Ur-Mak's guards. "I suppose you are right." Kunza turned to face the giant. "Incidentally, let me offer my condolences for the loss of Toth and Stone Queen Togatha. What an unforeseen tragedy. I can't imagine what that must feel like." He kept his voice flat, dripping with false sympathy.

Ur-Mak's smile faltered and, for the first time Kunza had ever seen, the giant's composure crumbled enough for Kunza to see through the courtesy and falsity. Ur-Mak's eyes darkened beneath his knitted brow. It took only a moment for Ur-Mak to regain his composure, but in that moment Kunza had seen to the heart of the giant. No obfuscation, no subtleties. It was hard for Kunza to not smile.

"Thank you," Ur-Mak said, his voice still and rough like a bed of volcanic rock. "I still struggle to believe my Stone Queen is gone." He stepped away from the low wall. "I cannot believe something such as that could happen so suddenly." He said the last sentence pointedly, a statement of fact.

Kunza relaxed a bit at the giant's candor. "It is unbelievable," he said plainly. "If you or your people require anything from a lowly man such as me, please do not hesitate to ask." He reached his hand out.

Ur-Mak's guards drew the heads of the maces from the stone and began toward Kunza but Ur-Mak waved them off. Kunza held out his hand, unfazed, and Ur-Mak smiled. "Thank you," he said. The giant's hand swallowed Kunza's in a loose but firm grip. "Perhaps I will have to take you up on that offer." He smiled again. "If you would like, I can send an apprentice of mine with you back to Kalaro. I believe he would prove to be quite helpful."

Kunza smiled as they shook hands. *He knows much,* Kunza thought as Ur-Mak and his guards departed. *Perhaps our goals are aligned after all.* He did not trust the Grand Mason but he was intrigued. The giant's anger had been genuine and that could prove useful.

Despite his aversion to rumors, Kunza heard things as well. A messenger from Toth had come to Noyo weeks before Toth was lost with word of fog and sickness. Azka could have aided his ally but he hadn't.

When the roots of dusk began spreading along the western horizon and fires were being lit in the tent city outside the worksite, Kunza left his vigil over the construction. Walking along the parapet to the stairs cut into the wall's interior, his thoughts had drifted from Ur-Mak back to the suffering happening just outside the walls. How many people had died already in the construction of a tomb for a godling rotting in a chamber beneath the palace? How many would have to die before the construction was finished? How many mortal lives were equal to that of a single godling?

One of Azka's freemen standing guard at the head of the stairway glared at Kunza as he passed. Kunza could feel the man's eyes on his back as he descended the wide stairs. They resented him and his faith. They resented his station and the blessing Talara had bestowed upon him. They would stare and snicker but none of them could look him in the eye. The unworthy averted their gaze.

At the bottom of the stairs, he turned and crossed the limestone road running along the wall. A narrow road ran between two dome-roofed buildings. Kunza entered the dimly lit alley and his Shadow soon fell in behind him.

"Where did the giant go after he spoke to me?" Kunza whispered, still walking with his back to the Shadow.

"To construction," the Shadow rasped. Kunza's personal Shadow was the only one he had made that was capable of speech after the myriad procedures. "Followed as far as open plain. Watched from tall grass." The Shadow's speech was littered with small pauses. Each word was painful but it spoke nonetheless.

"When I leave tomorrow, you're to stay here. Follow the giant. Listen to every word he says."

The Shadow assented without a sound. Its obedience was absolute.

Kunza crossed a wider avenue, passing tightly packed storefronts with tall doorways. Many giants lived in the northern quarter, a small, densely packed area only marginally more affluent than the slums where freed men and women lived. He walked unfazed by the glances and hushed snarls as he passed into another alleyway. His Shadow followed close at his heels, hooded robe barely tousled by the wind blowing down the avenue and into the mouth of the alley.

Halfway down the alleyway, Kunza spoke again. "I will return in one week. Meet me outside the city. I will again stay the night in the house of the farmer, Azedola. The night before I enter the city, find me. Report to me what you have gleaned." Kunza stopped abruptly and turned to face his Shadow. "Do you understand?"

Beneath the hood, the Shadow nodded. From the slit of its face wrap, it averted its clouded gray eyes. It stood more than a head taller than Kunza, even slouching as it was wont to do. The sickly sweet scent of rot and incense wafted faintly from its body. The scent of Talara.

"Good," Kunza said. "Very good."

Kunza continued down the alley and his Shadow followed, footfalls silent on the cobblestone.

CHAPTER 7

Farther south than Odessa had been in a year, the jungle was more vibrant than she had seen it in months. Abuzz with the faint sounds of life, she crept through the undergrowth, thighs burning and back aching. It had taken her all morning to reach the still-beating heart of the jungle. Her body cried for rest with myriad pains and aches, but she had to forge ahead. Had her hunger not weakened her so, she might have been able to resist Talara's intrusion the night before. She would have been spared the look of unease and discontent on Yakun's face. The fear and resentment in his eyes as he set the circle's magic to pin her to the floor. Even Poko looked at her warily. Poko had seen what she could do, and they walked about her as if she would explode in flames at any moment.

And perhaps she would. There was no telling what havoc the godsblood was wreaking upon her body. There was no precedent for what she was or what she would become in time. But the fire was always there. In her blood. She knew that much. She was an inferno barely contained in the flesh of a woman.

Tiny beads of sweat dotted her forehead. A slight fever and exhaustion working in tandem made her whole body burn hot. Weak tremors rattled her hands. Her feet moved clumsily through the brush. Often she found herself having to blink soft, weighty drowsiness from her eyes. Sleep beckoned. She had slept no more than a few scattered hours since Talara had snuck into her mind.

The jungle was dense. She could barely see a few paces in front of her for all the palm and vine. A misting of rain from the day before made the air pleasantly damp. Small hoofprints in the soft jungle floor led her down a slight ridge. She steadied herself with a shoulder or elbow against passing trees. Her bow was nocked and ready. Desperation quickened her beleaguered steps.

Amid the heady scent of the jungle, she could smell the pungent, sulfuric stink of marking peccaries. The tracks were still sharp and defined in the wet, leaf-strewn jungle floor. The scent was strong enough to tickle and sting her nostrils.

She slowed, pushing cautiously through the jungle. Peccaries had poor vision. If she could move through the jungle unheard, she had a chance.

As she followed the tracks, a coldness seeped out from within her chest. Her blood ran hot but her core was frigid. The cold, pitiless abyss that was her hunger opened wide.

Ahead of her, she heard a bark and then a rattling chatter. She froze mid-step. *Shit.* The chattering of an alarmed peccary's tusks came from little more than a dozen paces ahead. In her mind, she could see the peccaries taking off and fleeing through the jungle. But the chattering persisted, no farther away than it had been when it began. She held her breath and dared not move a muscle. Even blinking seemed to her too conspicuous.

She strained her eyes, trying to peer through the thick foliage to no avail. The chattering tapered away, overwhelmed by the faint buzz of the jungle. She exhaled through her nose. On the balls of her feet, Odessa slowly picked her way forward. Every step deliberate. She moved behind a cluster of stunted papayas, hiding her bulk behind a clump of broad-leafed, spike-flowered heliconias.

Leaning to peek around the ridged trunk of the papaya, she could make out the shapes of three peccaries through the foliage. They looked like Egende's diminutive relatives. Standing as tall as her knee, the peccaries farthest from her rooted in the soft dirt. The one nearest stood still in a patch of bromelias. Its head was raised. Its round ears flicked to and fro, attentive and cautious.

Odessa froze again, not taking her eyes off the peccary. She feared that if she took her eyes off it for even a second it would disappear. Lost to the jungle. If she moved too quickly or missed her shot, that would be the end of her. Her strength was dwindling. Only the dregs of vigor remained. She wasn't even sure if she had the strength to make the trek back to the grove.

Slowly, she raised her bow. So slowly the muscles in her arms twitched with impatience. So slowly it seemed the sun would set before she aimed. The peccary stood, watching her as she steadily eased the bowstring to her cheek. Her shoulder screamed with the strain of such a gradual draw.

A soft exhalation, and she released. With a squeal, the peccary turned to bolt but collapsed after two panicked strides, its front legs giving out and sending it sprawling. The two other peccaries disappeared into the foliage, but Odessa had forgotten all about them. Before the fallen peccary had even breathed its last breath, she was on top of it. It kicked and bucked with the last of its quickly draining life. It squealed again, a loud, pitiful scream that faded to a wet gurgling as Odessa slashed its throat open with her knife.

Blood poured onto her bandaged hand, soaking the linen in red. Hot blood into her scarred flesh. The smell of iron was in the air, heady and intoxicating. Cupping her hands beneath the spurting stream of blood, she drank all she could. Heat kindled in her chest. Her own blood ran hot and fast in her bulging veins. Her right arm thrummed on the verge between pleasure and pain. The dark lines pulsed, drinking in the peccary's life.

When she was done, blood dripped from her chin and the disgust that followed a feeding came in force. The peccary's innards lay strewn in a pile on the ground beside her. Her arms were bloodied to the elbows. The taste and texture of the peccary's heart lingered like a thick film. Coppery and tough. The urge to vomit bubbled at the back of her throat.

As the blood dried on her skin and seeped into the ground, she sat on her knees, waiting for the loathing to pass. *I hate this. I hate this. I can't do this anymore.* When the smell of blood was in the air, she lost control of herself. A primal fury overtook her and left in its wake disgust and self-loathing. In those moments, when her blood ran hot, she relished the squeal of terror and pain. She never felt stronger than in those moments. And that fact scared her as much as it revolted her.

Poko's right. I need to be rid of this. Talara's rasping voice grated in her mind. She was running out of time. As long as she had godsblood in her veins, she would never be safe. Never be normal. *I have to go to Asha-Kalir. Sooner rather than later.*

Allowing herself a few more minutes' respite, she rose and searched for her arrow. It had entered the peccary in the hollow of its shoulder and exited through its belly to bury its shaft in the dirt. She pulled it from the dirt and wiped the arrowhead clean. Before putting the arrow back in the quiver, she noticed a crack starting behind its bronze head. Her arrows had trouble matching the power of her bow no matter what she did. The bow she had made not long after arriving in the grove was a brutish thing, a compliment to her increasingly savage strength. Made from the red-tinged heart of a fallen massaranduba and backed with rawhide, Yakun could barely draw it a quarter of the way back.

Reinvigorated, she took the peccary by its hindlegs and started dragging it back the way she had come. Before long, after repeatedly untangling the peccary's body from vines and brush, she was forced to sling it over her shoulder. It was heavy but not nearly as heavy as she would have thought. The modicum of renewed strength she had gleaned from the peccary made the trek back to the grove quite a bit easier than the journey south had been.

She arrived at the grove in the late afternoon and hung the peccary by its back legs on a rope dangling from the branch of a jungle cedar just behind the house. She had just enough strength left to limp to the house on blistered feet and numb legs. When she made it inside she dropped to the floor in the middle of the front room and lay on her back.

It was a strange feeling. Her entire body was exhausted and sore, but she felt livelier and more alert than she had in weeks. Her limbs had turned to jelly but her mind was clear.

"Looks like you were successful," Poko said, looking down at her from their perch. They lay sprawled out like a cat, their head and one arm dangling over the edge of the table.

Odessa's head lolled to face the fairy. "How can you tell?"

Poko pointed to their chin. "You've got a little something on your face."

Odessa snorted. "Oh yeah. I forgot. Once I get feeling back in my legs I have to take a bath. And butcher the hog."

"You're running out of daylight then, lady."

"Come on, I've earned the right to lie on the floor for at least an hour."

"I'll give you ten minutes," Poko said.

"Thirty."

"Ten," Poko repeated.

"Twenty."

"Ten."

Odessa frowned. "Jerk."

"Look, we all have a job to do, Dessy." Poko smirked as obnoxiously as they could. "That's just the way it is."

"Call me Dessy ever again and I'll squash you," Odessa growled, trying her best to hide her grin.

Poko's arm dropped to dangle and swing limply beside the other as they leaned farther off the perch. "But I'm all the way up here," they sneered.

"If I could move my arms you'd be so dead right now."

Poko laughed but Odessa thought she saw in their black, bug-like eyes a twinge of reticence. Some reservation dulling their laughter. Odessa told herself she was being too sensitive and making something from nothing, but it nagged at her from the recesses of her mind.

Twilight was descending into the grove as Odessa washed her hands in the spring, then returned to the hanging peccary. As carefully as she could in the dwindling daylight, she skinned the peccary, alternating between slicing silvery connective tissue and pulling the slimy hide in rough yanks until it hung from around its neck. She sawed through its neck and carried the fleshy bundle to a debarked log lying a few paces away. She laid the coarse-haired side of the hide on the log, the peccary's head dangled off the side. It was silly, but she had never liked cutting an animal's head off before skinning. Ever since she had been a little girl watching her father at work, she hated seeing an animal's lifeless eyes as its head was removed from its body. When it was connected to a slab of hide it was easier somehow. It wasn't an animal, it was more like a rug that needed trimming. She sliced the hide and let the head fall snout-first to the dirt.

After wiping the knife clean on her pant leg and sliding it back into its sheath, she left the hide draped over the fleshing log and went to take the peccary down from its rope. Night had sunk into the grove, settling in deep pockets of shadow. She carried the skinned peccary over her shoulder. The growing dark was heavy on her skin. There was just enough light in the grove for her to find her way to the spring and lay the peccary in the springhouse, a stone-walled box near the mouth of the spring where they stored their perishables. She would have to flesh the hide and roast the meat tomorrow.

After submerging the skinless peccary in the cold water and letting it sink to the tiled bottom, she replaced the heavy wooden lid and then dried her dripping hands on her pants. Fat and dried blood still clung to her fingers and palms after she had dried them. The bandage around her right hand was ragged and stained a ruddy brown. Even in the gathering dark she could make out the bloody rags wrapped around her hand. Beneath the trees of the ravine, shadows deepened, oozing out from beneath the foliage to mass around her.

She walked hurriedly, climbing the slight ridge out of the ravine to the edge of the tree line. An anxious chill pricked the back of her neck, needling her to turn around. Her nerves sparked in bursts of uneasiness that accumulated with the passing of every tree and bush, for within each of them could be a predator lying in wait. Malevolent spirits obscured in shadow. Reanimated corpses shambling out from shallow graves. She imagined Obi charging soundlessly through the grove, half-rotten and furious. He would fall upon her, his hulking frame desiccated and maggot-gnawn, pummeling her with bony fists and tearing her to shreds until there was nothing left of her but gore and broken bones pounded into the dirt.

Why didn't I get the skinning done right when I got back? I knew it was getting dark. She walked faster, almost to the tree line now. Her hand had found its way to the handle of the knife on her belt and held on to it for reassurance. *A grown woman afraid of the dark. It's pathetic.* But her hand did not release the knife, and she did not slow her hurried pace. Some part of her was still trapped in the Night Jungle. Still waiting for rotfiends or the Bruka to return. Still lost in that never-ending dark.

She emerged from the tree line and trotted across the clearing toward the house. In her mind, Obi was still barreling through the grove, about to burst out from the forest at any moment.

It was not until she was inside the house and had slammed the door shut that she felt safe. The oil lamp beside Yakun's empty chair had been lit, giving Odessa enough light to see by.

"Well, you stayed out late tonight," Poko said, sitting beside the lamp with half of a woody nutshell on their head as a hat.

Odessa flopped into Yakun's chair with a huff, giving her heart time to slow its racing. "Yeah, well," Odessa said dismissively. "Nice hat, by the way."

"I know you're trying to be mean, but I worked very hard on this."

Odessa smirked weakly. "We all have a job to do, right?"

"Well, I have to stay busy somehow," Poko said. "Do you have any idea how boring it is when no one's around? I used to at least have the bird to talk to, not that he was much of a talker, but now I've got no one. I'm all by myself all day. I'm about to lose my mind."

"How about cleaning this place up? Make yourself useful."

"Useful? I'm nothing but useful." Poko gestured to the flickering flame of the lamp. "What's this then? Do you think this lit itself?"

Odessa clapped her greasy, blood-stained hands slowly and quietly, letting derision fill the air between claps. "What would we do without you?"

"Hey, you should be proud of me!" Poko said. Odessa thought she heard a bit of genuine defensiveness in their voice. "I'm getting better with fire."

Odessa's weak sneer faltered for a moment. "No, you are getting better," she said, the derision gone from her voice. Her hands fell to her lap. "You're doing well. Truly."

In the jungle and plains, she hadn't noticed how averse Poko was to the fire that had kept them safe from malevolent spirits. How they shied away from the flames and eschewed its warmth. Both Odessa and Poko had lost parts of themselves in that jungle. Poko remained in the firestorm she had created. With the roaring flames and the screams of their fellow fairies filling the smoke-choked air.

Sometimes Odessa wondered if Poko still resented her for what she had done. She had not meant to set fire to the fairies' court. Her flames then had been unbridled and furious with no means of control. But if it had been her family caught in those flames, she knew she could never forgive the one who had started them. Accidental or not. Justified or not. It wouldn't matter. She would hate them until her dying breath. Even in the eternal perdition that awaited her, her hate would remain.

How Poko could joke with her and be kind to her, Odessa could not understand. Poko said fairies did not abide by such moralities as humans did, and Odessa knew that to be true. But she also knew that fairies held grudges the way a miser hoards coin.

The night wore on, darkness deepening outside. They ate a dinner of beans and fried plantains. Conversation between Odessa and Poko was sporadic, thinning as the night dragged on.

Odessa paced, her fingers drumming along the handle of her knife. "Do you think he's still working on the wards?"

"Unless he's got cat eyes, I don't think so," Poko said, standing at her feet. "He's probably still on his way. He's old. He moves slow."

Odessa shook her head. "He would have made it back by now." Her pacing stopped. "What if he's hurt?" In her mind, another question emerged. *What if he's dead?*

"He's not hurt," Poko said. "He'll be coming through that door any moment now." Their words were soft and hollow.

What will I do if something's happened to him? What then? There's no cure without him. Her fingers wrapped around the knife's handle, the index finger nervously bouncing along the pommel. *Without him, I'm dead.* She could almost feel the dank cold of Talara's breath on the back of her neck.

Her body was in motion before she realized it, taking her bow from where it leaned against the wall. She was stringing her bow when Poko stopped her.

"You're not going out there, are you?" they asked.

With the tip of the bow's lower limb pressed against the side of her foot, she hauled the upper limb down enough to slip the bowstring's loop onto the grooved tip. "I have to," she said, her voice small. She did not have to explain why. Faint as it was, they both could smell the stench of rank decay on the air and feel the grave-cold chill about them. A familiar sensation like a recurring nightmare made manifest.

CHAPTER 8

Beneath the grove's thick canopy, it was pure darkness. Odessa loped along the ravine floor, reeling and stumbling through the oppressive dark, her torch barely a flicker. She could scarcely see the ground beneath her feet. All sound but the pounding of her feet against leaf litter was muffled in the dark. Nothing existed beyond the scant light of her torch.

Poko peered out from the top of a game bag hanging from her belt, holding on to the hemmed rim with white knuckles. Once the fairy had realized Odessa could not be persuaded to stay, they had insisted on coming. And she was glad for it. Had she been alone, she was certain she would not have been able to go on. *No spirit can get inside my head when Poko's by my side*, she told herself. She hoped with all her heart that was true.

Muddy water splashed up the back of her legs as she stumbled through the end of the stream. The mountainside emerged from the darkness without warning, torchlight failing to reach the stone until she was only two paces from crashing headlong into it. She slowed enough to careen into the cleft and dashed through the pass. The wet slap and suck of her footfalls through the muck echoed off the slick walls. Torchlight danced along every niche and nook.

She expected to find the end of the pass blocked by some twisted, corrupted beast, but she emerged into a silent jungle. Talara's presence was almost tangible. Stronger than it had been before. It cut through Odessa like a cold wind. A rank, defiling sensation seeping through every pore. Filling her lungs with putrid breath. Pressure like a whole world bearing down upon her stopped her in her tracks.

"We gotta go back," Poko whispered from where they now hid in the bag. "We gotta run."

Odessa wanted to run. More than anything she wanted to run back to the grove. Back to Kalaro. Back home. But she couldn't move. Not a step forward or back. A primal fear paralyzed her limbs. The torch's flame sputtered and shrank against the overwhelming strength of the fetid dark.

"Now that I've found you, girl," Talara's voice brushed against the back of her neck like the coarse, slobbering tongue of a carrion eater. "Your trials begin anew." The pressure bore down on Odessa's shoulders, and her knees threatened to buckle.

From the dark, she heard leaves rustling and branches snapping.

"You will grow strong or you will die," Talara said. "There is no alternative."

The pressure lessened and the darkness receded, allowing her torch to flare to life. In the torchlight, she made out at least five figures obscured in the shadowy jungle. But directly in front of her was Yakun on his knees, the side of his face swollen, discolored, and steeped in blood from a gash on his forehead. Behind him, with a hand on his shoulder and a curved blade to his throat, stood a figure in black robes. Beneath the figure's hood glittered a dark metallic mask in the shape of a skull.

"Do you wish to see more of those you love killed before your eyes?" Talara whispered in her ear. "Is it your desire to see your mother's throat opened as well? Your sister's?" Odessa's eyes misted and she bit the side of her cheek to still the emotion roiling within her chest. "Spurn your destiny further and I will see to it that you live to see all those that you love bleeding at your feet."

"Odessa," Yakun said through swollen, bloodied lips. "Run!"

"There is no running from me," Talara whispered. Although the goddess's whispering came from every direction, her words were meant for Odessa's ears only. "Do not reject my gift. Prove yourself worthy. Test your mettle against your ka-man's creations. Kill them. Kill them and take the first step on your path to absolution."

The skull-faced figure stared at her from beneath the shadow of its hood. Holding Yakun by the hair, it wrenched his head back and pressed the curved edge to the bulge of Yakun's throat until it drew blood. Yakun moaned, his hands clawing at the figure's robed arm. The figure did not move no matter how Yakun scratched and tugged.

A sick taste in her mouth, Odessa was drawing an arrow from her quiver and nocking it before she had time to think. Before her dropped torch hit the dirt. All she could think of was her father's throat open and bleeding. A sputtering burst of sparks from the torch as it hit the ground. In one fluid motion, she drew the bowstring back and let the arrow fly.

The figure's head snapped backward, its hood thrown off. The arrow was buried in its skull, the shaft piercing the mask above a cloudy white eye.

The knife-wielding hand sagged from Yakun's throat and he lurched forward, away from the tottering figure. The figure swayed and stumbled back a step, but it did not fall. Its blank eyes met hers. Yakun was all but forgotten as the jungle erupted in pandemonium.

CHAPTER 9

The torch guttered at Odessa's feet as the figures in the jungle charged. She loosed an arrow at a shadow moving in the swollen darkness.

A shape bumped into her, hands blindly grasping at her arm. "Run!" Yakun mumbled. "We have to run!"

She pulled away from his grip and loosed another arrow at an ill-defined figure charging toward them. It halted, two sets of yellow fletching barely visible in the dark. One in the figure's chest and one above the eye.

Odessa dug into her game bag and drew out Poko's wriggling form. "Take Poko and go!" Odessa thrust the fairy out to Yakun's indistinct shape.

A moment's hesitation, a moment enough for the figure to begin stumbling toward her again, and Yakun took the fairy. He ran, soft footfalls becoming wet slaps.

She tossed the bow away as five shadowy forms took shape in a semi-circle around her. The one that had held Yakun by the hair was but a few paces away now, warily creeping forward, two arrows still sticking out from its body.

Her heart pounded in her ears. Her blood ran hot. She focused on the heat. On the throbbing sensation coursing down her arm. With her left hand, she drew the knife from its sheath. Her bandages began to smolder, edges turning red and then falling to the ground in flakes of ash. With a single deep breath, she let the flames pour out. Her hand bloomed in rusty-red fire and then burst upward in a rush, engulfing her arm to the shoulder. As scared as she was, deep within herself there was a harsh, brutal euphoria. Like scratching at a healing wound. The scant, dirty light like a sooty lantern lit the jungle in a circle a few paces around her.

Three masked figures in dark robes stood in a loose triangle in front of her, each of them brandishing a curved bronze blade. The figure she had put two arrows in wobbled a step closer. Nearby she heard a crashing of branches.

As the flames roared from her arm and her eyes drank in the faded darkness, the world slowed for a fraction of an instant. Her fear was a frigid prickling along her nerves and a tightness in her chest.

Kill them? Yes, I'll kill them. I'll kill them all. A voice not altogether her own whispered in the back of her mind. *I'll rip their hearts from their chests.*

The triangle broke in an instant. The figures charged, blades flashing with the red glow of her flames.

Odessa backpedaled, ramming her back against the edge of the rocky cleft as she launched herself into the pass. A blade grazed the mouth of the pass with a shower of stone.

The walls around her were a kaleidoscope of fire and shadow. A figure filled the pass's mouth, arm raised for a short swing.

Odessa met the shadowy figure before the blade could fall. Her knife plunged into the armpit of its sword-wielding arm. Blood spilled over her hand, pleasantly hot. Her flaming hand wrapped around its neck. The robes and hood burst into flame, surging to swallow the figure's chest. Flames poured from the eyes of the skull mask.

She ripped the blade from its armpit and kicked the burning figure back. Its sword arced lazily as it fell in a fiery heap at the mouth of the pass. The figure, engulfed in lashing tongues of flame, writhed and tried to rise, but its limbs gave way as its skin and flesh sloughed off.

The figure with an arrow in its mask made to leap over the writhing body but tripped as it tried to rise again. The hem of its robe caught flame as it toppled over.

Odessa slowly backed away as the fallen figure crawled toward her, its bottom half entirely aflame. She breathed slowly, concentrating on restraining the inferno roaring in her arm. Her flames clung to her arm in a thin sheen of licking fire, allowing darkness to seep again into the pass's mouth.

Don't burn yourself out, she told herself. *Control. Control the burn.* But the temptation of the unbound pleasure of hot, unfettered fire railed against the thready grip of self-control. The thick, acrid stench of burnt flesh filled the tunnel. But in the harsh, foul stink she found a worryingly sweet note in the smell of singed hair and rendered fat.

The crawling figure stopped and collapsed to the mud, its entire body fully aflame. Another one of the masked figures leaped over the burning bodies.

Its robes singed but refused to catch flame.

Odessa swung her knife in a wild arc, putting a bit of space between her and her attacker. The figure snapped forward its wickedly curved blade. She leaped back, a swing following her in a flash of bronze.

With a jerk, she stumbled back a step. The blade slashed diagonally across her chest, blooming in white-hot pain from collarbone to lower rib. A gasped cry slipped from her mouth. Blood poured down her belly.

Another downward swing came before she could fully regain her balance. Fast as a whip, she had only enough time to raise her flaming arm and catch the blade. It bit into the meat of her forearm, striking bone and sending sharp, blinding pain reverberating through her arm.

Fire burst from around the blade sunk deep in her arm. She jerked back as the figure wrenched the blade free. Focus lost, flames boiled from her wound, roiling along her arm and wreathing it in bloody tongues of gold fire.

The figure stepped back, the fire reflected in its polished mask. Its sword raised warily. The edge of its blade, where it had hacked through her flesh, glowed a dull red.

The air in the pass grew hot. Her vision alternated, darkening and blurring. Her arm hung limply at her side. Droplets of blood dripped from her deadened fingers, burning like oil until they fell sizzling in the mud. The robed figure in front of her knew well enough to fear the flames. But what would happen when her flames fizzled out? Or when the masked figure realized that her arm was practically dead?

Her cleaved arm throbbed sharply, as if her beating heart was forcing shards of obsidian through her veins. She focused on the pain, gaining control of the flames and giving them purpose. The flames along her arm shrank, converging at the edges of the bone-deep laceration, an amalgamation of flesh-rending, bone-grinding agony.

She barely leaped back in time to avoid another arcing swing of their sword. It was targeting her right side. Her deadened side. Her focus wavered each time she had to dodge or knock away a slash, but each time it faltered she would redouble her efforts. Gathering the flames again and packing them deeper into her wound.

Her lungs burned. An acidic weariness delayed the speed of her movements. The figure was emboldened, hacking and slashing in the cramped pass. The narrow tunnel limited the figure's swing, but its momentum drove it forward and spurred it on. Odessa's arms and legs bled from a slew of grazes and cuts. The length and curve of its sword made it hard to deflect with her knife. A few half-hearted stabs and slashes were all she could do to keep the skull-faced figure from overwhelming her and driving the sword through her belly. She would not be able to keep dancing away from its blade forever.

Her fingers twitched as the flames along her arm flickered weakly. The mass of fire around and inside her gash dwindled.

The figure's foot planted in the mud, its sword low, it looked ready to lunge. About to skewer her through the middle. She was too close to dodge, not close enough to go in for the kill. Her arm jerked back and she threw her knife as the figure's sword leaped into motion.

The knife spun, end over end. The handle struck the figure's shoulder with enough force to knock it slightly off balance. The point of the sword turned, slicing deep into Odessa's side as she darted close.

Her arm bloomed into flame once more, a sputtering sleeve of red fire. She barreled into the figure, lifting them off the ground for a split second before slamming them into the mud. Her fists pummeled the figure's head and chest, its mask quickly becoming misshapen. The hood caught fire as her flames dwindled further and began to die. Its sword flailed wildly, desperately trying to plunge into her back or side. Before it could do more than poke and prod, Odessa had beaten in its mask, blood spilling out from the eyeholes. The pinned figure's thrashing came to a weak, spastic end.

Only when the flames along her arm had sputtered out and the figure pinned beneath her was fully ablaze did she stop. Her knuckles were torn and ragged, her own blood mixing with the dark, putrid blood that stained her hands. She staggered to her feet, fingers trembling from pain and exhilaration. She had killed Obi in much the same manner. Brutal and bestial. But it satisfied her hunger in a way that no other manner could.

It did not take long for the infernal fire consuming the corpses to gutter and die. These flames of hers were weaker. Colder. Without the flames, pitch black poured back into the pass. Darkness came to take her again. Odessa bent, scrabbling by the last flickering tongues of flame licking at charred robes and skin until her splayed fingers brushed metal.

I'm all burned out. Blindly searching, she found the sword's coarsely wrapped hilt and rose. She winced and steadied herself against the stone wall, the gash along her side a furious pain like a wasp's nest had been packed in it. Both her chest and side were slick with blood. *I'm all bled out.*

She cast a glance over the last flickering flames toward the darkness of the jungle and then turned and ran. Her legs felt about to buckle with every other stumbling step. The mud clung to her feet, threatening to not let go.

She found me. Odessa's mind revolved around that singular thought, endlessly like the flow of time and space around the draw of the void. *She found me. I was stupid to think I could hide from her. She's a god. A godsdamned High Goddess.* A sick feeling was sinking in her stomach. A feeling, heavy and cold. She didn't know if any of the masked figures had followed Yakun into the grove. It had been so dark and there had been so much happening all at once. One of the masks could have slipped past her. Talara would not spare Yakun or Poko. The goddess had already taken so much from her, but Odessa knew now that there was no end to a god's avarice. Talara would take everything from her again and again. As long as she lived.

As she barreled out of the pass and began splashing blindly through the ravine, her thoughts spun, spiraling through the dark recesses where her misery resided. She saw Ubiko's lifeless body. Her father's head wrenched back as the blade sliced through his throat. The blood that had poured down his chest, gurgling and bubbling as his last breath whistled through his open windpipe. The ka-man's hellish eyes were on her always. Talara's eyes buried in the old man's head.

Tears spilled from her eyes. She could already envision what awaited her at the sod house. Poko's small body crushed, a smear of blood and guts on the floor. Yakun broken and frozen in the rigors of torment. His body riddled with stab wounds and his throat sawed wide open. Blood, so much blood. Everywhere. Their blood on her hands. Staining them forever.

CHAPTER 10

"Yakun!" she shouted, pounding on the door of the sod house with the sword's rounded pommel. "Poko!" The locked door rattled on its hinges with every strike. "Are you in there?"

She glanced behind her, searching the darkness but finding nothing. She couldn't hear anyone approaching, friend nor foe, but there remained a prickle of unease at the back of her neck all the same.

Another pound on the door with no reply. It was locked from the inside, so Yakun and Poko had to be in there. "Open the godsdamned door!" She could imagine a masked figure slinking through the doorway as Yakun and Poko waited for her to return. The figure turning to lock the door behind itself before it set about its gruesome work. She battered the door again, cracking the pommel against the door hard enough to splinter the wood.

Waiting again for a reply, the silence became unbearable. *Godsdamnit, someone open this door!* She wished the door would swing wide open. That Yakun and Poko would quickly usher her inside and tell her everything would be fine. But the door stayed shut. The pitch-black grove was silent in the wake of her booming knocks.

She could take the silence and the mounting fear no longer. With a crash, she kicked the door at the latch. Pain erupted from her side as the gash tore wider. She stumbled back a step, clamping her numb right hand over the wound.

The door was split and splintered where her foot had struck it. She shouldered it open and hurried inside.

The fire had burned low, lighting only half the front room. She slowed a few paces inside, her sword raised. Her eyes searched the stacks and piles that littered the room, scouring the space for anything amiss, but found nothing.

Now that she was inside, she found it hard to raise her voice. "Yakun?" she ventured, almost hesitantly. As if she feared a reply now. The house was too quiet. Too still. "Poko?"

The squeak and groan of wood beneath her feet seemed much too loud as she moved cautiously through the room. The front room was empty. She was afraid to go farther, terrified of what she might find. But her feet kept moving. One step. Then another.

Halfway across the room, her ears caught a faint noise. A low whirring almost like a cat's purr. The farther she ventured, the louder it became. Coming from Yakun's study. It was hard to keep herself from running to the door and throwing it open. Her overwrought heart could hardly bear the stress.

The whirring was a dull roar when she reached the door. Her sword wavered as she reached her unfeeling hand out to the door. The wood vibrated in time with the ebb and flow of the roaring rush on the other side. The shuddering door stayed firm when she pushed. She slammed her hand against the door, impotent rage flaring. Frustrated tears misted her vision. "Yakun!" Another slam. The door rattled against the drawbar. "Poko! Are you in there?"

The roaring continued, oblivious to her shouting.

"No point in running." A garbled voice both wet and rough came from behind her. Odessa whirled around.

"No point in hiding." The slurred, mumbling words came from the slavering, blood-stained maw of a thin-snouted dog. A dog's head grafted to the slouching, monstrously muscled shoulders of a man wearing nothing but a loincloth and a layer of ash upon its skin. A loop of rope hung from its neck, snapped length of pole dangling from it. Myriad scars made a patchwork across its ash-daubed body. The stench of rot radiated from it like days-old maggoty meat. "Goddess's love is mine. Not yours." It spoke with a pronounced, spittly lisp.

"Her love is all yours," Odessa said, side-stepping cautiously from the door. Her sword held out across her chest. She had no more fire in her. Her wound, still not cauterized, was losing too much blood, too fast. The dog-headed man was smaller than Obi's monstrous form, not much taller than she, but its thin frame was wiry and hard like a gnarled old willow. And its jaws, stained red with fresh blood, were packed with rows of fangs. Far too many sharp teeth filled its mouth, causing some to spill crookedly out from beneath its lips. "I want nothing to do with your goddess."

The dog-headed man took a step closer, its gangly arms hung, letting long, bony fingers drag upon the floor. The broken pole hanging from its neck swung. "Only one can deserve Goddess's love. I kill you and I am loved."

There's going to be no reasoning with this thing. She kept slowly edging toward the fireplace. *Of course not. It's Talara's hound, for gods' sake.* In the dog head's bulging, white-rimmed eyes, there was an intensity that unsettled her to the core. A frenzied sort of ecstasy. Whereas Obi had been driven by hate and rage, this abomination was driven by an infallible reverence. By love.

She stopped before the fireplace, its warmth pleasant against her calves. "So it's kill or be killed then?" Odessa asked. "That's how she wants it?"

"Yes," Talara's hound growled. "Kill or be killed." It took another step forward, ears flat against its head and crooked teeth bared. Its head was low, a line of fur down its neck bristled as it took another slow step forward. The whirring roar from the other room had grown louder. Its flat ears twitched.

Her half-dead hand found the iron fire poker just as the dog-headed man lunged. She threw the poker end over end and leapt to the side. The poker bounced ineffectually off its shoulder.

Undeterred by her distraction, it barreled into her, its jaws clamped onto her forearm. As they fell, she swung the sword a glancing blow against its thick, muscled neck.

The back of her head cracked against the stones of the fireplace as they crashed to the floor. Teeth buried deep in her scarred flesh, she had enough sensation in her arm to feel the crushing pressure upon her bones. The hound shook its head, ripping and tearing her flesh.

She screamed. Her head, ringing from striking the stone, was filled with bright, overwhelming pain. Her arm felt broken, shattered into a million shards of pure agony. Hot blood poured from her arm with no flame to accompany it. The hound's bony fingers dug into her sides as it snapped at her arm, readjusting its grip before it shook again.

Swinging awkwardly from beneath the hound's frame, she hacked at its neck, slicing through tough hide into hard muscle. Rancid blood dripped onto her chest and neck. The scent of blood was a guiding light in the pained murk addling her mind.

The floor shook beneath them as the roar rose in pitch and power. The hound bared down on her arm. Her bones cracked.

It's going to rip my arm off.

Strength pouring from her in rivers of blood, she swung hard, burying the sword in corded muscle. The hound released her and knocked the sword from her hand as she pulled it free. It skittered into the dimly lit edge of the room.

The hound was lunging for her neck when the rushing roar abruptly stopped. She rammed her broken, blood-slick arm into its mouth until it was wedged against its back molars. Her other hand gripped the back of its neck as it bit down upon her arm. The pain was overwhelming. Black seeped into the periphery of her vision. With all the fading strength she could muster, she hauled the hound's head close to her cheek. It tried to pull away, but it was too late. She sank her teeth into its neck.

Its fur was greasy and tasted like death. Its thick hide hung loose from its neck. Her teeth were ill-suited but, with enough force and enough thrashing, she was able to break through the skin and rip into its jugular. Her gnashing teeth tore through hard muscle until a heavy spurt of blood filled her mouth. It tasted like rot and copper. She drank like a newborn on a teat. It tried to pull away. Its fingers raked her skin. But her grip was like iron. She kept the hound close, its head twisted to the side and its jaws still clamped on her arm.

She barely noticed the floor lurch and buckle beneath them. In a fraction of a second, they were thrown across the room in a roaring gale of power, crashing through tables and chairs, baskets and boxes, until they slammed against the opposite wall with a heavy thud.

CHAPTER 11

A sharp pain against her cheek and the smell of ammonia burning her nostrils woke Odessa with a start. Through bleary eyes, she saw Poko kneeling on her chest, hand raised for another slap. Their other hand held a small earthen vial of vinegar and smelling salts.

"Don't slap me," she mumbled, vision shifting back and forth, doubling and reforming.

Poko's hand cracked across her cheek.

Odessa blinked and tried to focus her blurred vision. Her cheek stung. "What was that for?" she murmured.

"You worried me near to death, that's what!" Poko rose to their feet, their movement barely felt upon her chest. "I can't take sitting next to your limp body, not sure if you're ever going to wake up. It happens once, well, that's understandable. But this is turning out to be a real lousy habit of yours, Dessa."

Her head was split and spinning. She could barely make out what Poko was saying. There was a delay between the sound and when her brain could glean meaning from the words. Poko hopped off her chest before she could form a response.

"Old man!" Poko padded past the dog-headed man's crumpled corpse and shouted toward the back of the house, their voice hoarse. "She's awake!"

Stomping footsteps and a soft thud. "See if she can stand," Yakun called from the study.

It felt like she had shards of glass between the vertebrae in her neck, so every time she moved her head the shards ground against her bones and flesh. She turned her head slowly, the muscles in her neck tight and sore. Odessa's vision still swam. With concentrated effort, she could force her vision to focus but she could not hold that focus for long before the images began to double and sway. Focusing the best she could, she tried to rise with Poko's gentle encouragement, but just raising her shoulders from the floor made the room spin and sent a wave of nausea up from her stomach. Collapsing back to the floor, she rolled to her side and vomited bloody bile.

Spitting the vile taste from her mouth, she pushed off the floor and tried to get up again. She got onto her hands and knees and swayed. The room pitched and tilted and spun all about her. She closed her eyes, trying to get her bearings, but a building pressure in her head made it hard to resist the pitch and spin of the room. It was as if her brain were pushing against the walls of her skull, cracking the bone with each throbbing swell and oozing out the back of her head, where the pain was most concentrated. If she moved too fast, her brain would rattle against those walls, and she thought she could feel her skull splinter and crack.

Her arm gave out and she fell back to the floor.

"Odessa!" Poko was at her side, putting a hand to her cheek. "Odessa, it's fine. Don't rush it. Just stay here. Stay right here." Poko hurried away, shouting for Yakun. Cheek pressed to the floor, Odessa watched Poko disappear behind a toppled stack of baskets before her eyes shifted to the dog-headed man's dead body only a pace or two away. It lay in a heap, one of its legs bent awkwardly beneath its body. Its head, turned away to expose its blood-matted neck, was beaten to a gory pulp. One of Yakun's walking sticks leaned against the wall beside the corpse, the carvings at its top filled with dried blood and bits of hair. Odessa closed her eyes and tried to slow the room's spinning.

The boom of approaching footsteps. Her eyes shot open to see Yakun's boots passing by. He took his bloody walking stick and hurried out the door into graying darkness.

"Yakun?" Odessa called after him as the door slammed shut.

"He'll be back," Poko said, padding to her side. "He's just getting things together."

"Things?" The pressure in her head had receded but Odessa's thoughts were still cluttered and ill-formed. "What things?"

"The wagon. The goats and llamas." Poko crouched in front of her face. "How are you feeling?"

"Bad." Odessa pushed herself onto her elbow and paused, letting the pain in her head swell and fade and the nausea rise up her throat and recede again. When she spoke again, the words came in a slurred mumble. "What's he doing with the wagon?"

Poko glanced toward the door leading into the fading night. "We're leaving. We have to get out of here. The grove's not safe anymore."

Odessa blinked, the two fairies in her vision becoming one. Her memory of the night was a blur of darkness, fire, and fear. She looked at her arm and finally noticed the thick bandage wrapped around it. The off-white linen was spotted with patches of dull maroon, making it hard to see all the hastily scrawled runes that covered the bandages. "What happened?" Her bandaged fingers moved clumsily, not entirely responsive to her direction. "How'd they get in?"

"Wards aren't much to a High God."

Odessa's stomach turned and she thought she might vomit again. "I thought we'd be safe here." *No matter where I hide, she'll find me eventually.*

"The old man was able to buy us some time, but we need to move fast," Poko said.

"What did he do?" Odessa could still hear the thrum before it had sent her and the dog-headed man flying.

Poko paced. "He made one final ward to push the rest of them out of the grove and hopefully sever Talara's connection here. I'm sorry you got caught in it, but it was all we could do to put some space between us and Talara."

"He can do that?" Magic aimed specifically at the divine and the ethereal was unheard of. It was seditious and exhilarating. Where would he have learned something like that? Then she remembered the magics he had taught her father, and it did not seem as exciting.

"Apparently," Poko said. "It's not much but it was enough to break her connection with the material for a bit. But we're running out of time." They reached out a hand and touched her shoulder. "Can you try getting up again?"

She managed to slide to a seated position against the wall. Her throbbing head lolled away from the lamplight in the center of the room—the light burned behind her eyes and drove spikes of molten pain into her skull through her eye sockets.

"That's good," Poko said. "Really good." Their eyes kept drifting toward the door, which hung slightly ajar. As if expecting another dog-headed man to appear at any moment. Their hand took her elbow. "Can you get on your feet?"

Odessa swallowed, pushing down a wave of nausea. "I just need . . . need to let my head settle." Her eyes closed, she let the back of her head rest against the wall. A brilliantly sharp pain sent her head jerking forward with another jolt of pain from her neck. Tentatively, she reached a hand to touch the back of her head. The hair was stiff with dried blood. Curls, plastered together, crackled against the wall. *That's not good.* The entire back of her head was a mess of matted hair and tacky blood. *Combing this out is gonna be a pain.* Her hand reached no farther, and fell instead to her lap, fingertips faintly brushed with the red of half-dried blood.

"I don't feel right," Odessa said, the words tumbling from her mouth without her meaning to say them.

"I know," Poko said softly. "I know. You took a pretty bad hit to the old braincase. But it'll clear up quick." Through the swirling tilt and pitch of her thoughts, Odessa could hear the uncertainty in their voice. "He said you would be fine. If I knew it was gonna hit you this hard I would have stopped it somehow. I would have done something."

Odessa nodded with a grinding of vertebrae and a jolt of pain. Her eyes drifted over Poko, who had taken her hand and was holding it, then around the shifting room until they fell upon the dog-headed corpse again.

She pulled her hand free of Poko's gentle, reassuring grasp and clumsily leaned over them. The muscles in her back pulled tight and spasmed. Pain shot through her neck and spine.

"What are you doing?" Poko asked, moving out of her way as she leaned too far and spilled onto the floor, her hands stretched toward the corpse.

The dog-headed man's foot was a twisted lump of callus and bone, giving the vague impression of a man's foot if that man had walked only on the balls of his feet all his life. Odessa took the foot in one hand and pulled it toward her. The black canine claws atop its permanently splayed toes scraped against the floor. Her deadened hand wrapped around its ankle and she hauled it closer, clenching her jaw against the pain arcing up her spine and neck and filling her nebulous mind. She twisted and jerked until she had yanked the body close enough that she could reach the loop of rope around its neck and haul its body in front of her. The smell of blood and death was strong.

Odessa crawled atop the corpse, swallowing hard as a chill widened like a cleft in her chest. "A knife," Odessa said to Poko as she came face to face with the dead abomination. Its dog's head was tilted to the side, its mouth hanging open and its purple tongue lolling out overcrowded rows of fangs. "I need a knife."

Poko wrinkled their nose in disgust but said nothing as they left to search the room.

Kunza-ka. She looked over the ka-man's handiwork. The ribbons of scar tissue and bulging lumps of ill-gained muscle. The layer of ash that stained its skin. The dog's head was thin and emaciated, the skin clinging to the curves of its skull. Kalaro had not seen a dog in years, and yet the ka-man had seen fit to make this monstrosity. *How could anyone do this?* She thought again of the mountaintop and coal-red eyes. *What kind of freak must you be to do this to your fellow human?* She thought of Obi and his twisted body. *To pervert people like this—it's disgusting. It's wrong.* She thought of her mother and sister living in the same village as the ka-man who had created these monsters. More than a year since she had last seen them. While Kunza-ka was perverting Ogé's creations into these abominations, she had been hiding like a sick dog.

He's been making monsters while I've become too weak to even stand up. Poko returned with the wide-bladed kitchen knife as Odessa rose to her knees, straddling the corpse's waist. *Talara, that rotten bitch, is right. I have to be stronger.*

She took the knife from Poko and told them to leave her alone. When Poko had retreated to Yakun's study, Odessa steeled herself. She held the knife awkwardly in her left hand, raised above the center of the corpse's chest. Staring down at the body beneath her and the knife poised to open its chest, she could not banish the clamoring memories of the men she had killed in the jungle and of Obi's perverted corpse at her feet. Death was no longer some external happening that came like a force of nature, taking what it wanted from her and those she loved. Death was a part of her. It had seeped through her bloody hands to stain her soul indelibly.

I have to be stronger, she told herself. But she did not want to be stronger. She wanted to be who she had been before. But the Odessa Kusa of those bygone days had died with her father and Ubiko and the rest of the hunters. They were all she could see when she closed her eyes, screaming at herself that she had to be stronger. All of them cold and dead at the base of the stone altar. Their blood filling a cauldron for Talara's gruesome magic. That blood staining the mouths of all those she had known and cared for.

Damn you, Kunza-ka. She raised the knife level with her chest and then took a deep breath and held it. *Damn you, Talara, I won't be your godsdamned lapdog.*

With all her weight, she plunged the knife into the corpse's chest, punching through tough skin and breaking through ribs. She sawed through cartilage and bore down upon the blade until each rib she came across snapped with a wet crunch. When she had sawed through four ribs, she pulled the blade loose. She took each broken rib and pried it back until it snapped again.

She carved its heart from its chest and held it in her bandaged hand. The heart was a bit larger than her fist. The blood soaking through her bandages was thick and stunk of decay. When it seeped through the linen to wet her skin, it tingled. Her fingers tightened around the heart. Blood squirted from its severed arteries and veins and ran down her hand in dark red rivulets.

She was disgusted by how much her mouth watered at the sight of it. When the heart reached her lips, she gagged but continued, digging her teeth into the hard muscle and ripping it apart. It tasted like rotten flesh, and she couldn't stop a surge of vomit from coming up. But she chewed and swallowed it all, then tore into the heart again. Biting, chewing, and swallowing until it was gone. By then the bloodthirst had her fully enthralled. She licked the blood from her hands, slurping up rancid clots. A fire bloomed deep in her chest, and her blood felt as if it were ablaze. Her heart pounded in her ears. Her heart was the same as the tainted heart whose putrid taste clung to her tongue. She gagged and then spat a glob of bloody bile into the corpse's open chest.

Her entire body pulsed with foul vigor. Her wounds radiated a scalding heat that teetered on the cusp of pleasure and pain. Whatever filthy magics had gone into the creation of this abomination edified her like nothing she had ever experienced. Her hunger relished the power in that rancid blood, but within the ecstasy of having her hunger sated, there was a lingering feeling of dissatisfaction. Satiation was so fleeting a feeling. When it faded, the hunger would only want for more. Gluttonous, the hunger deepened. The crack within herself split wider.

Nausea sat heavy and viscous in her stomach. As her vision cleared and the pounding of her heart replaced the pounding pain in her head, she pushed off the corpse and rose. She swayed and tottered, using the wall to brace herself as she stumbled to the door.

Her limbs were heavy. Her body was so weak she felt she could topple over at any moment. *More. I need more.* She leaned against the doorway and fumbled with her bandages until she had freed her hand from the loops of bloody linen.

An unlit torch rested in a sconce beside the door. Its twin on the opposite side of the door was empty, the torch lying in the mud outside the grove. Loosely, she grasped the torch's head, where the grease-soaked piths of multiple rushes had been looped through the quartered end of a green branch. Still leaning against the wall, she focused on her hand, letting the thrumming of her arm quicken and swell. The pulsing sensation moved, draining from her shoulder down to her bare hand, where it gathered, growing hot and throbbing horribly.

Her breathing hastened as she restrained the revitalized fire smoldering in her veins. Gathering more and more heat in her hand, she did not even have to bring forth a flame. The twisted knot of rushes caught fire readily.

She took the torch and shouldered the door open. The air was cool against her searing hand.

She stood, easing her grip on the heat within her arm and letting it seep back into the rest of her body. Yakun's voice came from the woods behind the house, cursing at one of the goats.

Vague thoughts of Kalaro and family and fire and blood slipped in and out of her mind as she stumbled down the slope, catching herself on a tree when she swayed too far in one direction or another. The strength she felt permeating the cracks in her battered body was so much more than that from a peccary or monkey. This strength ran deep, sinking into the depths of her hunger and arousing something. Something like a starved beast awakened by the putrid taste of Talara's blessed blood.

As the starved beast began to stir, she thought of those she had left behind. Those who had killed her father and uncle and tried to kill her. Her mother and sister trapped within Talara's grasp. And the ka-man at the center of it all. *If I was stronger,* she thought. *If I was stronger I'd kill him. Take Ayana and Mama away and kill anyone in my way. Kill them all.* Grease dripped from the torch and cinders drifted to the ground behind her as she staggered to the pass beneath the mountain. *I have to get stronger.*

The cramped tunnel of stone stank of death and burned flesh. The mud had soaked up much of the rotten blood that had poured out of the masked figures, reclaiming what Kunza-ka and his foul goddess had perverted. Odessa held the cooking knife high, anticipating another attack. The torchlight bouncing off the slick walls blinded her to what lay farther in the darkness. But nothing came from the dark. She tottered through the pass unopposed.

When she came upon the masked figure that had assailed her with the sword, she kneeled beside it. Ramming her torch into the mud, she set to work by the flickering light. Its mask was pounded nearly flat and tarnished by blood and gore burnt or congealing in the valleys left by her fists. Cutting a slit down the middle of the corpse's robes exposed ashen flesh marked with knurled scars. A wide line ran down the corpse's sternum and the point of Odessa's knife followed its guidance, slicing and sawing open its chest. Focused unerringly on loosing the heart from its rib-barred prison, the revulsion she had felt before was much easier to quell. Like stamping out tendrils of flame trying to escape the confines of a campfire, her hunger for the strength within that heart easily extinguished the sparks of her discontent. Disgust had no time to breathe before it was snuffed out. All that mattered was the rush that came with the blood. The thrumming in her veins and the soft droning thump of her heart in her ears. With no hesitation, she dropped the knife to the mud and sank both hands into the open chest cavity. Chasing bloody ecstasy.

CHAPTER 12

The front of Odessa's tunic was stiff with dried blood when she returned to the house. She had stopped at the spring and washed her face and hands, but the blood remained smeared here and there, dried in the creases of her knuckles, and caked beneath her fingernails. Her hunting knife was back in its sheath and her bow was looped over her shoulder, retrieved from the dark. Her bloated stomach churned, the sum of five tainted hearts thrumming through her veins and reverberating through her bones like a bolt of lightning continually coursing up and down the length of her body.

Her mind was clearer, only a dull ache in the back of her head remaining. Her wounds still throbbed furiously, and when she moved a certain way, the throbbing would solidify into a sharp, stabbing pain. But she felt alive. A current of stolen life pulsed and raged within herself. It was good.

Scant lamplight spilled out from the open door as she approached. Yakun's small cart had been pulled in front of the house, the two goats hitched to the cart busy eating the orchids growing outside the house.

Yakun emerged through the doorway, stooped over and straddling a cauldron filled with bundles of dried herbs and jars of oils and tonics. Odessa hurried past the cart and took the cauldron before he dropped it.

"I was managing fine myself," he said as she hoisted the cauldron over the cart's side panel. "You're feeling better, then?"

When she turned around, Yakun looked pointedly at her blood-soaked tunic. Shame bloomed like a weed in the pit of her stomach before it was crushed by elation. "Much better," she said, letting the subtle rhythm of her blood drown out the echoes of guilt and revulsion lingering in the back of her mind. "We're leaving the grove?"

"Yes, and there's no time for idle chatter. Help me load the wagon and we'll be gone before sunrise."

Odessa opened her mouth to speak, but Yakun was already shuffling back inside, a hand pressed against the small of his back. She closed her mouth and followed, caught up in the sudden swell of activity.

At Yakun's direction, Odessa loaded the cart, piling it high until the bed had become a precarious mountain of sacks and baskets, pots and pans, ewers and jars. The bulk of the cart's load had come from Yakun's study. The tools of his spellcrafting trade were invaluable and irreplaceable, he had told her, but still, she would have preferred more blankets or more fodder for the goats rather than arcane baubles and esoteric trinkets. So much of what she had hauled outside had been bundles of rune sticks or stacks of sigil-scrawled barkcloth or jars upon jars of oils, salts, and powders. She had convinced Yakun to delay their departure long enough for her to slice up some of the peccary and put it in a cask of salt and brine so that it wouldn't go entirely to waste.

"Is that everything?" she asked after stretching an old, moth-eaten blanket over the load. Poko lounged on the top of the blanketed mound, appearing unconcerned by their exodus, but Odessa still noticed the fairy's occasional glances into the dark grove below.

Yakun stood in the doorway with a stub of a tallow candle, glancing back inside the front room. He had walked through each room and surveyed what they were leaving behind, but Odessa could see his hesitance clearly now in the torchlit threshold. "I believe so. We've meager provisions but it should be enough to get us out of the mountains." He blew out the candle and flicked it with a jerk of the wrist, letting melted tallow splatter on the ground before he stuffed the candle and pan into a pouch on his belt. Odessa's torch was back in its sconce, its glow reflected in his eyes as he turned his back to the home he had built so many years ago. "Take the goats. I'll lead."

She took the lead ropes draped over each goat's back and hauled them into motion as Yakun closed the door behind him, torch in hand. Odessa was about to direct the goats down the slope when Yakun walked around the sod mound and motioned her to follow.

"Where are we going?" Odessa asked, leading the goats around the house. The wooded area behind the house led only to the sheer slopes of the mountains. If they were to escape, they were headed in the wrong direction.

Yakun hurried through the woods ahead, a subtle limp impeding the rhythm of his gait. "You'll see soon enough. Now get those beasts moving, Talara's presence is still too near to delay. There's much too much night left. She'll be back and I don't wish to be here when she returns." He cut through the trees, torch bobbing with every limping step.

When Yakun had pulled farther ahead of the plodding cart, the torchlight coming through branches and bracken for a moment brought to Odessa's mind images of the Night Forest and of the inferno she had made. A tug on both lead ropes and the goats hastened, the cart lurching forward. Poko pitched backward, taking hold of the blanket to keep from tumbling down the misshaped mound.

"It's never a smooth ride with you, is it?" the fairy said.

Odessa's nerves began to itch, the thrumming in her blood giving form to a fluttering anxiety. "Where is he taking us?"

Poko crawled to the top of the peak again. "I don't know. It's a dead end up here." They squinted, peering into the dark. "Goats can climb really steep cliffs though. Maybe we're taking them over the mountains."

"Can a cart scale a cliff?" Odessa said, a bit curtly. Her mind was abuzz. Beneath the thick canopy, the darkness was suffocating. *Why is he leading us to a dead end?* She slowly felt her thoughts melting into memory. The trees and the torchlight and the overwhelming dark. She was being marched through the Arabako Forest again. Marched to her death in accordance with Talara's will.

Something touched her from behind. Like the hand of one of the ka-man's followers shoving her toward the mountain and the doom that awaited her. She jerked forward and spun around. The goats watched her placidly. One nudged her ahead with their nose. Heart still racing, she realized she must have slowed to a creeping pace while lost in her memories.

"Dessa?" Poko ventured. "Are you all right?"

Odessa licked her lips and swallowed a knot of fear caught in her throat. "Yeah, I'm fine. Just thinking."

Poko knew she was lying. They knew her too well. She turned and yanked the goats onward, leaving the fairy reeling atop the pile. As the cart picked up speed again, Yakun began calling her name from a fair few paces ahead. She hurried, weaving the cart between trees and crashing through thick undergrowth.

"Hurry, now, hurry! We've no time for dawdling!" Yakun called as she neared.

"Sorry," she said quickly, trying to mask the irrational worry in her voice. *Stop being so damned paranoid*, she told herself, but she couldn't banish the thought of her trek to the mountaintop altar. The people she had grown up with and cared for all her life leading her to a brutal end. *It's fine. Yakun wouldn't do anything. I can trust him. Papa trusted him.* She followed close behind Yakun through the forest, trying to relieve the tension building up within herself. The mountains loomed high overhead, their immensity bearing down on her. A sense of dread akin to claustrophobia squeezed her chest. Her unease remained like a splinter lodged in her brain. Her father had once trusted the people of Kalaro as well, yet his throat had been slashed open all the same.

The forest ended at the foot of the mountainside. A sheer wall of rock towered above them, reaching up toward the murky black of the night sky. Slowing the cart to a halt before the cliff face, Odessa watched Yakun with unwavering intensity. Her body was tense. Her hand drifted to the knife at her belt.

"Just over here," Yakun said, moving along the cliff face. His fingertips brushed against the rock as he walked. Torchlight exposed nothing Odessa could see. She eased a sliver of blade from the knife's sheath and followed Yakun.

"What're we doing?" Poko asked nonchalantly.

Yakun stopped and gestured to a spot in the cliff at chest height. "Odessa, dear, break this sigil for me, will you?"

Odessa looped the lead ropes loosely around a tree and then slowly made her way forward. "What sigil?" Approaching, she could see nothing but bare rock.

"Right there." Yakun brought the torch closer to the cliff and pointed to what looked to be a shadowy divot. "Just give it a blow or two and that should dispel the last of the ward."

As Odessa neared, she saw etched into the stone and stained with rusty smears an elaborate series of bisecting lines and rows of runes surrounding a spiderweb of script. "Just hit it?"

"Yes, and make sure to destroy that cross in the center where the core lines converge." He pointed to the middle of the sigil. "Once that's gone, the ward should dispel immediately."

Odessa scrutinized the sigil a moment longer, trying to decipher the scrawl, but it was no use. Runes and sigils were all nonsense to her. Disorderly chicken scratch that, without reason, somehow guided the intangible, immeasurable energy of the cosmos to the service of a particular design. She drew her bandaged fist back, reticence staying her hand for just a moment. She imagined striking the sigil and her arm disintegrating in a bloody, pulpy mist. With a glance at Yakun standing expectantly beside her, she drew a short, hasty breath and sent her fist rocketing forward, squeezing her eyes shut just before impact.

Chips of stone struck her face, and dust tickled her nose. A shiver ran through the air, and a great pressure swelled and then dissipated in a sudden gust, but there was no disintegration of limbs. She opened her eyes to see her fist in a small crater in the rock. It had taken only one punch to destroy the sigil. Withdrawing her fist, large flakes of stone clattered to the ground.

The air around her still quivered like a mirage on the horizon. She stepped back as the wall of rock above the broken sigil shook and fluttered. Before her eyes, the stone flickered in and out of existence to reveal a path leading up along the true cliffside.

"Come," Yakun said, starting up the steep path. "The goats may need some coaxing, but they'll go up sure enough. And watch the cart near the edge. It gets narrow near the top."

Odessa followed, leading the goats up the ledge running along the cliff face. The slope itself was not as sheer as the illusionary ward had shown. *This path's been here the whole time?* Following Yakun up the path into the inky black, she could not think of a reason why he wouldn't tell her about the path. Wards didn't always work on her—she couldn't believe she never noticed something amiss.

The goats plodded up the path, pulling away from the ledge so the cart's right wheel scraped against the slope. Looking down, all Odessa could see was darkness, but she knew the grove was far below now. Yakun's limp worsened as the path grew steeper.

She could only think of one reason why he wouldn't tell her. *He doesn't trust me.* She thought of being pinned within the circle in his study. The look on his face as his magics restrained her. *Of course he doesn't trust me. I brought Talara to his doorstep and forced him from his home. Why would he trust me? I'm a godkiller. I'm a godsdamned monster.*

CHAPTER 13

The path cut through a saddle at the northeastern edge of the grove and then dipped down, skirting a ridge overlooking the slopes of the mountain range proper.

"This was once a path pilgrims took to the Stairs of Ascension," Yakun said, his voice dry and brittle with exhaustion. "Back when mankind was young and the Low Gods were yet warring."

The cart rattled along the rocky path, its wheel a few finger widths from the edge. Morning's pale blue-gray light was seeping into the dark clouds above the mountains. With morning came a modicum of safety. Talara's connection with the physical world was weakened in the daylight. They could put some distance between them and the grove before night reared its head over the horizon again. But they had been walking all night and Yakun and the goats seemed on the verge of collapse. Fatigue had begun to nestle in Odessa's muscles, and her wounds ached and stung more furiously, but she persisted, too caught up in her own feelings to worry about her physical well-being.

Poko stretched and rose from a nest they had made in the blanket. "Where are we going anyway?"

"Asha-Kalir," Yakun said. "Talara's left us little choice. My friend Azdava might not be happy but I'm sure she will help us. And Khymanir won't allow another god to encroach upon his sovereignty. High or Low, it matters not to him. If we can make it to Asha-Kalir, we should be out of Talara's reach."

If I had told him about Talara we'd already be safe in Asha-Kalir. Or he would have cast me out and I would be dead. Odessa shook her head. *There's that lack of trust again. If I had just told him about Talara's fixation with me, none of this would have happened.* Yakun's limp seemed to be getting more pronounced every other step, and when he turned his head she could see the side of his face was swollen and mottled in purple and red, the color of overripe acai berries. Occasionally she would see him repeatedly wipe his forehead with the back of his hand when the gash above his brow began bleeding again. *I lecture Poko about trusting him, but look at what my own distrust has done.*

"I thought you said getting to Asha-Kalir would be near impossible," Poko said. "That we wouldn't even get to the Severe Gorge or something."

"The Severed Gorge. And yes, the fact remains, it will be treacherous. Most everyone on the road to Asha-Kalir will be beholden to some god or will be themselves a god. But if we're cunning and exceedingly lucky, we may reach Asha-Kalir in one piece."

"You sure know how to inspire confidence, old man," Poko said.

"I just want to stress the direness of our situation."

"You don't have to. Last night was plenty dire. I think we get it."

"How far is Asha-Kalir?" Odessa asked, drawing herself from her rumination with a bit of effort. The words seemed to scrape and scratch her throat as she forced them out.

Yakun was getting winded, and it took a fair few moments for him to respond. "Twenty days' walk maybe. If we are quick."

Twenty days is a long time. A long walk through godly land and harsh desert. Her spirit sagged even further. They were going to die, and it was her fault.

Morning had fully taken hold when they finally stopped to rest. The trail had dipped into a narrow valley replete with rough scrub for the goats to pick at. Mountains loomed high above on either side of them as they nestled into a slight hollow between them. The goats had been freed from their yokes and hitched instead to a spike driven into the rocky soil. They nuzzled at the shrubbery beneath them, plucking hard, waxy leaves and twigs from spidery branches. Such dry, unappetizing forage was foreign to them, having lived their whole lives in the lushness of the grove.

Yakun had curled up on a blanket spread out on the scree, occasionally tossing and turning whenever sleep eluded him. Poko slept soundly in the cart, snoring softly from within a nest of blanket. But Odessa found no rest. Anytime she closed her eyes she thought she could feel Talara there in the dark behind her eyelids. She had gotten too complacent. Too stupid. And she had done exactly as the goddess had wanted.

Her bow lay unstrung next to the curved sword beside her as she sat, her back against a rocky outcropping next to the path, sharpening her knife with a round, coarse stone. The blade's edge was nicked and notched from the night before;

it was tedious work sharpening such a damaged blade, but she was glad for the distraction. Glad to busy her hands and clear her head. The rhythmic scrape of stone against metal and the rustling rush of wind down the mountainside were all she could hear. The ash-gray cloud cover above was soft and thin, allowing her a chance of reprieve from the dank dark that lingered in her mind. Everything awful in her life had come from the dark. The night was a time of loss and sorrow and there was no avoiding it. Her life was dictated by the tidal force of the night, tossing her to and fro until it succeeded in crushing her beneath its inky black tide.

The rhythm of the scraping stone paused only when she had to add more spit to the stone's face. The nicks in the knife's blade grew shallower with each pass of the stone, bit by infinitesimal bit. A chip nearer the handle was deeper than the rest and meant she would have to remove quite a bit of metal. She wondered how much more damage it could take. Would the cycle of damage and sharpening continue until it was little more than a sliver of bronze, or would it break long before then?

She would never know rest now. She understood that. Her time in the grove had been a sojourn in delusion, but it had come to an end. Peace was a faraway thing. Unattainable by her sullied hands.

She sharpened the knife until all the nicks and chips were gone. With a palm-sized, oblong piece of jasper, she honed the edge until it was as close to obsidian-sharp as it could be. Scrubbed clean of the rancid blood of the masked figures and honed to a keen edge, the iron gleamed. The blasphemous metal shone in the scant light filtering through the gray clouds above. Ogé's gift to mankind, the knowledge of ironworking, had doomed her and her people. Had they not had iron, Egende would still live. But even still, iron was a beautiful thing. She could not deny that.

With a blood-stained fingernail, she scraped at a blemish near the spine of the blade, a spot of dried blood or rust. So prone to rust, iron was easily tarnished and yet it could withstand so much abuse. Once she'd scraped away the blemish, she applied a thin layer of oil to the blade and then sheathed it.

Odessa knew she should try to sleep for at least a few minutes, but her blood was still abuzz, and the boom of her heart still droned in her ears too loud to ignore. There was no telling what horrors awaited her in the night. She couldn't force herself to sleep. She knew what awaited her in her dreams and, in her present state, she could not bear the nightmares. Instead she took the curved sword and set to sharpening it as well, letting her mind slip fully into pleasantly monotonous routine.

Poko was the first to wake since they had been sleeping off and on during the nighttime trek. "A privilege of the weak and tiny," Poko had called their naps atop the cart. They hoisted themself over the side panel and dropped onto the rim of the wheel. From there they slid down the spokes of the wheel, bounced off the hub, and landed in a patch of short, scraggly grass beside the road.

"What I wouldn't give to have wings again," Poko said as they came to sit beside Odessa. "Even just one wing. I could get by with one wing."

Odessa was honing the sword's edge, coaxing a razor's sharpness from the metal. "You'd be flying around in circles," she said, trying to put a touch of humor in her voice but it came out flat and lifeless.

"At least I'd be flying," Poko said. "You don't know what it's like."

"I don't have wings and I get by just fine."

"But you never had them to begin with! You don't know the joys of flight," Poko protested. "It'd be like if you lost both your legs and had to crawl everywhere. It's the kind of thing you only appreciate after it's gone."

A few more passes with the stone, and the sword was sufficiently sharp. She couldn't think of a thing else to say. Merely listening took a great deal of effort. All she wanted to do was hide away in her own mind. To isolate herself in the solitude of her own soul. Taking the soaking rag from the jar in front of Poko's crossed feet, she oiled the blade, letting herself drift away again. Feeling the distance between mind and body grow. In pulling away from the world, there was calm.

All that existed was the droning thump of her heart. Everything around her blurred, landscape and sound dissolving into vague shapes and whispers.

Something pushed her knee and she was jarred from her dissociative calm. "Dessa!" Poko called. "Dessa, are you there?"

It felt as if a bubble had burst, and the world came rushing back into focus with overwhelming intensity. "Sorry," she said, swallowing a sudden lump in her throat. "I drifted off for a moment."

"Yeah, I noticed," Poko said. "You need to get some sleep. You're exhausted."

"I'm fine," Odessa said. "Just a little shaken from last night still."

"More of a reason to get some rest then," Poko said. "Put the sword away and find yourself a soft patch of rocks to sleep on."

Odessa had no will to fight. She did as she was told, wrapping the sword in a bundle of cloth and stuffing it in the front of the cart bed so its hilt poked from beneath the blanket.

I should at least get a little bit of sleep, she thought as she dug another blanket out from beneath the heap. *To keep me going a little longer.* Her aches and pains had worsened since she had gotten up, the movement rekindling the embers of agony lying dormant in her wounds. Wrapping herself up in the thin blanket, she returned to the outcropping and lay down beside Poko. *I don't have the luxury of stubbornness. Have to get what I can when I can get it.*

"Is your head still . . . rattled?" Poko asked as Odessa shifted uncomfortably on the rough terrain.

"No, no, my head's clear now. I'm just tired," Odessa said, her body abuzz in defiance.

Poko leaned against the outcropping by her head. "We'll be fine. You know that, right? The road to Asha-Kalir can't be that dangerous. We'll get there and get you cured. I've got a good feeling about this. A blessing, that's what this is. A good kick in the ass to get us going."

Odessa smiled despite the sick feeling in her stomach. "Yeah," she lied. "Yeah, I'm sure you're right."

She shut her eyes, sleep held at bay by the thoughts running amok inside her head. The road to Asha-Kalir was a treacherous one. She knew that as surely as she knew there was no curing her tainted blood. There was no escaping Talara.

We'll be lucky if we live to see tomorrow morning.

CHAPTER 14

The sound of holy labor came from the distance like the steady thud of a god's beating heart. The sharp staccato of chisel on stone and the thud and grind of massive blocks set in place was clear even from outside the gates of Kalaro.

Looking down the wide dirt track, Kunza could make out the gate in the distance. Since clearing the old road, a trek that had only a year ago taken almost a week of hard travel took only three days. Clearing the road and making it safe had taken numerous hunting and logging parties and months of work, but now the higher reaches of the jungle had been tamed. They had cut and burned a wide swath through the jungle all the way to Noyo and placed a series of rudimentary forts along the path to ensure travelers had a place to rest at night. Kunza's first Shadows now patrolled the road, day and night, keeping the beasts of the jungle at bay with bows and spears.

Kunza and retinue emerged from the jungle in the midafternoon, crossing the rough open plain to the blaring of a horn.

Atop their watchtowers, the gatesman waved his party in. The gates cracked open and then swung outward to embrace them.

Kalaro, how I've missed you. Kunza had only been in Noyo for a short time, but the incessant bustling of that hornet's nest of a city never ceased to exhaust him. Home was a salve for the soul. Even though he was to leave for Noyo again in a few short days, he was glad to be back for now.

His high spirits were short-lived. A cluster of villagers stood just inside the gates, and when he drew close he could recognize the stooped forms of the Elders at the front of the cluster. For a moment, he debated turning around and heading back to Noyo.

I'm not allowed even a moment's respite before they resume their pestering, he thought. Passing through the gates, he consoled himself with a false smile. *What is a home without its pests?*

The guards holding the gates open bowed their heads as Kunza stopped before them. "Welcome back," Elder Kusa said. "I hope your journey was pleasant."

"Yes, it was pleasant," Kunza said, waiting for her to drop the formality.

"I see no army of Shadows behind you, so I assume Azka approved?"

"Do you require something from me, Elder Kusa?" Kunza asked sharply.

Elder Kusa and Elder Cuchal exchanged glances. "It's Ajatunde. She is making us take the blood every day now," Kusa said. "I told her that you assured us we could take the blood only when necessary, but she won't listen. She practically poured it down my throat the day before last."

"It's too much," Elder Cuchal said. "Every time I take the blood I spend the rest of the day with my guts in a fervor. She doesn't understand that we elders don't need as much as the others."

"Ajatunde is Bearer of the Cup. If she says you need to take the blood, then you should do as she says. Hers is the hand that dispenses Talara's elixir; she acts in accordance with Talara's will. If you refuse her, you refuse Talara." The Elders looked away from Kunza's eyes. "Your body follows the will of your spirit. If your body rejects Talara's gift, I implore you to reevaluate the depth of your faith."

Kunza pushed past the group of Elders and those of weak faith. Their skin was muddled gray, resistant to the ash. If they refused to drink their share of the blood, he would cut them off entirely. Let the boils return and choke them. Talara's blood was only for the strong of faith.

Coming down the hill into the basin, Kunza's irritation broke like a fever. The temple had grown so much in the short time he had been gone, the foundation of stone already set north of the village. Not far from the foundation of the temple, a massive hole opened, plunging so deep into the earth that one hundred men standing on each other's shoulders could not reach the top. The entrance to the temple's subterranean sanctum, ringed by a wide and shallow pit, was further surrounded by a slew of hastily constructed thatch-and-mud buildings. Teams of workers hauled huge slabs of stone from the mountains to the edge of the pit where those slabs would sit, waiting for placement below.

In the basin, Kunza followed the beaten track down to the site of the temple's construction. No one dared gaze at him as he descended the ramp down the pit. Ashen workers hauling or splitting stone averted their eyes and hurried their work.

The worksite elevator straddled the entrance, a hulking, almost skeletal thing, like a timber-limbed beast had sunk its legs to the dirt and now crouched above the entrance. The elevator was braced by whole logs rammed into the clay, which shuddered as the elevator's platform jerked into motion from below. A team of Shadows with bulging muscles turned the huge wheel that spun the hoist. Kunza had first seen use of the elevators in Noyo on his first foray as emissary of Talara. When the temple's construction had amounted to little more than a hole in the ground.

As the elevator's platform rose on its thick ropes up the central shaft, Kunza descended down the narrow, stone-lined stairway carved into the shaft's walls. His retinue followed in a line behind him, silent despite the fatigue that most assuredly plagued them. Even Kunza had begun to feel the insidious weight of exhaustion seeping into his muscles.

Around the first loop of the spiraling staircase, the platform passed them on its way up, carrying three wagonloads of spoil to be taken to the waste heap now towering a few spans from the temple.

They ventured deeper, winding down the spiraling stairs. Below, the chasm yawned in the scant light. A handrail would be added when the temple's subterranean necropolis was finished, but for now there were much more important matters to attend to.

A cool, pleasant darkness soon came to swaddle them in its reassuring grasp. Only the distant light above remained, peeking through the gaps between elevator and shaft. By the time they had reached the bottom of the shaft, they were submerged in total darkness. But their eyes were well-suited to the inky depths. Kunza's eyes, most of all, relished the dark. Soaking it in like scorched skin dipped in cool waters.

The staircase terminated into a wide thoroughfare stretching out from the elevator's platform. The sounds of chisel, hammer, and pick echoed off the walls and rattled in his ears. A raised path of stone ran from the staircase along the wall, allowing Kunza and his entourage to journey deep into the temple's sanctum without getting in the way of the wagonloads of spoil heading toward the elevator.

The open space in front of the elevator was wide enough to accommodate four wagons. When the temple was finished, this was where he would do his work. This was where Talara's army would be assembled.

Walking along the path, Kunza passed braziers burning softly. Threads of smoke rose to the high vaulted ceiling and filtered through small ventilation holes. Shadows, slaves, and wagons led by uneasy goats milled about farther ahead in the long antechamber, coming and going through narrow hallways into the labyrinth of catacombs or into the inner sanctum beyond the wide doorway at the end of the antechamber. Everything was rough and unrefined still. Every wall and floor marred with chisel strokes to resemble the knap of a stone blade.

If Ur-Mak's intentions are true, perhaps he could lend some artisans, he thought, running his fingertips along the uneven wall. *Talara's temple must be perfect. It must be a work of art, unrivaled by all. This is only the beginning. The foundation of what will become her greatest monument.*

Once the remaining rock was cleared and they began the more delicate masonry, the construction of the temple's aboveground complex could begin in earnest.

Before Kunza reached the inner sanctum, he was stopped by Kufu, a woman of astounding intellect from Asha-Kalir whom Azka had given him. To Azka, she had been little more than a slave under the guidance of his master architects, but to Kunza, she was an artist with stone.

"Kunza, *shah-kahn*," Kufu said with a bow. It was an Asha-Kaliran honorific she refused to put to rest. "The last tunnels will be cleared by the end of the week and then we will be finishing the hall."

"Very good," Kunza said. "And the inner sanctum?"

"I will let you judge for yourself." Kufu led him past carts half-filled with flakes and chips of dark rock. A thin, stoop-backed boy pushing a handcart laden with rock chips jerked to a halt and bent his head as they passed through the wide, arched doorway.

The sanctum was a huge, circular room lit by myriad small fires set in regular intervals in the walls. Their flames flickered, reflected by alcoves of polished basalt the color of the purest night. In the center, separated from the rest of the room by a dry moat of stone, was a wide circular pedestal where the grandest statue of Talara's visage ever seen would be placed. Halfway between the doorway and the empty pool and its pedestal was an altar just like the one atop the mountain and a large hearth set in the floor in front of it.

They crossed the room, following a trench carved into the floor. Grooves ran on either side of the trench, bending away and turning back in a serpentine shape that ran behind the pedestal to the other side of the trench, and back again to worm closer to the pool in the center of the room. The channels in the floor were so narrow and evenly spaced they were nearly imperceptible to the foot. Kunza followed the channels with his eyes as he walked, making sure the labyrinthian grooves spiraled and turned in perfect symmetry. Men and women on their hands and knees worked with thin chisels and small hammers, chipping away at the floor and perfecting the grade of the grooves.

"They're following the diagram precisely?" Kunza asked. "There's no room for error. Anything short of perfection is unacceptable."

"They're following your specifications exactly, *shah-kahn*," Kufu said, lagging behind Kunza as he walked. "It is flawless."

He slowed to watch a small woman polishing a groove with pieces of quartz. "How much longer until the floor is done?"

"Not long. Not long at all," Kufu said. "The channels are very close to perfection. Once the correct grade is achieved it will take only a few days to finish polishing."

"Good," Kunza said, moving on toward the altar. "But once it is done, no one is to consecrate it save for me. Any tests shall be done with water."

"Of course, *shah-kahn*," Kufu said quickly. "I would never dream of consecrating the sanctum. That honor is yours alone."

Kunza reached the altar and placed his hand upon the stone. It was cold and smooth like a sheet of ice. Its face was covered in spiraling grooves leading to the four corners of the altar. Circling the altar was a wide but shallow channel that fed the trench that branched out toward the doorway.

It's coming together. He smiled and breathed in the dank earthiness of the sanctum. "You've done well, Kufu. Very well." He took his hands from the altar and turned to face her. "This temple is proof that men and women can create works worthy of the divine. The truly divine. We are not beholden to any god but our one true goddess."

"Thank you for your high praise." Kufu bowed her head. "I am grateful you've allowed me such honor. I never thought I would build anything of this magnitude."

"This is only the beginning," Kunza said. "Your works will be many and they will stand long after everything else has fallen to ruin."

Leaving the temple's subterranean level, the true weight of his exhaustion bore down upon his shoulder. As he walked down the long antechamber with his retinue in tow, he caught sight of a Burrower, as he had named them, exiting one of the many tunnels branching off from the hall. With the knowledge he had gleaned when crafting Obi's more perfect form and his subsequent experiments, he had been able to push the human form even further. His Burrowers were short and hunched over with backs bulging with corded muscle. Their arms were long and their hands dragged when they walked. Their hands were wide and their long fingers bore wide spade-shaped talons made of hard bone and braced with scar tissue. Bronze tips were embedded in their talons to break through the bedrock. After the creation of his Shadows and the stroke of genius that had been Obi's rebirth, the creation of the Burrowers was one of his proudest achievements.

The first Burrower had been definitive proof that man could be something greater than lowly creatures at the whim of greater powers. Obi had not been a fluke. Even simple men and women could be reshaped and perfected. With Talara's blessing, humanity could be so much more.

His legs ached and burned as he climbed the winding staircase up to the surface. The pain was not entirely unpleasant. Pain was proof of living. Pain was faith.

The light grew brighter as he rose higher up the stairs, and he wished he could stay belowground. *Once the sanctum is done most of my days will be spent below.* After seeing the progression of the sanctum, he was almost giddy. Like a child in the days preceding a festival, his excitement bubbled below the surface. *There is so much to do. Soon enough Talara's empire will take shape in earnest.*

Once they were aboveground, he made his back to his hut, making sure to dismiss his attendants at the edge of the village. Having a large Shadow at his back was great when walking about Noyo, but in Kalaro with his people, it made certain things difficult. It was hard for his people to speak with him candidly when a Shadow's blank, milky eyes were staring at them over Kunza's shoulder.

At the edge of the village, a mass of new mud brick-and-wattle huts stood, the rejuvenating lifeblood of Kalaro. On the way to his hut, Kunza could make out on the western edge of the village the huge adobe structure that his Shadows called home. When Kunza arrived at his hut, Ajatunde was outside, waiting for him. She bowed as he entered the wattle-fenced yard.

"How was Noyo?" Ajatunde asked. "Was our gift well-received?"

"There was resistance of course, but Azka seemed interested in what our Shadows can provide him." Kunza approached her and put a hand on her shoulder. "All looks well. You've done well in my stead."

"Thank you, Kunza. I am sure not everyone would agree with you, but your word is Talara's and I am honored to hear your praise."

Kunza smiled. "The Elders are fools. They wish only to glean the benefits of Talara's mercy without any of the commitment. But that will change very soon, one way or another." He gestured for her to follow him inside the hut, eager himself to be back within the simple comforts of his home.

His hut was mostly empty, the cauldrons and bloodletting tools that had taken up most of the hut's space now occupied Kalaro's central plaza.

The smell of burnt stinkweed had seeped into every surface, and its lingering fragrance was a welcome scent. He could feel Talara more clearly than he had in days. Unfelt tension in his muscles eased in her comforting presence. He lowered himself to the floor to sit cross-legged in front of Talara's shrine and sagged in relief. "I've been on my feet since dawn," he said. "And the stairs down to the inner temple are torturous on the legs."

Ajatunde sat beside him. "You should rest for a few days. Gods know you deserve it."

"Now is now the time for idleness. We're on the cusp of a new world. So much still must be done."

"And it will be done. But you cannot take all the burden upon yourself." She waited for him to reply, but he said nothing. She did not understand the breadth of the burden he bore. "How many nights did you spend working flesh and bone to make the Shadows? For weeks you sequestered yourself in this hut. Until you could barely stay upright. You cannot keep doing this. Your faithful are here to aid you. Please, let us bear some of your burden."

"Once the temple is built, there will be more than enough for all of you to do," Kunza said, watching the flickering of Talara's shrine. Ajatunde had kept it well-fed in his absence. "How many Shadows did I shape? One hundred for Azka. Two hundred here in Kalaro. That is nothing compared to what Talara requires. Our labors are only just begun." He looked at Ajatunde. "We have less time than Talara had predicted. The Stone Queen is dead. Toth is consumed by the Gray and its cancer is spreading eastward. If we hope to save our people then our work must be hastened."

Ajatunde was quiet for a moment, her mouth ajar but giving no voice to the thoughts racing through her mind. Then she nodded, composing herself. "I suppose that is all the more reason to share your burden," she said, her voice muted and somewhat strained. "In the coming days you will have too much to do to burden yourself with the minutiae."

"Perhaps you're right." Kunza smiled, his teeth as red as rubies. "I chose well, appointing you as Bearer of the Cup. You serve Talara well." He rose, his legs steady again. "When the sanctum is complete you will be the first to be baptized." He added a bundle of stinkweed to the fire and inhaled as the flames singed its edges. "If you wish, that is."

"There is nothing I wish for more."

Kunza let the smoke from the shrine tickle his nostrils and seep into his road-grimed skin. "Once we take this step there is no turning back. Right now we stand on the threshold of Talara's domain. Once we do this, we are hers. Wholly and absolutely."

"Decay is inexorable and inescapable. To become one with death is to become one with life. To become one with rot is to become immortal," Ajatunde said with solemn reverence. "Talara is my life. No matter what comes, I owe my life to her."

CHAPTER 15

Night sank into the mountains like a wave of frigid darkness seeping into the valley. The first two nights, Odessa had been able to get a few hours of sleep despite the distant shrieks of spirits on the wind. Their fire kept most of the spirits far enough away that they could not worm inside her mind, but still they screamed and cried with the voices of her father, mother, and sisters.

The third day, as day began to darken into a twilit dimness, Odessa led the goats along the steeply sloping cleft of a ridge leading into the foothills of the western slopes. Grass and shrubbery had gnawed at the path until there was almost nothing left but the occasional hoofprint of a wandering goat or llama.

Grassland stretched from the foot of the mountains, first bunched in steep ridges and hills and then leveling out into open plains reaching toward the distant horizon. Yakun led Odessa and the cart down the mountainside into a shallow valley dotted with acacias. They set up camp beneath a wizened acacia, snapping limbs off it to start the night's fire.

The goats, tied to the trunk of the acacia, grazed contentedly on the waist-high pampas grass as Odessa set about starting the fire. Striking the spine of her knife against a palm-sized piece of chert, she cast a small shower of sparks onto a pile of crumbled hoof fungus. The sparks glowed bright, singeing the dry fungus before blinking out like distant stars lost to the void. She struck the stone again and again, gently blowing to coax flames from the sparks before they were snuffed out.

She did not dare start a fire with her scorched arm. Removing the bandages would alert every nearby god and god-fearing being of her presence. Even baring her fingers could be enough to draw Talara's attention.

It took only a few minutes to get the tinder burning. Odessa fed the fledging flames twigs and bits of bark until they were large enough to climb up the scaffolding of branches and consume it. Watching the fire grow larger and brighter, she sat back amid prickly pampas grass. The thrumming vigor in her veins had died yesterday morning, and all that remained was a dull aching throughout her body. Her wounds were halfway healed, but she still suffered the occasional bright, stabbing pain when she moved too far in a certain direction.

Her body felt as if it was worn at the seams and that she could come apart at any moment. It was not the bone-deep exhaustion she had felt before. She was raw and ragged, but she was still moving. Still alive.

Yakun was making a perimeter around their campsite with stones bearing warding sigils. While he prepared the wards and charms that would keep them safe and hidden through the night, Odessa rose and took from the parked wagon enough salted peccary to keep them from starving and a small, mostly empty ewer of water. Their supply of water was draining faster than she would have thought and they had not even reached the desert.

There was little to talk about during their meager dinner. Poko prattled on about deadwood and woodpeckers for a short while before tapering off and leaving the party mired in silence yet again. Each of them ate quietly as night sank deeper and darkness thickened around them.

Odessa was done eating before the others. Her stomach could not bear too much food in one sitting. Poko leaned against her thigh, gnawing on a nut as she peered out into the growing darkness. Out of the mountains, there was a strange sensation in the air. A familiar feeling, recalling memories of the Night Jungle.

It was the feeling of being watched.

"Everything all right?" Yakun asked, still chewing on a mouthful of tough, hastily roasted meat.

"Will we be safe out of the mountains?" Her eyes scoured the valley steeped in inky night. All she could make out was the black silhouette of the mountains and foothills against the murky dark of the night sky.

Yakun swallowed. "If we stay to the foothills, we should be fine until we reach the Cleaving Road." His gaze followed hers into the night. "I don't quite fancy being in the open like this either. And I wish we didn't need such a large fire. But hiding in the foothills, we will be fine. My wards will hold strong during the night and by daybreak we'll be gone. Nothing will find us, divine or otherwise."

Odessa pulled her eyes free from the arresting grip of the unknown dark. "I believe you," she said to Yakun. "It just feels strange being out here. It's so vulnerable." She could still feel the chilling sensation of spirits clawing into her mind when she and Poko had escaped the Night Jungle. The terrible things those spirits had said as they burrowed into her head. Without her realizing it, a primal anxiety had settled in her gut and set her nerves ablaze with jittering nervous energy. Like a cornered rabbit, she sat blindly scanning her surroundings. Heart pounding against her ribs.

"It'll be fine," Poko said, wiping crumbs from their gossamer tunic. "If anything nasty comes our way, I'll know." With a finger, they tapped their nose. "I've a good sniffer for stuff like that."

"I wish you'd warned me about the other night," Yakun said with a thin smile. The bruises on his face had taken a sickly yellow hue, and the firelight accentuated the browning purple undertones still lingering at their centers.

"That's not my fault! The grove's too busy. Everything's fuzzy there. Out here, now that's where I shine. If a spirit even thinks about coming our way, I'll know it."

Odessa wanted to believe Poko. She wanted to believe both Poko and Yakun. But the chill buzz in the air would not allow her.

Not long after eating while Yakun and Poko slept, Odessa retrieved the sword from the cart. She paced quietly around the fire, careful not to disturb Yakun or Poko. In the dark, time wore on but Odessa was oblivious. She kept her watch on the dark swelling at the edge of the fire's light, feeding the fire when it began to shrink. Weariness pricked at her eyelids, looking for purchase to sink its hook into them.

Don't sleep, she told herself. *Can't sleep. Something's coming.* She paced, sword dangling in her grip. *There's something out there. I can feel it.*

Poko slept soundly, nestled in a folded blanket. The goats lay beside the acacia, their heads rested on one another. All was quiet in the valley. But Odessa could feel an ominous chill on the wind.

It started with the voices. Whispered pleas stretched into shrieks of torment. "Odessa!" they said, a chorus of stolen voices, quiet at first then dragging the last syllable out into a harsh, hair-raising scream. "Odessa! Odessa!"

Odessa backed up close to the fire as Yakun and Poko began to rouse from sleep. The goats bleated, shifting and pulling against their ropes.

The voices were closer and louder than they had been in the mountains. In the dark, Odessa could make out the shifting, mirage-like shapes of spirits careening through the air.

"Odessa!" her father's voice called above the rest. "Come out and take your punishment like a good girl!"

She took a handful of branches and tossed them on the fire. A plume of sparks rose, whirling in smoke.

"Pay them no mind," Yakun said to her over the cries of her family and friends. "They can't get through the wards."

Despite Yakun's assurances, she kept the sword raised at her waist and slowly circled the crackling fire. Spirits dove and spun through the air, shrieking and crying. Diving toward the edge of the fire's light in a flash of phantasmal hues and then disappearing back into the night like fish breaching the surface of a still pond. Their shimmering, translucent forms, when close enough to the firelight for her to make out, bore tortured faces. Weak facsimiles of those she knew and loved. Poorly constructed death masks to goad her from the safety of the fire and wards.

"Look at you," her mother hissed. "Running away like the petulant brat you are. Such a disappointment. You were always my least favorite child. You take too much after your selfish ass of a father."

The goats bleated louder, kicking and jumping in the air. One of the goats spun with its head down, its horns slashing through the air. A rotfiend's mucous form clung to the goat's hindleg as the goat bucked and spun.

Shit, Odessa cursed, running toward the panicking goats. The goat's leg jerked away as she neared, the rotfiend's needle-teeth raking into its flesh. Odessa grabbed the rotfiend. Her fingers sunk into its slimy body until they gripped something solid. She hauled the rotfiend from the goat's leg, hacking at its vine and tendrils until it finally came loose.

The goats were still frenzied, pulling against their ropes and bleating, as Odessa carried the writhing glob of moss and sludge toward the fire. Its tendrils wrapped around her fully extended arm and lashed at her face. When she was next to the fire, the rotfiend's thrashing became desperate. It squealed like sizzling fat when she plunged it into the flames, holding it against the embers as it screamed. The delicate hairs on its mossy exterior were immediately singed. Its slimy body blistered and popped. The stench of burning hair and rotten flesh filled her nostrils.

When the rotfiend stopped thrashing, she lifted its still-burning body and with a heave sent it sailing back into the pitch-black night it had come from.

Yakun had untied the goats from the acacia and dragged them toward the fire's glow. The goats dug their hooves into the dirt and jerked backward. Odessa shook the cinders and ash from her singed arm and helped Yakun drag the goats well within the campfire's light.

"It should not have gotten past the wards," Yakun shouted in her ear over the increasing din of spirits. "The wards are weaker than at the grove, but they're not that weak."

They fear Talara more than they fear the sting of the wards. A sick feeling stirred in her stomach. *How long before the spirits start getting through? Before they start getting in my head?*

"Stay by the fire," she said to Yakun. "Stay as close to the fire as you can." She noticed Poko poking his head out from the pouch at Yakun's waist. There was worry in their eyes. Not worry for themself but worry for her.

She pointed to Poko and said to Yakun, "And keep them safe. Don't let anything happen to them."

Before Yakun or Poko could reply, Odessa was gone, barreling into the dark past the fire's edge. *As long as they're by the fire, they'll be okay. These spirits only want me.*

Before she'd even left the warmth of the fire's glow, the spirits descended upon her in a swarm of screaming faces.

They can have me.

The sword cleaved through a swathe of spirits, the bronze blade glinting in the firelight as it split through ghostly faces like thick fog. A dozen grave-cold talons dug into the soft meat of her brain, dragging sharp claws across the delicate flesh. A dozen voices echoed in her mind.

"I never loved you," her mother spat. The words reverberated through her skull, becoming more real the further it seeped into her mind. "I despised you the moment you dropped out of me."

Odessa bit the inside of her cheek and swung the sword again. Any spirit she cut reformed a moment later and continued assailing her. More spirits came from the dark to swarm around her like hornets. So she swung the sword faster. Cleaving spirits in half again before they could reform. She bit her cheek until she had sheared off a wide scrap of flesh.

Keep going, she told herself over the incomprehensible din in her mind. *Keep going. Keep swinging until there's nothing left!* Internally she screamed, trying to keep her sense of self intact. The spirits pulled at her mind, ripping and tearing at her. Shredding her very being. But she would not let them break her. They could scratch and claw, but they could not take away who she was.

"I am Odessa Kusa," she growled through gritted teeth turned red from her bleeding cheek. Her sword arm came alive, moving faster until the blade was a blur. "I am my father's daughter. Egende's blood runs through my veins. And no wretched little ghosts are going to drive me mad. I'll drive you mad. I'll make you wish you'd never crossed paths with me. I'll have you praying to Talara for mercy from me."

The spirits only burrowed deeper into her mind, clawing their way in like rats. The screaming grew louder. More frenzied and hateful.

"You abandoned me!" Ayana shrieked. "You left me with the ka-man and now I'm a mask-wearing monster. All because you left me behind!"

Images flashed in Odessa's mind. Her sword arm hitched, hesitating for a moment and allowing more spirits to swarm her.

She was outside the grove again. Peeling the mask from the dead figure's crushed face to find Ayana, her sweet face a bloody pulp. Her face was a mess of blood and bone and meat. Her lips were split open. Teeth broken or missing. Her nose was smashed flat, the skin ruptured where cartilage met bone. But her eyes were unmarred. Cloudy and lifeless, they held an ocean's worth of sadness and betrayal.

In her mind, Odessa watched as Ayana's shredded lips twitched. They began to move. Trying to form words.

Odessa swallowed hard, watching helplessly as she cocked back her fist, her bloody, godsforsaken fist, and sent it hurtling into her little sister's face.

Her fist closed one of Ayana's eyes, turning it into a bloody crater. Her other fist came down, knocking her jaw askew. Her fists continued pummeling Ayana's face again and again.

Despite the bloody gurgling coming from the broken pulp that had been her mouth, Ayana spoke clearly in a high-pitched wail. "You and Papa left me. You could have saved me but you didn't. You didn't just kill me. You left me to something worse than death. You left me and Mama with the ka-man and let him cut us open and turn us into monsters. And for what? So you could live with some old pervert in the woods?"

Odessa found herself leaning into the punches. The more Ayana talked the further Odessa would go to make her stop. Her fists made wet thuds against Ayana's shattered skull, drops of blood and bits of brain splattered Odessa's face.

"Running away won't change what you did. No matter where you go, I'll still be here. Still dead because of you."

Tears ran through the viscera splattered across Odessa's face.

"This is all your fault and you don't even have the decency to take responsibility for what you did. You're the worst sister ever and I hope you die. I hope you die screaming." Ayana's wail turned to an inhuman screeching. "I hate you. I hate you. I hate you! I hate you! I hate you!"

When the sun's rays spread over the mountains and the spirits dissipated like morning dew, Odessa was screaming. Her voice was hoarse and her throat raw.

"I hate you," she croaked as the last of the spirits slipped from her, a shimmer in the air before it disappeared. As she regained herself, her legs gave way and she tumbled to the rocky dirt.

In the shadow of the mountain, caught in predawn dimness, Odessa's mind reeled. She laid her forehead against the dirt, scrabbling for disparate thoughts, piecing together where she was and who she was. Parsing through the lies the spirits had left embedded in her mind. The false memories that had been seared into her brain.

Ayana wasn't there. She's home. I didn't do any of that. I would never do that. But her knuckles ached with the impact of so many punches. It felt as real as any pain she had felt before.

Strewn about her were the parts of multiple rotfiends, stomped and slashed apart. The night was a remote memory, but vaguely she recalled her body moving nearly autonomously, hacking apart spirits and rotfiends as her mind was torn asunder.

Odessa rolled onto her side. Sharp-edged grasses scratched her and rocks stabbed at her aching body. The sword was still clutched in her bandaged hand. A slurry of blood and mucus from the dead rotfiends dotted her arms and legs. The wound in her side had broken open and welled with blood. Her limbs throbbed as if they'd been ground down to marrow. Her entire body had become much too heavy to move. Her eyelids closed without her realizing and she slept, too exhausted to even dream.

CHAPTER 16

Poko sat atop the cart as it bounced and rattled along the base of the mountains. Odessa was nestled in a blanket beside them, sleeping like a corpse. Every once in a while, Poko had to check that she was still breathing, just to reassure themself.

During the night, the foolish girl had run far into the valley, and when the old man found her, it had taken him more than an hour to drag Odessa back to the cart. To fit her in the back of the cart Yakun had to leave a fair few bundles of rune sticks and earthen jars of oil with the buried remains of their campfire, but he did it willingly enough. Odessa was clearly in no condition to travel, but they had to move on.

Neither Yakun nor Poko had gotten much sleep during the night. The spirits and rotfiends had, for the most part, given up trying to overwhelm the wards once Odessa left the safety of the fire, but some spirits had lingered, diving from the pitch black above whenever Yakun ventured too close to the edge of the fire's reach. Holding onto the goats so they did not run, Yakun had still tried to get Odessa to return. Calling her name until his voice was hoarse.

Leading the goats up the slight ridge of the mountain's outer roots, Yakun walked like a man half-asleep. The goat that had been attacked by the rotfiend limped on its back leg. A shallow crater was hidden beneath its long hair where the rotfiend's many teeth had dug into its leg and the rotfiend's acidic slobber had gnawed at its skin. The medicinal scent of one of Yakun's salves smeared onto the goat's hind leg tickled Poko's nose.

As the cart crested the top of the ridge, Poko could make out over the rolling hills to the west a flat plane of dull brown and yellow. Seeing such wide-open spaces still struck Poko with a tingling prod of anxiety. The world was so much larger than they ever could have imagined. The jungle had been all they had known. Gods and such grandiose things had never mattered much to Poko and the rest of the Court. Although Odessa said the god Azka owned the Night Jungle, for Poko, it had always been a joyously godless place. Now that Poko was far from home and they could see how much the humans feared the gods, Poko felt truly small. A fairy without wings was nothing in such a vast world.

As the cart crested the ridge and tilted to descend, Odessa's sleeping form shifted in her blankets. Poko could never save her if she went tumbling over the side of the cart, but they put a tiny hand on her anyway.

Beneath the blankets, her chest rose and fell so subtly. Breath whistled through her nose so quietly Poko's keen ears could only hear it over the cart's rattling wheels if their ear was practically pressed against her nose.

Her sleeping face had an almost beatific calm to it. The stress and pains she bore had melted away. *What could you have done that deserves this?* Poko wondered. She had killed a god, but to Poko it seemed if a god was able to be killed by lowly little humans then it wasn't much of a god at all. So why was she to suffer so much?

The cart jounced over a half-buried stone as it straightened out at the bottom of the ridge. Odessa's brow furrowed for a moment, a sudden wince. Even in unconsciousness, her pain reached her. *I've seen you like this too many times,* they wanted to say to her. *And I'm afraid that one of these times, you just won't wake up.*

Poko wasn't sure what to call the feeling they had for the girl. The fairies of the Night Jungle had been bound by necessity and tribalism. Fairies were born from earth, morning dew, and the rustling of a gentle breeze. There was no familial bond between fairies. There was only the bond of mutual survival and camaraderie. The fellowship of those who danced, wrestled, and tricked together for many, many years. But when food became scarce, that camaraderie was the first to be cannibalized.

With Odessa there was something else. Whether it was pity or obligation or a mixture of the two, they could not be sure. But Poko felt something for the girl. That much they were sure of.

As Odessa slept, Poko combed the tangles from her hair and continued to check that she was still breathing. It was nearly dark by the time she woke up.

The foothills directly below the mountain had become too steep and treacherous for the cart, so Yakun had led them over a rise and closer to the open expanse of Azka's plains. He had stopped the cart just outside a small copse of trees at the foot of a loping ridge hours before the sun was to set. He was roasting mushrooms and salted peccary over the fire when Odessa first began to rouse.

It was a mumbled murmur. Barely a sound. But Poko was there to hear it. "I'm sorry."

She began tossing and turning, her eyes fluttering beneath her eyelids. More murmurs came. More mumbled apologies.

Poko scrambled to her side to console her, but as soon as their hands touched her face her eyes snapped open and she recoiled. Poko took a tentative step back as she blinked, bleary-eyed and confused.

"What's happening?" she asked, her voice husky and dry.

"You were just having a bad dream," Poko said.

Odessa's eyes drifted from Poko to the trees behind them. "Where are we?" She glanced at the darkening sky. "What time is it?"

Poko hesitated, not wanting to tell her that the horrors of the night were fast approaching again. But they had to. "It's almost nighttime. Yakun built a bigger fire and put more magic rocks around us, though, so we'll be all right."

Odessa shook her head. She struggled beneath the blankets wrapped around her until she was free. "It won't be enough to stop them."

"You don't know that!" Poko said as she hoisted herself up using the cart's side panel.

She didn't say anything in response. Clumsily, she hauled herself over the side of the cart and landed on buckling legs. Her limbs were still leaden with sleep. Yakun had risen to try to steady her, but she waved him away.

"Where's the sword?" she asked him, her voice flat and brittle like a dead leaf.

"Odessa, my dear, you have to rest," Yakun said. "Sit by the fire. Eat something, please."

"Where's the sword?" she repeated. Her words had an edge to them.

"Just sit down," Yakun said, soft but firm.

"I have to get away from here," she said. "I can't be here when night comes. Now where is the godsdamned sword?"

"Dessa, stop it!" Poko shouted as they climbed the side of the cart after her. "You can't do this! You're going to get yourself killed!"

Odessa whirled around to face the fairy and, for the first time in a long time, Poko was scared of her. Only for a moment they recoiled as she took a step toward them. "Do you want them to kill you too? Because as long as I'm here, they will! They'll get inside your head and tear you apart. I won't let that happen!" She charged to the cart, pulled aside the blanket, and rifled through odds and ends until she found the sword.

Yakun sighed and came beside her as she took her bow and quiver from the back of the cart as well. With some effort he climbed onto the hub of the cart's wheel, leaned over the side panel, and dug into a half-empty basket. "At least eat something before you go. You can't fight on an empty stomach."

"She shouldn't be fighting at all!" Poko interjected. "How can you just roll over like that? She's been passed out all day. She's in no condition to do anything. This is reckless and stupid!"

From the basket Yakun took a handful of stones and a knotted length of thin hemp cord. "She's right, little fairy. We stand no chance against those denizens of the night when they come in force as they did last night." He turned to Odessa, who had stalked away from the cart, and held out his handful of warding stones. "Have a fire burning all night and set these in a circle about double your height across. That should keep the worst of the night from getting to you."

She hesitated, then reached out and took the stone. He held onto one stone and looped the cord around it in a rough pendant knot. "Put this around your neck." He held the stone and rope out to her. Dangling from the rope, the stone spun, showing first a crude etching daubed with red and then on the opposite an eye of lapis lazuli. "It should keep the spirits somewhat at bay."

Poko stomped their feet like a petulant child. It was all they could do to keep from screaming. "You can't be serious!"

Odessa cast them a glance. Her eyes lacked the bright spark of vitality they usually held. That spark had been replaced with a worn, jaded dullness. She was tired and broken on the inside. It was so apparent to Poko, it appalled them that Yakun could be so oblivious. "I'm not a child, Poko," Odessa said as she tied the warding stone around her neck.

Muddled waves of emotion rippled from Odessa, strong enough for Poko to sense. Fear, guilt, doubt, and rage all mingled together. Her mind was in turmoil. Whatever happened last night had broken something inside her. Poko was on the verge of tears themself. "I'm going with you," they said with conviction.

"No, you're not," Odessa said flatly. She turned her back to Poko and walked to the fire. The pot with the mushrooms and peccary lay in the ashy coals at the edge of the fire. She reached into the pot, plucked out a hunk of sizzling pork, and ate it.

Poko hopped down onto the rim of the cartwheel. "I'm no child either," they said, their voice rising with indignation. "I'm coming and that's final."

"You're not coming. I'm not letting anyone else get hurt or killed or worse because of me. And *that's* final." Sword in hand, Odessa stalked away without another word. Poko did not try to follow her. They only watched her walk away, following her with their gaze until she disappeared into the woods.

As night seeped into the sky, a fire bloomed far on the other end of the ridge. Yakun and the goats fell asleep not long after night fell in earnest. The spirits did not bother them that night. But Poko could not sleep. They instead stared at the fire in the distance and hoped with all their heart that Odessa was all right.

CHAPTER 17

Kunza's time at home had yet again come to an end. He had done so much to ensure the safety of his village and his people, yet he could not enjoy the fruits of his labor. His work in Noyo required his full attention. Garnering the full support of Azka and his sons was paramount. Noyo was the key to the greater world. The foundation of what would become Talara's empire in the world that would remain after the Gray. As of now, Kunza and Kalaro were a mercenary and novel indulgence, but if he could ingratiate himself further there was no telling how high he could climb. He had already ascended to heights unheard of for a mere man. But he had shed the pretenses of a common man. His aim went far beyond Noyo. His aim was Talara's, and the goddess sought immortality. True immortality. Total freedom from the looming hand of death.

The night before he was to leave Kalaro, Kunza left his hut. The night air embraced him, cool and gentle against his skin. The vulture feathers of his cape rustled in the breeze like a hundred voices whispering on the wind. He followed the path to the plaza. The fire in the center of the plaza was small and placid as two of his younger disciples tossed offerings into the flames. A portion of their dinner went into the fire. Spirits danced in the thick smoke above the plaza.

A faint light glowed in the open windows of the Elders' lodge. He had been worried the Elders would have gone to sleep already, as stubbornly bound to the sun as they were. With Talara's blessing, most of Kalaro required less sleep than they had before, but the Elders and their obstinance kept them clinging to the sun's rise and fall.

Kunza rapped on the thatch door before he opened it. The Elders continued to view him as an equal, so to avoid unnecessary dissension he still abided by certain courtesies.

The front room of the Elders' lodge was small and suffocatingly cozy. The floor and walls were covered in thick, brightly colored rugs. A roaring fire burned in the bulb-shaped fireplace built into the back wall.

"Ah, Kunza," Elder Cuchal said, surprised. Awkwardly, he rose in a hurry from his mat in front of the fire. "I was not expecting you so late."

"It is not late at all for me," Kunza said, trying to inflect a bit of humor in his flat tone.

"No, no, of course not." He wiped dust and ash from his kaftan. "Would you like some matte?"

"I've come to see the Kusas," Kunza said.

"Yes, of course." Elder Cuchal nodded and gestured to the arched doorway to the left of the fireplace. "They're in their room."

Before Elder Cuchal could say more, Kunza made his way into the short hallway. He rapped his knuckles against the single door on the left side of the hallway. The rushes that made up the thin door rustled. "Excuse me," Kunza said. "May I come in?"

Elder Kusa opened the door. "Kunza," she said, bowing deeply before letting him into the small room. "It is always an honor."

Mutumi and Ayana, who had been sitting on the floor before he arrived, rose and bowed as well. Both of them kept their eyes averted as he entered.

"May I sit?" he asked Mutumi, gesturing to mats on the floor.

"Of course," Mutumi said, still not raising her eyes. "Please, sit if you would like. May I offer you some matte?"

"No, thank you," Kunza said. He lowered himself to the mat. The small room was crowded with four bodies in it. Nearly half the floor was taken up by the bed of rushes the three Kusas slept on. He gestured for Mutumi and Ayana to sit as well. Elder Kusa stood near the door, forgotten.

"How have you two been feeling?" Kunza asked Mutumi and Ayana.

Mutumi sat across from Kunza, folding her legs beneath herself and smoothing her kaftan across her knees. "We are very well. With Talara's blessing, we are better than we ever have been." Her eyes met his, and he could see the dark bags beneath them. They were bloodshot and dull. "Thank you for asking."

"Talara is good," Kunza said with a smile. Mutumi's gaze fell to her hands, clasped in her lap to still the slight tremble she thought he did not notice. Guilt haunted her. Kunza's mere presence summoned that guilt in full force. He pitied her. She had done the right thing, but still she could not find the strength to forgive herself for doing what had to be done. There was little he could do to mend what was broken inside her. Her body had taken to the blood, but her mind and soul could hardly bear the strain.

Ayana still had not lifted her gaze. Her skin was wonderfully ashen and her downcast eyes were bright. Youth often took to Talara's blood readily, but Ayana more so than any other.

"Ayana," he said softly, coaxing her attention from the floor. "How have you been enjoying your lessons?"

Her eyes rose but did not meet his gaze. "They're good," she said quietly. "I'm learning a lot."

"That's very good," he said. "Very good. You must learn all you can while you're young. Everything gets harder when you're old like me."

A small smile brightened Ayana's face. As forced as the smile was, Kunza was glad to see it. During most of his visits to the Kusa household, which had been quite infrequent as of late, Ayana would rarely say a word, let alone smile.

"Do you feel a connection with the goddess yet?"

Ayana nodded.

"What does it feel like?"

"Sometimes," Ayana started, then paused. Her voice was barely above a whisper. "Sometimes I feel like I can hear her. I can hear her whispering in the back of my head."

Kunza smiled. He leaned forward a bit, barely able to contain his excitement. "What does she say?"

"I can't hear the words. I just know it's her."

Tears filled Mutumi's eyes. The trembling of her hands worsened. Ayana reached over and held her mother's hands, steadying them. They both knew what this meant.

"This is wonderful," Kunza said. "I knew my faith was not misplaced. You are the Kusa family's redemption, Ayana. You should be very happy." He smiled. "Keep working hard and, when I return from Noyo, you will finally meet our goddess."

A choked sob escaped Mutumi's mouth. Elder Kusa came beside her and held her shoulders as she cried. Kunza watched silently as Ayana and the Elder Kusa consoled her.

She loses another daughter, but Talara will be kind to Ayana.

In the morning, the whole of Kalaro came to the plaza for their daily lamentations for the departed Kutali. Kunza stood in front of the plaza's fire, leading the lamentation.

Immediately after, Kunza departed. It took three days for him and his retinue to reach the outskirts of Noyo. They spent the night in the house of a farmer, Azedola, a woman of remarkable faith.

When night came in earnest, Kunza left the warmth of the farmer's cozy hut. The road leading north to Noyo stretched out into the darkness. Fields of stunted sorghum lay behind the hut, and a long path leading to the road divided two small paddocks. Between the paddocks, a few hens roosted in a wattle coop next to a squat silo. Kunza stalked through the dark to the far side of the mud-brick silo; he found his Shadow hidden in its shade.

"What have you learned?" Kunza whispered.

"Construction struggles. Sickness runs through work camps," the Shadow said.

"What of Ur-Mak? Who has he spoken to? What has he said?"

"Ur-Mak met with godlings. Godlings threaten to have him hauling stone if work does not hasten." The end of the Shadow's last sentence sounded like the words ripped its throat as they came out.

"Did he say anything to the godlings?"

"He apologized. Said work will improve once sickness passes and new workers come from the north."

New workers will only bring new sickness. Especially workers from the north where Toth's foul winds blow. Kunza nodded. *This could be quite advantageous.* "Who else has he spoken to since I've been away?"

"He complains to other giants."

"Complains about what exactly?"

"Azka and his godlings," the Shadow said, its words growing quieter and more ragged. "He says they are unrealistic and they care nothing for his people. He speaks brashly."

"Yes, those are bold accusations, indeed," Kunza said, his mind following a dozen threads of thought. A plan emerged from disparate threads. "You've done well. Very well."

The wind howled through the stunted fields.

"Go to Ur-Mak now," Kunza said. "Tell him I wish to meet tomorrow night. On the parapet. There are a number of things I would like to talk about."

The Shadow nodded and left, seemingly melting into the darkness. Kunza stood by the silo for a few moments, enjoying the soft embrace of night. He breathed in the dark and the silence. Night was a chance for others to rest and to dream. But for Kunza, night was when his goddess was the closest. When the sky darkened and died, awaiting the morning's rebirth, that was when Kunza was most at peace.

CHAPTER 18

Noyo was abuzz with its usual bustle and bedlam, but the nearer Kunza came to the palace, the more intense the furor became. The envoy from Asha-Kalir was set to arrive at any moment with Khymanir's reply. The main thoroughfare was lined with bright banners, and streamers of gold hung above the road, thin strips of cloth twirling in the wind. Merchants and peddlers mingled with those who came to watch the procession. It had been a while since an official envoy from Asha-Kalir had come to Noyo. The flow of caravans from Asha-Kalir had grown infrequent. Those working in the fields even craned their necks to catch a glimpse of the envoy's procession despite the crack of a whip that would surely follow.

Azka's freemen and giants lined the road leading to the palace's steps. His Chosen stood in the palace's front plaza.

Kunza took his place at the end of the stairs alongside Azka's Chosen. The Chosen stared at him and curled their lips, but they could do nothing. He had earned his place.

It was not long before the peal of horns rose in the distance and another horn joined the chorus, this one closer than the last. This continued until the streets leading to the plaza were filled with the blast of trumpeting horns. Bells rang as the procession approached the gates.

As the procession made its way down the thoroughfare, escorted by Azka's soldiers to keep the crush of onlookers at bay, Kunza smoothed his feathered cape and straightened the crow feathers atop his head.

Down the thoroughfare he could make out more than a dozen of their beasts of burden, the bazaks. Large fleshy beasts with a dense coat of silvery, amber-white hair that shone as they approached even in the overcast dullness. Their bodies were barrel-shaped with a sloping back segmented by rolls of fat. Like a massive, hairy slug held upright by six gangly legs lifting the beast to nearly a man's height. Its head was a lump of fleshy rolls. A protruding forehead angled down kept its puckering mouth with its flat, grinding teeth parallel to the ground.

At the head of the procession of bazaks walked Khymanir's envoy, a figure with the head of a hornbill dressed in a crimson and gold kaftan. The bird-man's head bobbed ever so slightly as it walked, its steps fluid and somehow delicate as it entered the plaza.

The line of bazaks and humans filed into the plaza and stopped as the bird-man approached Azka's Chosen and bowed before them. "I am Bukoris," he said, his voice high and warbling. "My eminence, Khymanir, the King of Bones, extends his kind regards to your sovereign, Azka of the Eastern Wind."

"Welcome," Tialta said. "If you would please follow me, our sovereign awaits an audience."

"Please," Bukoris said, bowing again. "Lead on."

Tialta led Bukoris up the wide stairs. A pair of Azka's Chosen flanked him while the rest followed behind. Kunza trailed behind them all.

"Greetings, Azka of the Eastern Wind," the bird-man said, prostrating himself before Azka and his godlings. He rose and brushed the dust from his kaftan. "I, Bukoris, come in peace under the auspices of my eminence, Khymanir, the Exalted Hand of Aséshassa and King of Bones. My eminence extends their regards to you and yours."

"Welcome, Bukoris. Noyo accepts you and yours with great hospitality," Azka said, his voice loud and booming through the streets. "I wish your eminence many years of splendor and peace and I extend Noyo's kindest regards to them and theirs." Azka closed his eyes slowly and bowed his head a touch, as much as was allowed a great god. Too much humility was weakness.

Bukoris bowed in return. "To thank you for your hospitality, my eminence has sent many gifts."

"How very kind." Azka said. "What else has your eminence sent with you? What say he to our proposal?"

Bukoris straightened, his long neck extending higher. "My eminence respectfully asks what benefit would this arrangement present Asha-Kalir? It is of my eminence's mind that they stand to lose a good number of slaves and the valuable expertise of numerous soulweavers. My eminence does not have the time nor resources to devote to such impractical endeavors. Asha-Kalir will continue to stand after the Gray has passed without the use of your so-called Shadows." Bukoris shifted on their bird feet. "That is not to say that we will not continue to supply Noyo with the slaves necessary to build young Kutali's tomb, but my eminence will not spare any more slaves for Talara's purposes. Aséshassa is the guide by which Asha-Kalir will prosper and flourish."

Azka's lip twitched but his eyes remained impassive. "Are the High Gods not in league with one another? Your eminence makes it sound as if Talara's and Aséshassa's purposes do not align."

"There are differences in their means that Asha-Kalir cannot condone. To attempt to perfect the human form to weather the Gray is a waste of time and resources and also an affront to the divine. Humans are tools for the exultation of the gods. To think humanity can be elevated beyond that is ludicrous blasphemy." Bukoris's eyes flashed to Kunza for a moment. Cold, spiteful eyes.

"Humanity will always serve to venerate and bow to the divine. To perfect the human form is to perfect how they may serve us," Azka said. "Did your eminence not allow humans to work his magics? That is no different than what we propose."

Bukoris blinked blandly. "Your justifications make no difference. My eminence cannot agree to your terms."

"I understand," Azka said. "Devils wreak havoc along your borders every day. Sak-Tor gnaws upon the fringes of Asha-Kalir like a cancer. I am sure your eminence cannot spare a soul at the moment."

"Devils have never been a threat to my eminence and his domain and they never will be," Bukoris said sharply. "They are gnats on a bazak's ass. They are nothing but a nuisance, easily quashed and forgotten."

"If I may," Kunza said. The Chosen and Bukoris glared at him as he took a step forward. "Perhaps if you have a provisional force of, maybe, one hundred Shadows to join your eminence's formidable Red Clay Warriors in ridding Asha-Kalir of the devils, then your eminence could see firsthand the utility of our Shadows. As a lowly human, I believe there is much to be gained in perfecting the imperfect human form. There is much for both Noyo and Asha-Kalir to learn from one another if they work together. I may be bold in saying this, but I foresee this confederation standing the test of time. Talara and Aséshassa will lead us from perdition together."

Bukoris looked at Azka. "Does this man speak for you?"

Azka glanced at Kunza, then back at Bukoris. "Yes. Yes he does," Azka said. "Tell your eminence Noyo will pledge one hundred Shadows to fight the devils. Each Shadow is the equal of ten devils and will root them out and send them scurrying back into the mountains."

"If my eminence's warriors have not been able to slaughter these devils, what makes you think your twisted humans will fare better?"

At Kunza's signal, twenty Shadows slid down from the arched ceiling or from behind colorful columns to line up on either side of the hall. Bukoris spun to face them. "Shadows can go where warriors cannot. They are silent and furtive and, most of all, ruthless. If you would like, you may take these twenty back to your eminence as a gift. Loose them on the devils and the Darrood will run red with devil blood."

It was dark when Kunza reached the city walls. Negotiations with Bukoris and what soulweavers he brought had lasted far longer than he had anticipated. When he reached the top of the stairs he saw Ur-Mak was alone on the parapet, leaning against an embrasure, his ring-laden hands folded over one another.

"Grand Mason," Kunza said. "It's good to see you."

"Kunza," Ur-Mak said, rising to his full height as Kunza came to stand beside him. "Your Shadows are deserving of their name. I scarcely noticed it in my bedchamber until it spoke."

"I apologize," Kunza said.

"You could have sent a letter, you know?" Ur-Mak's gold teeth glinted as he smirked.

"I believe in discretion," Kunza said.

"One can never be totally discrete in this city," Ur-Mak said. "There are eyes and ears everywhere."

"If one has to gouge a few eyes and pierce a few ears in the name of discretion, then so be it." Kunza looked out into the darkness. "May I ask you a question, Grand Mason?"

Ur-Mak glanced at Kunza. "As you please."

The fires of the distant worksite guttered as a cold breeze blew over the dark plains. "Do you believe all gods to be equal?"

"Of course not."

"Of course not," Kunza repeated. The night air was sweet and pure. "Our High Gods reign supreme, and even among our Low Gods there are some that stand lower than others. That is just the nature of the world. It is right and good."

"It's funny how truths from the lips of a man can sound like terrible blasphemies." Ur-Mak's smile remained, but there was wariness in his squinting eyes.

"Your Stone Queen is dead. Sak-Tor threatens Asha-Kalir. The days of peace in the world of the divine are gone. Whatever tenuous calm held their weapons at bay is broken. Ripples of discord spread, growing ever larger. In the coming days, I am afraid we will see which gods are truly peerless. But I ask you, Grand Mason," Kunza said, turning to pierce Ur-Mak with scorching eyes. "How are mortals to survive when gods wage war?"

"You speak as if there has not been war since the Age of Divine Blood. Mortals always die in the gods' wars. That is why we exist. To be proxies in their squabbling."

"The Gray mists and the beasts that they birth took your Stone Queen and they will continue to take life until there is not a soul left alive," Kunza said. "And there is only one goddess who can ensure the survival of our peoples."

"I take it you are not speaking of our peerless sovereign?" Ur-Mak said, a smirk hidden within a coy scowl.

"No," Kunza said. "No I am not."

Ur-Mak smiled. "You speak such sweet sacrilege."

"There is only one goddess I will not profane. One goddess who has my heart and my soul, totally and utterly."

"I don't think I have ever heard such brazen blasphemy. And we were just speaking of this city's eyes and ears. What if I went and told Azka what you just said?"

"You won't. Because I know you have your own issues with Azka."

"I take some umbrage with most everyone I meet," Ur-Mak said. "That does not mean I am impious. A god is a god, no matter what offenses I may suffer."

"But as we've established," Kunza said, looking back out at the plains. "Not all gods are equal. And in the days to come, only the strong and the cunning will survive. Mortal and divine alike, the Gray and its bastard spawn will take indiscriminately."

Ur-Mak leaned against the embrasure again. "If what you say is to come to pass, then what chance do we lowly servants have to survive this looming catastrophe?"

"Talara," Kunza said. "Talara is all we need."

CHAPTER 19

By the time the paved road to the Severed Gorge came into view, Odessa could barely discern what was real and what was some spirit's forgery. She had spent the past four nights fighting until sunrise as spirits screamed and cried in her head. She tried putting candlewax in her ears, but the screams still resonated in her skull. There was no escaping them.

As the cart turned east onto the road, bouncing and jostling its load, Odessa lay motionless, unable to sleep yet too exhausted to move. Her family hid behind her eyelids, their faces twisted in agony, sometimes stripped of skin and flesh, sometimes only bloodied. Sometimes they were charred to the bone and still screaming. Most of the time her father spoke through his cut throat in a bloody, gurgling rasp.

Her eyes were half-open, and she stared blankly at the cart's side panel as it shook in time with the clatter of wheels against stone. The light filtering through the soft gray above stung her dry, tired eyes. Her mind was raw and every idle thought that came to her brought a sharp, grating pain along with it.

The cart rolled along the empty road for an indeterminate amount of time. Odessa did not register time in minutes or hours. Life had become delineated between night and day. Night was torture, but she hated day for its false reprieve. The dread she felt for the night made her days unbearable. How could she rest when another night of horrors awaited her? How could she possibly sleep when the terrors of the night waited behind her eyelids?

Quite a bit of daylight remained when they came to the adobe walls surrounding the caravansary. Mountains loomed high over either side of the road behind the gate. The last safe respite before entering the Severed Gorge.

The cart halted suddenly, jarring Odessa from the depths of her stupor. Poko had climbed higher up the blanket-covered mound, their gaze forward. With a weary sigh, Odessa followed suit, hauling herself up to peer over the front of the cart.

A woman in a quilted cotton tunic and a leather helmet worn low over her eyes approached Yakun, a spear held across her waist. A cyclops in hard leathers followed her. "What is in the cart?" she asked.

"Everything I have," Yakun said. "I lost all else. Now I head to Asha-Kalir to ply my trade there."

"And what is it you do?" the woman asked, eyeing the cart behind him. Her eyes met Odessa's. Odessa did not so much as blink.

"I'm a ka-man," Yakun said. "I deal in salves and poultices mostly. Sometimes prayers when things don't look good." The lies rolled from his tongue so easily Odessa almost believed them.

"I don't believe I've seen a ka-man with such pale skin," the woman said. "I thought you northerners to be a godless people."

"Not at all," Kunza said with an amiable smile. "Only those wretches in the ice fields are godless Forsaken."

The woman nodded, still eyeing the cart. "You travel with a pixie?" the woman asked, gesturing with her chin at Poko.

"The poor thing can't fly. I couldn't leave it. I've adopted it, you could say."

The woman nodded slowly, her eyes dragged from the cart. "If you wish to pass through the gates, I will need to search the cart."

"By all means," Yakun said. "You will find little more than salves and trinkets."

Odessa's hand slipped to the knife on her belt as the woman approached. She watched the woman's hands. The spear held loose in them. The spear was longer than the woman was tall, and its head was a wide leaf of bronze. Odessa's fingers tightened on the knife's handle. Her raw nerves exploded in bursts of anxious energy like sparks.

The woman walked around the cart, her cyclops companion standing by Yakun, making the old man look tiny and frail in comparison. The woman lifted the blanket and inspected a few baskets, but her eyes, half-hidden beneath the helmet and furrowed brows, kept drifting back to Odessa.

When the woman had done a full revolution around the cart, she stopped and tilted her head at Odessa. "Girl," she said gruffly. "What is your name?"

Her eyes fell from the woman's gaze. Her hands stayed affixed to the knife. "Odessa," she said quietly.

"Do you have a family name?"

Odessa shook her head. She had lost the right to call herself a Kusa the day godsblood tainted her body.

"Where are you from?" the woman asked.

"Noyo," Odessa said, trying to remember all that Yakun had told her when she had first begun venturing out of the grove. Trying to conjure up the lies he had given her to repeat. "Originally, that is."

The woman surveyed her a moment longer, then turned her attention to Yakun. "Did you adopt this one too?"

Yakun shrugged. "What can I say? I am a soft-hearted old man. All creatures living are loved by Matara and so too should I love all creatures, big or small."

"The pass and the desert beyond it is no place for the soft," the woman said. "Devils have been slaughtering whole caravans. You would be wise to find another place in need of healing."

"Oh dear," Yakun said, tapping a finger against his chin. "I did not know things had gotten that dire. Perhaps you're right."

The woman glanced at Odessa with sharp, narrow eyes, then looked back at Yakun. "You're welcome to stay here while you think on your future. With the devils strangling traffic on the other side of the pass, we have plenty of rooms."

"Ah, thank you," Yakun said as the woman approached him again. She took his name as she had taken Odessa's, and he gave her a fake one. Atli-ka. The two spoke of an entry fee and daily lodging rates, and after a short talk, he gave her a few copper coins from a pouch on his belt and she and the cyclops went to open the gates.

Yakun led the goats into the long, spacious courtyard. Opposite the entrance gate was another identical gate set within the walls. The whole of the caravansary wrapped around the courtyard with many empty stalls for animals lining the interior walls. A few stalls held strange, fleshy beasts or the occasional draft goat. There was a paltry group of market stalls around the periphery of the courtyard. Yakun led the goats into an empty stall in the corner of the stables, unhitched them from the cart, and then led them into another adjoining stall to keep them from eating the cart's blanket or anything within it.

While Yakun tended to the goats, Odessa crawled out from the cart's bed and rolled over the side panel. She held onto the cart as her legs buckled upon touching the ground. Her legs were numb and an electric prickling ran up and down them. After a moment she let go of the cart.

"That lady really was staring you down," Poko said.

Odessa rummaged in the cart for the sword. She had been lying on it. "She could tell what I am." She wrapped the sword and her bow in a blanket. "She could feel it probably. Feel something wrong."

"Or she was just jealous," Poko said. "'Cause you're young and pretty and she's all old and shriveled up."

Odessa didn't reply. She took Poko by the waist and put them in a bag on her hip. She had never felt less pretty in her life. She was haggard and tired. She felt like a dry, weathered branch about to snap at the first gust.

Leaving the stall with her bundle of weapons and a bag with her few possessions, Odessa walked out into the dry, dusty courtyard, averting her gaze when one of the peddlers caught sight of her. She had no energy to deal with some wayward merchant hawking bolts of linen and silk. Her thoughts were much too scattered. Much too vague and indistinct. It was as if she were detached from herself. Floating just outside her body, watching the world pass her by from a distance. Peering dazed through a hazy veil of torpor.

In the other stall, the goats greedily slurped from a water trough and ate what little feed they had left from the cart. While they ate, Yakun inspected the injured goat's gouged leg, following the goat's hind end as it side-stepped from his poking and prodding. When he was done, he joined Odessa in the courtyard.

Latching the stall's gate, he turned to her. "Let's see about getting a room, no?" he said before taking a bag from the cart. "You should be able to get a good night's rest here. In a room with a roaring fire, no spirit will be able to get in and harass you tonight."

Odessa followed him across the courtyard where a large doorway stood open, not daring to believe him. A merchant sitting on a rug by the western wall called to them as they passed, holding out a bolt of lustrous green silk.

The doorway was tall and wide. Yakun opened the heavy, dark wooden door and they stepped into a cool, dim room. The room was spacious with a high vaulted ceiling and a small fountain bubbling into a white stone basin in the center. Plush cushioned chairs and mats were spaced around the perimeter of the room. Their shoes sounded on the red tile floor as they walked around the fountain. From a door set in the center of the opposite wall came an old man dressed in a bright yellow kaftan.

"How can I help you?" the old man asked.

"We need lodging," Yakun said. "For one night. Maybe more."

The old man shuffled toward them. His thin fingers were adorned with glittering rings. "That can be easily accommodated. You have beasts that require tending, as well?"

"Yes, I stabled them in a stall in that far corner. I hope that is all right."

The old man paused. "There was no one to meet you and take them?"

"No," Yakun said slowly. "Not that I saw."

The old man's jaw flexed a moment before he spoke. "I apologize that our stablehand was not there to assist you. I personally will make sure your animals are well tended."

"Thank you," Yakun said.

The old man led them down a hallway that ran around the entire courtyard. Walking down the hallway, they passed many doors and niches with lamps or statues of Azka and the High Gods. They passed a communal bath and, as the old man prattled on about the water's medicinal properties, Odessa wanted very much to slink inside and soak in the water until she melted away. Her muscles ached for warm water. Her grimy, sweat-stained skin begged for it.

They were given a windowless room near their goats' stall. The room had a wide cotton mattress on a platform of wood and woven rope. There was a small hearth set in the wall, and floor mats surrounded a low table that held a lamp, two copper cups, and an ewer of water.

"Dinner will be ready just before sundown in the dining room," the old man said. "If you require anything at all, our servants are always close at hand." He bowed and left the room.

"Cozy, isn't it?" Yakun said, looking around the room.

Poko crawled out from the bag on Odessa's hip. "It's not bad." They leaned against the rim of the bag, half their body hanging forward in the air. "A view would be nice though."

Odessa set her bundle on the floor and then took the bag off and dropped it with a thump, leaving Poko to leap from it and land sprawling on the floor. "I'm going to the bath," she said, turning to Yakun. "It's the middle of the day. Talara won't know if I take the bandages off to wash, right?" Her bandages were nearly black with filth and stank of rotfiends.

"I have to replace those bandages anyway," Yakun said. "Go bathe. But be quick about it. There's no sense in tempting the gods."

Odessa took a change of clothes from her bag and left for the bath. Walking down the hall, a subtle anxiety tickled her spine. A servant in cream robes approached her from the opposite end of the hall and as they drew nearer, a frantic feeling frenzied inside her chest like a caged rat harrying at its bars. She thought about turning around and returning to the room but resisted. When the servant passed, their gaze down at the floor, the frenzied rat calmed, but she could still feel it in her chest, heavy with pointed nails digging in her heart.

She peeked inside the bath before entering. The bath's antechamber, a small room of white stone illuminated by a single large brazier at its center, was empty. The doorways leading to the left and right were marked, the figure of a man and woman carved into the stone beside either doorway. She took the left doorway, marked by a simple glyph of a sitting woman's profile with long hair and exaggerated curves, and entered a room of red granite tiles and pristine white stone. Stone benches ran along the walls, and stone shelves had been carved into the walls themselves. The shelves were all empty.

Set at regular intervals between the benches were shallow stone washbasins. A faucet in the shape of an open-mawed snake came out of the wall before each bowl and poured into a small slanted trough that let water pour gently into the basin. Odessa sat by the nearest basin, put the brass stopper in the drain, and then fiddled with the faucet's knob until water came bubbling from its spout. She had never worked a faucet before and the ease with which it worked was surprising. The basin filled quickly with clear, cold water.

She glanced back at the doorway she had entered through and at the lacquered door leading to the baths. The bath was quiet—not a sound other than the gentle splash of water in the basin. Tentatively, she took off her filthy tunic. Her linen breastcloth was stained with sweat, and peeling it off came with a wave of relief. After another furtive glance at the doorways, she slid out of her stained, grimy pants and her underwear, leaving them in a pile on the bench beside her. And then, carefully, she unwound the soiled bandage from her arm and let it fall, cascading onto the floor as she exposed her gnarled arm to the air.

When the basin was filled, she turned the knob and took a worn bar of marbled black soap and a rough, mostly dry washcloth from a shelf above the faucet. She lathered and washed her face and then moved down her body, scrubbing the dirt and dried sweat from her skin. Cold water ran down her body in icy rivers and her skin was soon dotted in gooseflesh. Carefully, she scrubbed the grime from her burned arm, taking care when cleaning the valleys of her furrowed scars.

Dirty water ran down a drain set in the center of the floor as she rinsed herself. After her body was clean she set about wetting her hair and taking her braids out. Her hair was knotted and tangled, and the whole endeavor took longer than she had wanted. But it was nice, losing herself in the minutiae of normal living. Like washday at home, it was pleasant. Combing her hair with her fingers, she untangled most of the knots and then washed it with a well-diluted lather of black soap. Unbraided, her hair hung down past her shoulder blades.

As she was rinsing her hair, the sound of footsteps approaching made her freeze. A sudden thorn of panic pricked at her heart.

Yakun entered the women's bath. Odessa covered her nakedness the best she could. "What are you doing?" he asked, his voice low and sharp. "I said be quick about it!" He was holding a loose bundle of rune-scrawled bandages in his hand. "Dry yourself off. That arm needs to be covered right now." Dropping the bandages onto a dry bench, he took a towel from a nearby shelf with one hand and grabbed her arm with the other, pulling her close. "What are you thinking, waving this godsdamned arm around? This isn't the grove. What if someone walked in and saw you? Anyone could look at your arm and know something isn't right." As he spoke, he rubbed the towel roughly against her arm until it hurt.

She didn't pull away from his grip even though she knew she easily could. She just stood there, both frozen and limp, as he mopped the water from her body. He moved from her arm to her chest. She could feel his hand through the towel, scrubbing and groping. She wanted to pull away. To shove him aside. But this was the man who had saved her. "I'm sorry," she mumbled.

When her arm and chest were dry he began hastily wrapping her arm in the rune-marked bandages. "I said be quick about it for a reason. Do you not understand how much danger we're in? To go around a public bath waving your cursed arm about. How stupid can you be?"

A lump growing in her throat, Odessa couldn't speak. Shame and humiliation choked her into silence. Breathing heavily through his nose, Yakun was silent as well as he looped the bandages up her forearm. When the bandages neared her shoulder, he sighed.

"I'm sorry for losing my temper," he said, his voice soft and calm. The sudden shift in his mood surprised her. "I never thought I would find myself running from a High God's wrath. I told myself a long time ago I was done running from them. That I wouldn't let them dictate the course of my life. But when their thralls have beaten you senseless and a sword is at your throat, you realize how powerless you are. When you divorce yourself from the world of the holy and god-fearing, you can lose sense of that. Even when the passion of youth has long passed, it's easy to delude yourself. Even for an old man, it's too easy to believe your own lies." He tied the bandage tight. "We cannot afford to be foolish. Do you understand?"

Odessa nodded, unable to look him in the eye.

His hand fell from her bandages to rest upon her waist. "I don't want anything to happen to you, Odessa." His other hand fell and took her own cursed hand, gently squeezing it. "You're too important to me."

A sick feeling sank in her gut. His hand wandered from her waist to her navel.

Odessa closed her eyes and thought about home.

CHAPTER 20

That night no spirits harassed Odessa. No rotfiends came from the shadows to ensnare her limbs and gnaw at her flesh. Yet even still sleep eluded her. With only one bed, she lay beside Yakun as he snored, turned away from him and nearly hanging off the edge of the mattress. She had offered to sleep on the floor but he refused. So she lay with her eyes closed and her thoughts turning in slow, torturous circles. Feeling filthy and sick to her stomach. All while he slept so soundly.

No spirits came the next night either. Or the night after that.

Each day, Odessa did not leave the room. She waited, hoping the caravan from Asha-Kalir would come soon. Each day that passed led to another night in bed with Yakun. Sometimes, while tight in the grip of insomnia, she wished some creature of the night would come. Nights spent hacking at spirits and rotfiends had been preferable to the torture of lying in bed with Yakun. During the night, he often would turn and rub against her, stiff with sleep. And not long after she lay down to sleep, his hands would invariably find her waist or her breast.

Yakun's hands had wandered or lingered occasionally during her nightly examinations, but he had changed after his assault in the bath. As if some barrier had been broken and now this groping and molesting was proper and right.

Poko had taken to sleeping in a deep wicker basket, so they never saw Yakun's nightly abuses. The fourth night at the caravansary, as Yakun and Poko slept, a voice came. Barely a whisper. "Get up," Talara's voice whispered in her ear. "I wish to speak with you."

Odessa slid out from under Yakun's arm draped over her and picked up her knife from beneath the bed. On the edge of the mattress, she waited, knife half-sheathed.

"Come to the door," Talara said. "My Shadow waits in the hall." Odessa's eyes stayed fixed on the door as she slowly rose from the bed, half expecting a knife to slash the back of her ankle. The tile floor was cold on her bare feet. The fire still burned in the hearth, but it burned low and in sputtering tongues of dark orange. All the heat had been drained from the room.

The door shook against the drawbar set against its center. A gentle rattle. Odessa backed away until her back was against the cold adobe of the opposite wall, her knife raised before her.

"Open," a rasping voice said from the hall.

"A peaceable dialogue is all I desire," Talara purred. "No harm will come to you or your companions."

"You're a liar," Odessa hissed.

"The truth is a vague, transient thing. But I will tell you one truth right now, Odessa Kusa. If you do not open that door, my Shadow will break it down, cut that old heathen's throat, dash the pixie's brains against the wall, and drag you out into the hallway. The choice is yours."

Odessa stared at the door, her knife wavering and beginning to fall. "Swear you won't hurt them."

"If you open the door, no harm will come to the old man nor the fairy."

"Swear it."

"I swear no harm will come to them by my hand nor the hands of my Shadows."

Every fiber of Odessa's being resisted as she hesitantly made her way to the door. Muscles tense, she lifted the drawbar from its slots and set it against the wall. She paused standing a bit away from the door, waiting for some brutish monster to come plowing through. Knife drawn back, she reached out and cracked the door open.

A metallic mask shrouded in darkness stared at her from the hallway. Her body ached to slam the door and retreat from its cloudy dead eyes, but it showed no signs of movement. It only stared blankly back at her.

"Come," it said from behind the lips of the mask. "Follow." The masked figure turned and headed down the hall. Odessa cracked the door wider, watching the figure walk a few steps before it stopped and turned, gesturing for her to follow. She took a tentative step into the hall and followed the figure, leaving a few paces between it and her.

The figure slinked through the shadows, braziers dimming as it passed. Its footsteps were silent on the tile floor. At the hallway's corner, it paused for a long time before turning. The figure led Odessa through a doorway into an outbuilding in the corner of the courtyard. Bags of grain and fodder filled the air with chaff and dust and a pleasant fragrance that was soon tainted with the stink of death as the figure lingered near the door leading out into the courtyard proper. The room was nearly pitch black, and Odessa knew if she took her eyes off the figure she might not be able to catch sight of it again until it was too late. Its robes seemed to melt into darkness like ink in water. As it peeked out a gap between the door and doorframe, she watched, not daring to even blink.

After a long moment, the figure turned to face her. As the mask stared expressionless at her, the stink of death grew stronger. A heavy, overwhelming pressure filled the room as the stench packed Odessa's throat. Dread unraveled in her chest like tendrils of ice coiling around her innards. Chilling her to the bone. She raised the knife and took an unsteady step backward.

"I did not lie," Talara's voice came hoarsely from behind the mask. The figure's arms spread in a placating gesture. "I've come in peace. I only wish to speak."

Odessa could almost feel Obi's dead hand wrapped around her throat again. "Every time you've wanted to speak to me, I've nearly gotten killed. Your monsters had a sword to Yakun's throat little more than a week ago. Why would I want to talk to you?"

The placating hands fell to the figure's side. "I do not care if you want to or not, but you *will* listen," Talara said. "I have left you alone to go fallow for long enough. You killed your ka-man's rejects but you are not ready to face the cruelty of the world alone. So I offer you an opportunity." Talara scrutinized Odessa through the figure's dead eyes, watching for any feelings, but Odessa only stared back guardedly. Talara continued, "I assume since you are here that you are bound for Asha-Kalir. There will be a caravan bound for Asha-Kalir arriving tomorrow. You will join it. Tell the leader, Bukoris, that you are the indentured mercenary he was told of. He will take you to Asha-Kalir and you will prove yourself to Khymanir. Prove to him that Talara's word is true."

"I am not indentured to you or anyone else," Odessa said.

"If you will not come willingly, there will be twenty Shadows here in the morning who will take you to Asha-Kalir by force if necessary. Will that be necessary, Odessa?"

"Your Shadows held a sword to Yakun's throat. He won't come willingly."

"I am not asking that he come at all. It is only you whom I require."

Odessa lowered the knife. The thought of being alone again terrified her. "What do you want me for?"

"I want you to become stronger. And Khymanir's war with Sak-Tor's devils is how you will grow stronger. Devils are blessed with diluted godsblood and that godsblood will be yours to take in battle."

"I don't want to go to battle," Odessa said. "I want to be rid of this tainted blood, not sully myself further."

"Your life will be one constant battle whether you like it or not," Talara said. "You've seen what the night is like for you. When your godsblood becomes too much for your puny wards to mask, your days will be much worse. I'm offering you protection. From spirits and gods alike. I'm offering you strength so you may yet live a peaceful life."

Odessa swallowed, her mind racing. "If I accept your offer," Odessa said, "will Yakun and Poko be safe too? Will they be under your protection?"

The corners of the Shadow's dead eyes wrinkled. Beneath the mask, Talara contorted the figure's face into a terrible, rictus smile. "If you wish it," Talara said.

"And my family. Mama and Ayana and everyone else. I want you to swear to keep them safe at all cost. If anything happens to them, this deal is off. If anything happens to them, I'll kill myself and be of no more use to you. Do we have a deal?"

The wrinkles around the dead eyes deepened. "I swear to safeguard your family from the cruelties of this world. No matter what happens, no harm will befall them."

Odessa relaxed a bit. Her face softened as she thought of Ayana and her mother. "How are they?" Her voice was softer and quieter.

"Your sister is growing into quite a young woman. She takes after your mother in so many ways. She and your mother miss you so much, Odessa." Talara's voice was gentle and soothing. "If you do as I say, perhaps you will see them again soon."

Odessa's heart ached. It had been more than a year since she had seen her sister and mother. More than a year since she watched her Papa die. "I'll do it."

The Shadow's ash-white hand extended out to her. "Shake on it and it will be done." Sharp nails grew from the end of each long, gnarled finger.

Reluctantly, Odessa took the Shadow's hand in her own. Its grip was solid and firm as stone. Then the Shadow's hand flexed and tightened. A sharp pain shot through the center of her palm and she tried to draw her hand back but found only more pain as she jerked. The Shadow's hand gripped hers and shook.

"It is done," Talara said. "A deal bound in blood." When the Shadow released her hand, there were three barbed points of bone retracting into slits in the skin upon the upper part of its palm. Blood seeped into the bandages wrapped around Odessa's hand.

"What did you do?"

Talara turned the Shadow's palm to face Odessa and flexed. Three barbed bones slid out from the skin again. "Very useful for scaling walls," Talara said. "Your old ka-man is quite the savant with flesh and bone." The Shadow turned halfway and cracked open the courtyard door. "Late tomorrow morning the caravan will arrive. Speak to Bukoris. Do not fail me."

Talara and her Shadow disappeared, melting into the night. The stink of rot and the overwhelming presence of the goddess dissipated before the door even shut behind the Shadow.

Odessa clutched her bleeding hand and went back to her room, disgusted with herself.

CHAPTER 21

The caravan rolled into the caravansary courtyard around midday. Odessa watched the gates open and the caravan's vanguard enter from the shade of a spice merchant's awning. Poko sat on her shoulder, wringing one of her braids between their hands.

"This is a bad idea," Poko whispered. "This is a very, very bad idea."

Odessa had told only Poko of Talara's offer. Since word of the caravan's arrival had reached the caravansary an hour ago, Yakun had been busy preparing to negotiate passage with them, unaware of what troubles brewed within its ranks. When he caught sight of the Shadows, Odessa was sure he would hide in their room or otherwise flee while she left with the caravan. That would work. "I don't have a choice," Odessa said. "This is the only way I can ensure nobody gets hurt."

"This is a bad deal. And fairies know a good deal about bad deals. We usually love them. But this one is all kinds of trouble."

"Well, you don't have to come," Odessa said, wincing internally at the sharpness of her words.

Poko seemed unfazed by her curtness. "You think I'm going to leave you alone in Asha-Kalir with a bunch of mask-wearing freaks? No way. You need me."

Odessa snorted, but she was happy that Poko wouldn't abandon her.

The spice merchant shuffled past her and Poko with a tall basket heaped with something red and pungent. He set it down beside the other baskets laid out in a row beneath the awning and wiped his hands on the front of his kaftan. "The fairy," he said to Odessa suddenly. Odessa had been watching the caravan's tall, gangly beasts being led toward the stalls, thinking of what she could say to this

Bukoris to convince him she was some sort of mercenary, but at the merchant's words she found herself somewhat startled. "Is it your pet?"

"Um, not really," Odessa said.

"Would you sell?" the merchant asked, his words almost liquid the way they flowed so melodically.

Reflexively, Odessa's hand rose to Poko's legs dangling from her shoulder. "Oh no, they're not for sale."

"Not even for a handful of silver?"

Having lived in Kalaro where deals were done in barter, Odessa knew little about currency, but she knew that was a lot. "Not for sale," she said emphatically.

The merchant frowned. "That's a shame. Wings or no, that fairy still makes dust." Poko crossed their arms and glowered but the merchant paid them no mind. "I would pay you for a coppersweight of dust."

"Keep your copper," she said, waving the merchant off and walking out from beneath the awning into the muted heat of a sun obscured only by a thin layer of gray clouds. She walked into the courtyard as the full length of the caravan began to pull into the gates. Dismounting, unharnessing, and unloading. The scant few people who had been occupying the caravansary had come crawling into the courtyard like roaches and mites skittering out of a rotten log. Servants and stablehands pushed past the crush of merchants now filling the courtyard, most of the peddlers having set up their stations near the gates. Only the spice merchant and an old woman selling jugs of fermented fish sauce stayed near the lobby, ostensibly not wanting to appear desperate.

As Odessa crossed the courtyard to the gates, Yakun's voice called out from behind her, calling her name.

"Odessa!"

She wanted to continue, to ignore him and make her way toward the mass of milling bodies, toward the clamoring servants and merchants and great sandy-haired beasts, but a part of her had also been hoping he would stop her. Hoping that someone, anyone, would stop her. She stopped and turned to see Yakun coming toward her at a brisk pace.

Equal distances between Yakun and the caravan, Odessa was, for a split second, frozen between the two. Her eyes met Yakun's.

She turned her back to him before he had gotten halfway to her, and she walked at a pace nearing a trot toward the caravan. Shoving past merchants and sliding between pack animals and people carrying saddles and sacks, she made her way toward a cluster of people near the gates.

"Excuse me," she called through the clamor, trying to keep her voice steady and firm. She was supposed to be a mercenary bound to Talara but she felt like a simpering child running away from home. But she had to get away from him. She had to get away from Yakun. "Excuse me. I need to speak to Bukoris."

A few faces turned to her but most ignored her. Yet one face was not like the others; it did not turn to face her directly. A bird's head turned and cocked so its beady eye was trained on her.

She noticed now the sandy-robed figure behind the group, the masked figures standing in a row behind them. The bird's eye blinked once and then the bird-man pushed past the group toward her. "But does Bukoris need to speak to you?" the bird said, its voice a raspy warble. "Who are you to interrupt me, girl? In Asha-Kalir, I would have you scourged for such impudence."

Odessa quickly bowed, her face flush and her guts gone cold and sinking. *Think before you speak, idiot.* Bowing, her mouth fumbled for words. "I apologize," she said. "Talara told me to seek you out when the caravan arrived. I am the mercenary. She told me you would be expecting me. I apologize for my impudence. I did not mean to offend."

Her head still bowed, she heard the bird-man sigh, a dry, throaty noise. "Raise your head," he said curtly. "I told the coal-eyed man we needed no more of his so-called 'gifts.' I thought he would have relayed that to his goddess." He eyed her again. "Talara told you to find me?"

"Yes," Odessa said.

"For what purpose?"

"To kill Sak-Tor's devils," Odessa said. "I'm to kill devils and prove my worth to Khymanir."

"Do not speak his name," the bird-man hissed. "That is your eminence. If that name graces your filthy lips again I will tear the tongue from your mouth. Do you understand?"

Odessa nodded hastily and bowed again. "I apologize."

"What is it you are to prove to my eminence?"

Odessa faltered for a moment, internally cursing Talara and the haughty bird-man. Desperately, she tried to recall all that Talara had said. "I am to show your eminence that Talara's word is true." The bird's face was impassive and she scrambled for more to say. "That Talara's soldiers are worthy of your eminence."

"You are not the same as the others the coal-eyed man has given us, I take it?"

"No," Odessa said, glancing at the dispassionate masks staring blankly forward.

The bird-man sniffed the air. "No, you are not. There is something different. Something I find even more unpleasant than the stink of rot that hangs off the others."

"I am just a Forsaken wretch whom the goddess Talara has taken pity on," Odessa said, finding purchase in her mind to form a half-coherent lie.

"And what could a Forsaken *zandun* hope to give my eminence? Just because your goddess has taken pity on you does not mean I shall. These Shadows at least have proven themselves to be sneaks and prowlers. In you, I see nothing that merits my eminence's glory and goodwill."

Shit. Odessa's mind raced, trying to find a way to convince him. She stammered, "May I show you what I can do, please?" She took the unstrung bow from the bundle.

"I suppose you may," the bird-man said. "But if I am not impressed, you will leave me without another word. You have taken too much of my time as it is. Agreed?"

"Yes," she said. "I agree." She held out the bow to him. "Will you string this?"

The bird-man looked at her, blinking slowly, then cocked his head at her. "Can you not string your own bow? And you hope to impress me this way?"

"Just try to string it," she said.

The bird-man sighed again and took the bow in his taloned hands. Suddenly her anxiety spiked. The bird-man was tall and skinny, but if it carried within itself some unbelievable strength, then this gamble would fall flat and everyone she cared for would still be in danger. And she would return to Yakun's side. The bird-man set the strung tip of the bow in the dirt and stepped a leg over the bow so he could bend it over his hip. Holding the looped end of the bowstring in one taloned hand and the tip of the bow in the other, he twisted and the bow's arm bent slowly. Bit by bit, bending until the loop of string was nearly to the notch. Beneath the thin brown feathers at its neck, a thin cord of muscle and ligament pulled taut and stuck out from beneath the skin.

The loop jerked toward the notch but fell short. The bow's arm relaxed halfway, the loop even farther from its goal. The bird-man tried once more but failed to string the bow.

Odessa let loose her bated breath when the bird-man finally relented and held the bow out to her. "Let us see you string it," he said.

With the tip of the bow beneath the arch of her heel, she pulled the bow's arm down and slid the loop into the notch, doing her best to give no sign of the exertion it took to string the bow. "There," she said, unsure of what to do next. Among the merchants gathered around them, she saw an elderly woman with a basket of slightly overripe marula fruit.

"May I borrow one of those?" Odessa asked the woman. The woman glanced at Bukoris.

"Give it to her," Bukoris said. "And quickly. I grow tired of this."

The woman dug into the basket and took out a marula fruit the size of her palm. It was a waxy yellow and marred with dark brown blemishes. Odessa took it from the old woman, wishing she would have given her one of the large ones at the top of the basket. "Thank you," Odessa said before turning to Bukoris. "If one of our masked friends behind you would like to hold this, I will demonstrate how well I can use this bow." She tried to channel some of Poko's nonchalance into her own voice but to her ears it sounded false and paper-thin.

Bukoris pointed a finger at one of the Shadows and then at the fruit in

Odessa's hand. The Shadow came forth with effortless haste, moving like a breeze and plucking the fruit from her hand. "Stand over by the wall and hold out the fruit," Bukoris said, gesturing flippantly before turning his attention to Odessa. "That Shadow was bequeathed to my eminence, so let this be a warning. If you so much as graze my eminence's property, you will be dragged behind a bazak to Asha-Kalir and brought deep beneath the Gravefather's Skull to the Pits. There you will receive a thousand cuts and in each of those thousand cuts shit will be smeared and flies and wasps will leave their maggots to burrow into your flesh. Squirming and gnawing beneath your skin."

The Shadow stood in front of the wall, the marula fruit held aloft in an open palm. The mass of people began to move to the edges of the courtyard as Bukoris continued, "If you miss but do not strike my eminence's Shadow, then that will be proof that you are not worthy of my eminence nor your goddess. But if you are able to strike the fruit at, perhaps, twenty-five paces, I will let you have your fill of devils. That fruit is just a shave bigger than a devil's eye, I should think, so it should make for a good measure of your skill. Is that suitable?" The bird-man's voice dripped with heady contempt.

Twenty-five paces? Her plan had been to put the arrow cleanly through the marula fruit at ten paces. At twenty-five paces the fruit would look to be the size of her thumb. But she had no other choice. It had been her idea. "That sounds grand."

Her stomach twisting in tight knots at the bottom of her abdomen, she went to the Shadow holding the fruit and turned to take her twenty-five paces. The center of the courtyard was now empty save for Bukoris and the knot of bird-men and humans from his caravan who stood off to the side, watching her. The other Shadows stood lined up in rows behind them. From the doorway of the caravansary lobby she saw Yakun's face, confusion and worry clear in his sun-reddened features even from a distance.

She never really knew how long her legs truly were until she took her first step. Counting them off, her stomach sank even deeper as her strides took her farther and farther. She tried to shorten her stride but the scrutinizing eye of Bukoris kept her from shortening them too much. She could not give him a reason to deny her a victory.

Another stride. *If I miss, Talara's protection is gone. If I miss, there's no telling what will happen to Mama and Ayana.* Her thoughts raced in a spiraling descent to the depths of despair. Bukoris's threat of torture in Asha-Kalir buzzed in her mind like gnats, but what scared her even more was the thought of what would become of her family and friends if she failed. *This was such a stupid idea.*

At twenty-five paces, she stopped and sighed before turning around. The marula fruit was even smaller than she had anticipated. From twenty-five paces it was smaller than her thumbnail. The Shadows stared at her, its skull-masked face watching her dispassionately. The eyes of everyone in the courtyard felt sharp and needling. In her mind the picture of putting an arrow in the Shadow's head was so vivid she thought it might be a premonition.

With a trembling hand she slid a long arrow from her quiver and looked down its length. The arrow was straight and true. Its point was a simple bronze bodkin, uniform and sharp. She took a moment to straighten the guineafowl fletching and then nocked the arrow and positioned herself, scuffing the dirt with her heel and setting her feet with her lead foot pointed toward the Shadow and its fruit.

I've made harder shots, she told herself to quiet the furious buzz in her head. *I can do this.* But the spiraling fervor persisted. A hive of despair set her nerves on edge and put a slight tremor in her hands.

She searched within herself for some respite from her despair. Some safe harbor from the storm of unease. And she found it in the pounding of her racing heart and in the thrumming of her tainted blood. It was always there, that core of vicious fire smoldering within her chest. She closed her eyes and breathed in, giving way to the subtle throbbing and letting it seep into her extremities. Her right arm soaked up the thrumming strength.

"My patience grows terribly thin," Bukoris called.

Odessa opened her eyes, focused solely on the marula fruit. The eyes trained on her from around the courtyard seemed farther away now, their prodding gaze less intense. She raised her bow and took a slow inhalation. As she drew the arrow back, she let out a half breath in a constrained whistle, and when her hand reached her cheek, she held the rest in her belly, stiffening her torso until her entire body was still as stone.

Her narrowed eyes stared down the arrow's shaft and did not stray from the tiny yellow fruit in the palm of the Shadow's hand. The gentle thrum in her veins calmed her mind until it was as still as her body.

She released the arrow.

Juice, pulp, and fragments of seed sprayed into the air as the arrow found itself buried nearly a quarter of its length into the adobe wall. Odessa exhaled, tension melting from her shoulders.

Bukoris went to the Shadow standing with its palm raised as if it still held more than juice and bits of fruit flesh in its ashen hand. He looked at the Shadow's palm and then at the arrow in the wall. Odessa did not dare move. Even in victory, her fate was not assured.

"I suppose you will be joining the caravan then," Bukoris said. "With your skill with a bow, you should be able to kill a devil or two before you get your head crushed in with a club."

And Bukoris moved on, rejoining his group of caravanners heading toward the lobby. Odessa stood in the center of the courtyard, unsure of what to do.

Unsure exactly of what had even happened. Her next steps were shrouded in uncertainty, obscured within the machinations of a god.

She thought Yakun would surely talk to her after Bukoris and his Shadows went inside, but he was nowhere to be seen. Poko squirmed from the bag.

"I still think this is a bad idea," Poko said. "But I'm glad you're not getting dragged and gnawed on by maggots."

"For the time being," Odessa said flatly. The relief she thought would come was hollow. Safety found beneath the auspices of a cruel and terrible god was little comfort. She was indentured to Talara in truth now. A pawn in a god's grand scheme. Just like Kunza-ka.

CHAPTER 22

As the temperature began to dip with the coming of dusk, Yakun found Odessa sitting in the goat stall, sharpening her blades again. Poko sat on the edge of the goat trough, dipping their feet in the chaff-strewn water.

"Odessa?" Yakun said, cracking the stall door open.

Fine stone scraping against stone was her reply.

The stall door opened farther. "Do you want to talk about what happened today?"

Another honing scrape along the sword's edge. "No."

He stepped into the stall and closed the door. Odessa paused her sharpening, set the stone down beside her, and clutched the sword. The goats chewed grain contentedly, oblivious.

"Why did you talk to that Bukoris? Why did you tell him such a foolish story?"

"I need to join the caravan," she said, watching him from the corner of her eye and from beneath her downcast brow.

"You could have gotten yourself killed," Yakun said. "Asha-Kalir does not view humans as kindly as Azka. If you're not a soulweaver then you are just cattle to them."

I'm going to be seen as less than cattle just about everywhere I go, Odessa thought. "It worked though."

"They think you're some devil-killing Talaran!" Yakun snapped, his voice edging past the bounds of a whisper. Odessa's muscles tensed and her grip on the sword tightened reflexively. "Everything that we've been working for, all that I've done, is in jeopardy now! You're supposed to stay out of view of the gods and now you're part of their damned army!"

"I didn't have a choice," Odessa said firmly, stopping Yakun as he advanced.

"What do you mean?"

"Talara came to me last night."

"In a dream again?"

Odessa shook her head. "One of those masked things, a Shadow. It came in the night and she talked through it. She told me if I said what I said and was able to join the caravan and kill devils, then my family and you and Poko would be safe."

"You made a deal with her?" Yakun's voice had dropped to a whisper, a somber, wistful sound.

"I had to," Odessa said. "Or those Shadows with Bukoris would have killed you and Poko and taken me to Asha-Kalir anyway." Odessa sat back against the adobe. "We live at the whim of gods and there's no avoiding it. Our lives are just threads to be weaved to their design."

"That was very pretty," Poko chimed in, like a songbird during a funeral. "Did you come up with that? That's good."

"You should have told me," Yakun said to Odessa, ignoring Poko completely. "We could have done something. We could have left. We had a head start; we could have outpaced the caravan and—"

"That Shadow was already here," Odessa interrupted. "There's no telling how many have been skulking around here that I didn't see. There would have been no running away. Those Shadows would have been on us before we even hitched up the goats."

Yakun's fingers drifted to his beard and began tugging at strands near the corner of his mouth. His eyes narrowed, cast toward the ground. "Shit," he whispered to himself. "There must be a way to get out of this."

"I have to do this," Odessa said firmly. She raised her hand and showed her palm and the round spot of blood staining the bandages. "I'm bound in blood. I don't know how binding that is, but I assume a blood pact with a High God isn't something that can be easily broken."

"Oh godsdamnit," Yakun whispered, his mouth hanging ajar for a moment. "That is not good. Not good at all." He began twirling his beard around a finger. "Why now of all times? This is no coincidence, this is the gods conspiring against me, the holy bastards."

Sticking the sword's point in the dirt, Odessa rose to her feet. "I'm going with the caravan, Yakun," she said. *And you're not coming*. The words skirted at the tip of her tongue for a moment and then were gone, a fleeting thought like ashes cast to the wind. She didn't know why it was so hard for her to speak her mind to him. Perhaps it had to do with her father. "I appreciate all that you have done for me. I truly do. You have done so much, but I need you to do one more thing for me. Please, take care of Poko while I'm gone."

Yakun's gaze had drifted away with his thoughts momentarily. "What?" he said. "I can't leave you now. You don't understand. Azdava's apprentice was among the caravanners. He's taking me to see her when the caravan reaches Asha-Kalir. She could help you, I'm sure of it. But now Talara has complicated matters and I'm not sure how we can proceed."

Odessa's heart dropped. "You still think I can be cured?"

"I don't know," Yakun said. "This pact, that is concerning. Talara's eye is directly upon you. There's no hiding from it now."

"But Azdava will still help me, won't she?"

Yakun's eyes softened. "We'll talk to her as soon as we reach the city. But you must understand, the wrath of a god is a terrible thing. A thing almost beyond comprehension. And that is to say nothing of the wrath of a High God. Talara is capable of horrors our human minds could not even imagine. The veil between this world and theirs is not thick enough to keep them from destruction. If she wanted, she could rot the flesh off the bones of every creature from the Slateseer to the Calamitous Straits."

Despair like a brutal ocean current ripping her feet out from under her. "So what do I do?" Odessa asked, forcing herself not to break down. Not in front of him. Anyone but him.

"You do as Talara bids you," Yakun said. "Become a devil-killer." His eyes glittered and gleamed with some emotion both bright and bold. In anyone else's eyes it would have looked like feverish madness, but within his wizened gaze it looked like inspiration and hope. "And all the while you are doing her bidding, you will be getting stronger. Maybe even strong enough to break the shackles she's placed on you."

Odessa nodded, unable to meet his gaze. It had been stupid to do what Talara had told her to without consulting Yakun. But she couldn't talk to him anymore. She could barely stand being in the same room as him. Her skin crawled with unease whenever he was around. She could ignore it when it was just the occasional lingering hand during her exams. But now, despite his nonchalance, there was no ignoring what had happened. He had broken the trust that had bound them together, and now all that held them was mutual need and her odd sense of obligation. "I'm sorry," she said. "I'm sorry I didn't tell you." She couldn't stop the words from coming out. It was as if she were a child again, telling her father she fell asleep during an early morning hunt. She was ashamed, and that disgusted her more than anything.

"Why didn't you tell me?" he asked placidly. As if she had no reason to be wary of him. As if he had done nothing to cause her to keep secrets or find some avenue of escape, even if it meant dooming herself to a life of Talara's bondage.

There was so much she wanted to say, but none of it came out. "I don't know," she said, still looking away. "I just wanted everyone to be safe."

Yakun watched her with a discerning glint in his eyes that unnerved her. He nodded as if her answer had assuaged some doubt in his mind. "You should have told me, but I suppose the end result is the same. But next time, please tell me when a High God calls upon you." He smiled warmly, trying to reassure her. It sent a shiver down her neck where his hot, stinking breath had lapped each and every night since they arrived at the caravansary.

"Of course," she said, forcing a smile.

"Now, when you're done sharpening your arsenal, I want to introduce you to Azdava's apprentice. He's really quite something. He said he's been thinking about your affliction for a while now." Yakun moved to the stall door. "I'll have him come to our room for tea after dinner. It will be good for you to have another soul to talk to. It's a heavy burden you bear."

After Yakun left and the stall door shut behind him, Odessa felt all the life drain from her body. Like she was a broken vase, and the entire time she was talking to Yakun she had been keeping the shards pressed tightly in shape with her bare hands. And now it came falling apart.

She didn't notice the tears at first. Her eyes grew blurry and she sniffled. A blink and they came tumbling down.

"It'll be all right!" Poko said, jumping from the edge of the trough and bounding to her side. "You heard him! We're closer to getting you cured than ever!"

Odessa shuddered, trying to stop the sob rising from her diaphragm. A choked moan escaped. She clamped a hand over her mouth as more tears spilled down her cheeks.

Poko reached out to her shin, a gentle embrace to reassure her, but she stepped away from their touch. The last thing she wanted was to be touched. She swallowed back the growing lump in her throat and wiped her eyes. "I'm fine," she said, sniffling and barely restraining another sob. "I'm just overwhelmed."

"I understand," Poko said, and Odessa knew they did. Somehow, the fairy could almost always sense what she was feeling in some capacity. Poko may not know the particulars, but they knew that she was hurting. And that in itself was enough. She wasn't totally alone. "We'll get through this."

Odessa turned away and closed her eyes as another river of tears fell. She bit her lip and swallowed the returning lump. "Thank you," she said, her voice husky. "You're my best and only friend, Poko. In the whole world, you're the only one I have."

When she turned, Poko was smiling and wiping tears from their own beady black eyes. "You jerk," they said, sniffling. "Now I'm crying."

A soft smile found its way to Odessa's lips. "Why are you crying?"

"No one's ever called me their friend before, you big dumb human," Poko said, wiping their nose on the back of their hand. "And I . . . I just . . . well, you're my best friend in the world too."

"Stop it!" Odessa said, fresh tears wetting her eyes. "I'm trying to stop crying and you're not helping!"

"You started it!"

The goats, having finished licking the last dusting of grain from the bottom of their feed trough, stood and watched the two, fairy and Forsaken, crying and laughing. And for those few minutes, Odessa was almost happy.

CHAPTER 23

The fire roared in the room's hearth, warming Odessa's back as she poured cups of tea for her and Yakun. The cakes of dried dung burning in the hearth filled the room with a slight earthy, redolent scent that almost overpowered the smell of steeping tea swirling to her nostrils in ribbons of vapor. Steam rolled from her own cup as she finished pouring. She set the empty teapot on a trivet beside the water ewer in the center of the table and sat down across from Yakun, whose nose was burning in the vapor rising from his cup.

"There's nothing quite like a cup of hot tea in the desert night," Yakun said. "It's wonderful, really."

Odessa looked into the cup. The thin brown liquid looked like swamp water but smelled almost floral. "It smells nice."

"Human ingenuity at its finest." Yakun took a sip that most certainly scalded his tongue, but he showed no signs of pain. "If I could have gotten some seeds, I'm sure we could have grown some tea plants ourselves in the grove. It's a similar environment, I've heard."

Poko leaned over the lip of Odessa's cup and engulfed their head in steam. When they withdrew their face from the cup's maw, moisture dripped from their hair. "Wow, that does smell nice."

"Can you please not dunk your face in my cup? I don't want your snot dripping in my tea." Odessa forced herself to joke with Poko. She could not allow herself to become withdrawn with the apprentice soulweaver coming any moment. She needed to be genial and polite. This person could save her life. She could not afford to be cold or discourteous.

"You heard what the spice man said, right?" Poko said. "People will pay a lot for my dust. I'm sure my snot is just as valuable, if not more so. You'd be lucky to drink my snot!"

"You're disgusting," Odessa giggled.

A knock at the door cut Odessa's quiet giggling short. Her throat tightened and nervousness boiled in her stomach as Yakun rose and headed toward the door. She stood up and smoothed out the wrinkles of her clean tunic.

Odessa had not known what to expect in an apprentice soulweaver, so as Yakun swung the door open she was surprised to see a man who looked not a day older than her.

"This is Tarik," Yakun said, ushering the slim man inside. Tarik wore a high-collared plum robe with gold embroidery at the collar and down the front. His skin was like red ochre, and his shoulder-length hair was wavy and black as ink. "Tarik, this is Odessa."

Tarik bowed, his hands clasped together at his waist. "It is an honor to meet you," he said. His voice was soft and pleasant like a gentle stream over smooth stone. "I have been speaking with my master Azdava of your predicament for some time. I pray we are able to offer you some comfort."

"Thank you," Odessa said. He had high cheekbones and long eyelashes, and his face had but a whisper of stubble. Unsure of what to do, she bowed in return. "It is nice to meet you, Tarik. It's quite the surprise to find you among the caravanners. We did not expect to see a friendly face."

"I was not originally going to join the caravan but with this whole Shadow business, Mistress Azdava insisted one of her soulweavers be in attendance. I suppose it must have been fated that we should meet." He smiled and Odessa found herself smiling as well.

"Come," Yakun said, gesturing toward the mats placed around the table. "Please, sit. Get comfortable."

Odessa waited for Tarik to sit before she sat down, as to be polite. He sat between her and Yakun, and looking at his profile she saw how prominently his nose jutted from his face. But it was not as bent and crooked as Yakun's nose.

"Odessa, brew Tarik some tea, will you?" Yakun asked.

As Odessa began brewing a pot full of tea for Tarik, he and Yakun spoke of Azdava.

"Has she told you how we met?" Yakun asked.

"No, she never mentioned it," Tarik said.

"That makes sense. It's ancient history," Yakun said. "Over thirty years ago, it must have been. I had been divorced from my homeland for maybe two or three years at that point and I found myself in the highlands, in Chanduria. It was a hard but welcoming city. The god that ruled Chanduria, I forget its name now, was one of the better ones. Allowed people to own slaves themselves. Quite progressive. It was another twenty years before Sak-Tor's armies came. They set up camp upstream on the Darrood and began slaughtering captives they had taken from the Chandurian villages and towns, drowning them in the river and letting their corpses rot and float down into the city. They made a dam of corpses and contaminated the water downstream. When Sak-Tor and his devils marched south into the city, there was barely anyone willing to resist them. But that did not sate Sak-Tor's appetite for blood."

Odessa listened intently as the water began to boil in the pot above the fire. She had never heard much of Sak-Tor in Kalaro, save for the fact that he had led a horde of devils to war in the name of conquest and bloodshed. Knowing where her path led, she wanted desperately to know more about the devils she would be killing. The tainted abominations of man and god. Her siblings of a sort.

"Anyway," Yakun said, realizing he had rambled. "I found myself in Chanduria, working on a boat hauling stone and ore down the Darrood. Terrible work that was. I felt the lash almost every day, I believe, for some reason, real or imagined."

Odessa shaved a small piece from the tea brick into the teapot and poured the boiling water in. The tea shavings swirled as the water filled up the small clay pot, ribbons of color diffusing as they tilted and spun inside.

"My first time arriving in Asha-Kalir, I was found to be lacking permit or stamp or some such nonsense and I was taken by your Red Clay men and locked away awaiting hard labor or death. But as I waited in a cold stone cell, drinking from a puddle and eating two-day-old porridge, Azdava came. She was not a soulweaver yet. As an apprentice she dealt in the examination and procurement of suitable flesh. And on that day, I was but another poor soul for her to examine."

Odessa sat down as the tea steeped. She had never heard this story, but the aloof way Yakun told it belied a certain grimness. He smiled, but there was little humor in it.

"In my delirious ranting and pleading, I told her I had expertise in magic, which was true but quite embellished in my desperation. And when she heard my ideas on the essence of divinity, I could see, despite her stony demeanor, a glimmer of something."

"Heretical delight," Tarik said with a soft smile. "I see it on occasion even today."

"Yes, it's exactly that!" Yakun said. "Heretical delight. I quite like that." He poured Tarik a cup of tea. Setting the teapot back on the trivet, he continued, "It was nearly four days before she returned to my cell. She asked me, a filthy wretch in rags sitting next to a bucket of his own shit, 'What is humanity's purpose?'"

"What did you say?" Tarik asked, leaning forward, his slender fingers wrapped around his cup.

"Well, by that time I was half mad from hunger, thirst, and isolation so it was not exactly eloquent, I'm sure. But to paraphrase as best I can remember, I said something along the lines of 'I don't know but I'll be damned if it's just to serve and die.'"

Tarik chuckled, a smooth, pleasant sound. "I'm sure she truly enjoyed that answer."

"She must have because two days later she had bought me. Or, that is to say, her office and station bought my services. Officially, I was Architect Istri's, but everyone knew it was she who had bought me and it was she whom I served."

Tarik lifted the cup to his lips, blew into it, and took a sip. "If you would indulge my curiosity, how did you gain your freedom then?" He set the cup back down on the table. "Mistress Azdava never mentioned how you came to leave Asha-Kalir."

"You will have to ask her that," Yakun said, smirking and taking a sip of tea himself. "It was her doing anyway."

Tarik frowned. "I do not know if she was different when you knew her, but she doesn't tell anyone anything."

"It sounds like she hasn't changed at all," Yakun said wistfully. "Always lost in her own thoughts. And whenever I was able to get her to talk, her thoughts moved so quick I felt as if I was always three steps behind and losing ground."

"Yes, exactly!" Tarik said. "Or she starts talking in the middle of a thought and I have to try and guess what she's talking about."

Odessa sipped her tea. It was growing cold. Her eyes met Poko's as they sat cross-legged by the ewer. In exaggerated pantomime, they silently jabbered on and on.

"As to your situation," Tarik said. Odessa turned from Poko to find Tarik's eyes, as dark brown as eyes could be.

"Ah, yes," Odessa said, suddenly struggling to find the right thing to say. "Yakun told me you've been thinking about what to do about me."

Tarik smiled. "It is quite the conundrum." He looked from her to Yakun and then back to her. "From the bird, I am to understand that you were party to the killing of a god, yes?"

Odessa's cheeks grew warm with something akin to shame, and she did not know why exactly. She had come to terms with what they had done, she had thought. "Yes," she said. "Egende."

"How were you able to do this?"

"We used iron. Sanctified iron."

Tarik nodded. "Interesting." He looked to Yakun. "And this Egende, you believe it to be an aspect of Ogé?"

Yakun glanced at Odessa and then back to Tarik. "Yes."

"So with its blood, Egende's and, in an indirect fashion, Ogé's divinity was bound to your body," Tarik said to Odessa. "Has engraftment begun?"

Odessa looked to Yakun and Yakun answered, "Yes. Her right arm is nearly entirely attuned to the divine. We've begun work to bolster her body's capacity for divinity but that is a slow endeavor."

"May I see your arm?" Tarik asked.

Something fluttered in her stomach. She lifted her bandaged arm and held it out for him to inspect. "I'm sorry the bandages are dirty," she said. Her bandages were only slightly dirty with dust and dirt and a bloodstain on her palm, but it set a bad precedent, she thought.

"It's fine," he said as he began to unwrap her arm. His fingers brushing her skin was like embers upon dry tinder, singing and smoldering with every gentle touch.

As her scarred skin was exposed to the air, she wanted to pull her arm from him and hide it. His discerning eyes on her marred flesh. Too ashamed of her arm, she had to look away as he moved up her arm, unwrapping the bandage from around her elbow and then her bicep.

When he was done taking the bandages off, he dropped them in a pile on the floor and took her hand in his, turning her arm back and forth, staring at her scarred skin. "These burns are from godsblood, yes?"

Odessa nodded.

"How were you able to keep the godsblood from killing her before engraftment could take place?" Tarik asked Yakun.

"That's the thing," Yakun said. "I don't know how she survived exactly. Her father was the one who was supposed to take the blood. He had been preparing his body for many years, but I don't know how her body was able to bear the strain."

"Incredible," Tarik said, his eyes never leaving her arm. They moved up and down, following the fissured and furrowed scars. "And your letter, it mentioned fire. Is that magic or just godsblood exposed to the air?"

"It is magic, but its magic is derived from the blood, so there is some bleeding and whatnot," Yakun said.

"So how do I get rid of this godsblood?" Odessa asked suddenly. The conversation had veered far from its course and she had to set it right.

Tarik seemed taken aback. "Ah yes, I'm sorry." He looked to Yakun. "You've tried bloodletting, you said. How much blood have you let in one session?"

"Nearly a liter."

"Oh," Tarik said. "That's quite a lot. And did it have any effect on her capacity as a conduit?"

"It had a similar effect as when she uses her flames. So the blood is still the medium for the divinity, but since engraftment it returns to full capacity in time with no permanent loss."

Tarik let go of her hand and sat back. "I wonder what would happen if we were to let all of her blood."

"I would die," Odessa said. "And I would prefer to avoid that if possible."

"Of course," Tarik said quickly. "You would be given fresh blood. We've made great strides in the transfusion of blood; it really is a wonderous thing. Along with amputation of the arm, that would be our most likely course of action."

Yakun rose and walked around to Odessa's side. "I'm afraid we may have lost our opportunity for amputation." He took Odessa's arm and, pushing aside the sleeve at her shoulder, pointed at the dark lines beneath her skin burrowing toward her heart. "Engraftment has spread into her chest cavity."

"Well, that complicates matters," Tarik said.

"Do you still think you can cure me?" Odessa asked.

Tarik met her gaze and took her hand in his. "I promise you, I will do everything in my power to make you whole again."

Odessa's heart skipped a beat staring into his eyes. She could tell his words were genuine.

CHAPTER 24

The caravan assembled in the courtyard while it was still doused in the shadow of the mountains. Yakun and Odessa hitched up the goats to the cart and led them out of the stall to join the rear of the caravan. The Shadows flanked them on all sides. Yakun was jittery around them despite both Odessa's and Tarik's assurances. Tarik was enamored with the Shadows and had faith in their loyalty to their master. Odessa had faith only in the steadfast bindings of a blood pact.

When the gates opened, the bazaks leading the caravan stretched their ungainly legs and lurched forward, their saddlebags and the large bundles strapped to their backs bulging with all manner of goods.

Odessa walked behind the cart as Yakun led the goats. Poko sat on the back of the cart, legs swinging idly. A dour uneasiness clung to Odessa's shoulders and hung like a lead cape. The day before, a stablehand had given the bazaks moldy fodder, and Bukoris had flogged the boy half to death. *I'm in bad company,* she thought. *This Bukoris is no good at all.*

"Do you miss riding with me yet?" Poko called to her as the cart jerked to a start and the end of the caravan began to follow.

"I'll gladly walk if it means I get to sleep at night," she said.

"You say that now," Poko said. "We'll see how you feel at the end of the day."

"I'm telling you, as long as I get to sleep at the end of the day, I'll walk as far and for as long as I have to."

They passed the eastern gates, and the mountains' high peaks loomed ahead. She could see the canyon ahead and the road winding through rough hills toward the gap between steep cliffs. The mountains on either side of the rift were shorter than the ones next to them, but they still towered over the road, massive walls of stone flanking the road for miles.

The terrain leading to the gorge was dry and the vegetation sparse. Short, gnarled trees and knobby shrubs clung to the hillsides in clumps, and coarse yellow grasses dotted the rocky soil. Far to the north and south the mountains' outer range flanked them, funneling them toward the gorge.

"What is a fairy doing riding a cart and not darting around the sky?" Tarik sidled beside them. Odessa had not seen him, although she had searched the milling crowd of caravanners for him.

Poko watched him cautiously as he approached. "I live a life of leisure." Poko crossed their arms across their chest. "I don't worry myself with such trivialities as transport."

"Ah, how I envy you," Tarik said, glancing at Odessa with a wide grin before turning his attention back to Poko. "I apologize—I did not get your name yesterday. By the time I saw you, the time for introductions had passed."

"My name is Poko. But you can call me Your Highness."

"Don't call them that," Odessa said. "I don't know if you've ever met a fairy before, but they are an arrogant bunch."

"Take that back!" Poko rose to their feet on the back of the cart. "Just because we're better than humans and we know it, doesn't mean we're arrogant!"

Tarik laughed. "I came to ask you a question, Poko."

"And what is that?" Poko asked haughtily.

"Do you want wings again?"

Poko narrowed their eyes and studied him. "Yeah. Yeah, I do. Why?"

"I thought, since we will be working on Odessa here, we could work on fixing you as well. Would you like that?"

"What's the catch?"

"There's no catch," Tarik said. "I promise. I just want to do what I can for you both. I'm afraid Asha-Kalir can be quite unkind, especially to outsiders. I want to at least help how I can."

Poko sat back down on the blanketed heap, looking pensive. "I was stripped of my wings and banished from my court. I don't know if I'm allowed to have new wings."

"Who's to stop you?" Odessa asked. "We're not going to run into any of Ishkinni's court out here, are we?"

"If there's any of them left," Poko said, their voice sullen now.

Tarik gave Odessa a worried glance.

She leaned toward him and said in a low voice, "There was a fire."

"She started it," Poko said. "But we tried to eat her, so we're even."

"Oh," Tarik said, taken aback.

Odessa shot Poko a nasty look, and they stuck out their tongue, their sullenness having passed. "It's a long story," she said to Tarik.

"No it's not," Poko said. "I just told it."

"There's more to it than that!"

Tarik laughed again. "You two argue like my sisters and I."

"You have sisters?" Odessa asked.

"Five of them."

"Five?" No one in Kalaro had been able to have six living children in decades.

"And I'm the eldest, so all the familial responsibilities fall to me," he said. "Do you have any siblings?"

"I have a sister," Odessa said, her smile faltering a moment. "I haven't seen her in more than a year."

"I can't imagine what it has been like," Tarik said. "Being Forsaken and away from home like that."

A warm sensation swelled in Odessa's chest. "It's not been easy."

"If there's anything I can do to help, just let me know," Tarik said. "No one should have to struggle alone."

Within a few hours, the caravan had reached the mouth of the gorge. The road through the gorge was relatively wide, and the caravan walked through, two bazaks abreast with room to spare.

Odessa peered upward at the stretch of sooty gray between the cliffs. The cliffs loomed high above their heads, jagged and harsh.

It was dusk by the time they reached the other side of the gorge, and it was later still when they reached the eastern caravansary. The eastern caravansary was similar in shape to the other but larger and grander. The walls were carved stone with parapets and towers. The gates were massive, made of thick timbers and bound with wide strips of brass. It was utilitarian but with subtle artistry here and there. The pounded brass strips across the door had intricate scrollwork engraved along its edges, and the corbels beneath its parapets were all fluted and curled at the top and bottom like rolls of parchment.

A group of soldiers met them at the gates and escorted them inside. In the growing darkness, Odessa did not notice until they were near the walls and the light of torches that half the soldiers were not giants or cyclopes, as she had assumed, but massive creations of hard red clay. They lumbered forward, leading the caravan into the safety of the caravansary walls, holding long-handled axes and polearms with heads like crescent moons in their huge fists.

Within the walls, the courtyard was wide with a large, placid pool at its center. Small trees grew in a garden encircling the pool, their thinning foliage brown and curled.

A veranda, extending from the caravansary's inner walls, surrounded the courtyard's northern and southern sides. Yakun and Odessa found lodging in a room on the southern side, but Odessa spent little time inside it. Feigning sleep as Yakun pawed at her chest and between her legs, she let him do as he would until finally, mercifully, he was snoring beside her. On bare feet, she slipped out of the room and onto the veranda.

The veranda was as wide as she was tall and made of smooth cream-colored stone. The roof overhead, with its thick columns and high arches, made the veranda's long hall a tunnel of dark from end to end. The courtyard beyond was lit only by the tiny bit of moonlight that managed to filter through the night's clouds.

The sound of the goats and bazaks rustling in their bedding came faintly from the stables. Yakun's goats were very wary of the bazaks and their grotesque appearance. Odessa was not entirely certain of them either. They were strange creatures, both gangly and blubbery with toothed beaks hidden beneath flaps of skin. To Odessa they looked like some deep-sea slug had been dragged from the depths and thrown onto land where, instead of shriveling up and dying, it had hastily grown not two, not four, but six legs.

Odessa leaned against one of the veranda's columns, its carved surface cool against her bare skin. She wore only a thin linen nightgown and the chill of the desert air easily seeped through it into her skin and down to the bone.

She glanced down the veranda to the door she had seen Tarik enter with his fellow soulweavers. She had hoped to find him skulking about the veranda as well. It was easy talking to Tarik. It soothed the raw unease that seemed ever present now. Talking to him was effortless and somehow familiar, as if she had known him all her life and not merely a few days.

"The night air is much too dry here," a raspy voice said from the darkness. "A lifeless place does not lend itself well to death and decay. Plants turn to dust in the sun. Bodies become dry husks. Little goes to the carrion eaters and the insatiable desert squanders what life is given in death."

Odessa's head snapped toward the opposite end of the hall to see a Shadow's skull glinting in the scant moonlight coming from the courtyard. "Death serves life and life serves death, but the desert serves nothing and no one," Talara said through the Shadow's mouth. "I much prefer the jungle where rot can take hold in living flesh as well as the dead. The cycle of living and rotting is so fluid in the jungles and swamps."

"What do you want?" Odessa said. "I did as you said."

"And you did well." The Shadow was totally motionless as it spoke, as if the words slipped from its open mouth without any guidance. "I am here only to give you praise."

"You have wanted to kill me ever since I was cursed with this damned blood and now you want to heap your praise upon me?" Odessa snorted. "I'm doing as you say, but don't take me for a fool."

"You misunderstand me," Talara said. "I am not like your former ka-man, I don't want your death any more than I want your life. My ambivalence is a scale for you to tip as you see fit. Do well and become strong and I shall want you to live and grow ever stronger."

"Why are you so intent on me getting stronger? What do you want from me?"

The Shadow was silent for a moment. "You are a curiosity to me." There was a strange earnestness in the goddess's rough, gravestone-cold voice. "You absorb life into yourself like desert sand takes water and blood. Greedily and entirely. I wish to see where your body's limit lies. How much life can a mortal body hold before it is torn asunder? This is what I want."

"So I'm just some experiment? I'm just supposed to kill until I start falling apart? And for what exactly?"

Talara's presence grew heavier around the Shadow. The darkness on the veranda seemed to solidify. "Have you seen what is left of the Nameless Ones in the sky?"

"Yes," Odessa said, now regretting the harshness of her words. *I've done it. I've tipped the scale.* She wanted to run away.

"Do you know how they died?"

"The Serpent and the old other gods killed them and ate their names so they could make the world."

"No," Talara said, sounding almost regretful. "I tell you this only so you may know the gravity of your role in what is to come. The Nameless Ones and the ones that came after them, they were consumed by the Gray. Everything was consumed by the Gray. It happens again and again. But life is ever resilient. It crawls from the corpses of fallen gods and starts anew only to be reaped later by the Gray. And another reaping is upon us."

"The Gray killed the Nameless Ones? That can't be."

"But it is. It comes and feeds off divinity and life until there is nothing left, and then it flees to the void where it resides until the world has grown fat enough to feed its hunger once again."

"How do you know this?"

"Because my siblings and I were there when the old ones died. When the World Serpent drew its last breath, we were given life. Just as the Gray was receding, we were born into that dead world. We inherited desolation and we've built this world for the sake of preserving it. Yet the Gray still comes as if all that we have done is for naught."

Odessa's mind faltered for a moment. "But what does that have to do with me?"

"The human body was built to withstand the Gray. But now that you carry divine blood in your veins, will your human body still resist it? If you continue to feed that divine blood, will it continue to resist the Gray? These are questions that need answered. For if life can be safeguarded in your mortal flesh and you can survive the reaping, then you will be a seed from which a new world can grow."

Odessa was speechless. Nothing made sense any longer. Talara, the cruel goddess that had cut her father's throat and poured blood down her mother's and sister's throats, now suddenly cared for the greater good of the world? It was illogical and wrong, and yet Odessa couldn't piece together how exactly it was wrong. It just felt so . . . impossible.

"Why didn't you tell me this before?" Odessa said quietly. "Why haven't you told everyone?"

"I did not tell you before because you did not need to know. You were not ready to know." The Shadow approached her in a few fluid steps. "No one else must know this. You are bound to me, so heed me well. You must not utter to another soul what I have told you tonight. If the world were to know how precariously it is balanced upon the precipice of oblivion, it would descend into utter chaos. Panic would rip what little unity we have into pieces. Then there would be absolutely no defense against the Gray. It would wash over this world like a cancerous tidal wave. And there would be no surviving it at all."

"Talara," Odessa said after a long while. "Answer me honestly. Do you truly think we stand a chance of surviving even now? Those of us down here, I mean."

One of the Shadow's hands reached out, its cold fingers brushing against her cheek. "Do not worry, Odessa," Talara said. "You must have faith in your goddess."

My goddess. The phrase sent Odessa's skin crawling as if a thousand millipedes were skittering up and down her spine. But it was true. Talara was her goddess and she was Talara's pawn.

It was not until Talara's presence had dissipated and the Shadow had slunk back into the darkness that she realized Talara had not answered her question.

CHAPTER 25

The mists have reached the southern reaches of Toth and now begin to creep toward our northern holdings," Tialta said. "Our scouts have seen nothing in southern Toth that would be cause for alarm, but they have not gone far into the mists for fear of exposure. I've increased our military presence in the border towns and slowed the flow of refugees."

"These refugees," Piata said. "How many are coming to our borders afflicted?"

"Nearly all of them now," Tialta said. "Although the flow of refugees has slowed quite significantly as the mist has drawn closer."

"Perhaps the stench of the burn pits is making them reconsider," Piata said.

"The giants who are fleeing what remains of Toth do not fear the burn pits," Tialta said. "They may beg and plead and fight for their lives but still they try to cross the border because they *know* whatever took Toth is much, much worse than a burn pit."

Kunza sat on his cushion, listening intently with a pit in his stomach. The Gray was coming much too fast. There was no time to make enough Shadows to hold back the flood of fog pouring from the northern shores. Kunza raised his hand to speak as Azka's Chosen grumbled over one another.

"Excuse me, Chosen Tialta," Kunza said. "Of the unafflicted who attempt to cross the border, how many are giants?"

Tialta cocked his head at Kunza. "Very few," he growled.

"And how many are humans?"

Tialta's lip curled a moment before he spoke. "The majority."

"What are you getting at?" Piata asked.

"I am only asking because my goddess says that the human body is somewhat resistant to the poisons of the Gray. And I wish to dispense with the ambiguity and say for certain that these mists are the coming of the Gray. The clouds that blotted the sky are coming down to smother the land and if we are not proactive they will soon enough smother us as well."

"Of course you would say that," Piata said.

"We have been courteous and we have indulged you enough, ka-man," Tialta said. "But do not presume a thing in the presence of Azka and his children. Allow me to say with certainty that there is nothing you humans can do that we, Azka's divinely appointed Chosen, cannot do."

"I did not mean to offend," Kunza said quickly. "I know humanity's place in the world, believe you me. I only wish to be useful. I only wished to ask that some human freemen be used as vanguard scouts in the mists to test my theory."

"I believe that can be done easily enough, yes," Azka's godling said to Tialta.

"Yes, Your Highness," Tialta said.

The godling met Kunza's eye, and before Kunza could avert his gaze, the godling winked an eye and then looked back out over the rooftops of Noyo.

Kunza left the meeting with Azka and his Chosen, unnerved and feeling small beneath an immeasurable dread looming above them all. But also he was emboldened. The godling's support was huge for his standing in Noyo.

He left the hall for his chambers at the far end of the palace. His rooms were dark and smelled of herbs. The window overlooking the city was covered with a thick curtain that drowned out any light but a dim corona around the edges. A makeshift altar stood beside the bed. The palace had a temple to the High Gods, but he had found it gaudy and impersonal. Here in the dark, smelling the stinkroot, he could clearly feel his goddess even in Noyo, where Azka's presence was so overwhelming.

He knelt on the stone floor in front of the altar, his knees finding the dry blood stains that had accumulated from his hours of prayer. His knees were calloused and constantly weeping blood. Kunza took it as a sign of his devotion.

In the daylight, Talara's voice could rarely reach him. But still he prayed. He prayed until the sun had set and he prayed until it rose again. He reported to her the day's events. She said nothing but he could feel her so clearly. Listening. Just listening.

It wasn't until the corona around the curtain had begun to seep into the room again that he heard her, answering his prayers.

"Patience," Talara whispered in his ear, raising the hairs on the back of his neck. "When the Gray comes, you will have your army. Your goddess provides in due time."

CHAPTER 26

The day after they left, the western caravansary was long and grueling. Early in the day they were surrounded by a plain of dry, rocky dirt scattered with sparse shrubbery, but by the time the sun was setting behind the mountains, the road had been swallowed by hills of sand.

The caravanners had donned head veils that wrapped around their mouths and nose. Odessa had not understood why they had done this until the first gust of wind hit her. Sand buffeted her face like a flurry of hot cinders and obsidian shards. After that, Odessa had bound her face in thin linen, but the spare bandage she'd used wasn't long enough to cover her face fully. and the wind and sand found its way through.

Conversation was at a minimum; the wind became so furious, the only way to be heard was to shout. Tarik stayed near the middle of the caravan with the other soulweavers, and Poko had hidden themself at the bottom of her bag, so she was left alone with her thoughts. Thoughts of a dying world and tainted blood.

The caravan traveled through dusk, hastening the exhausted beasts and men to cover more ground while the temperature was dropping.

They made camp on the leeward side of a high dune. Thus sheltered from the wind, the caravan made a circle near a rocky outcropping half-buried in the side of the dune.

As they set up camp, the bazaks, after being stripped of their bundles and bags, collapsed, folding their six legs beneath them and, on their knees, squirming back and forth until they, too, were half-buried in the sand. Odessa paused unloading the wagon to watch the bazaks sinking into the sand. It was a strange sight to behold all of them burying themselves in unison. Little more than a year ago, seeing creatures such as these would have been a once-in-a-lifetime opportunity. Seeing much of anything outside of Kalaro had seemed as remote a possibility as growing wings.

Talara's words echoed relentlessly in her mind. As the day wore on, and the more they were repeated, they had taken a sort of dreamlike quality. But that was a mechanism of the exhausted mind. The Gray had killed the world at least twice before. Each time she had looked at the gray sky had been further proof in her mind that Talara's words had been true.

She hated Talara. But still she believed the bitch.

In the circle of bazaks, the caravanners huddled around a series of small fires, each of them burning dry dung and any thorny scrub that the bazaks had not eaten. Over the largest fire, a pot hung from a tripod, and a soup of barley and dates simmered inside.

All the heat of the day was drained from the air, and the chill of dusk became a bitterly cold night. Odessa sat beside her and Yakun's fire, wrapped tightly in a blanket with Poko nestled in her lap. Being from the mountains, the cold was not foreign to Odessa, but she had always had a hearth and a family to keep her warm. Around them, smothered in night, the desert stretched in all directions, desolate and pitiless.

After an hour, the soup was doled out to all but the Shadows who skulked around the outside of the camp's perimeter, moving like dark mirages on the periphery of one's vision. Odessa sipped from her bowl of soup, not particularly hungry herself but glad for its warmth. The soup had little taste, but it was nourishing. While draining the last of her bowl, she picked half a soggy date from the dregs of barley and gave it to Poko, who took it greedily.

Not long after everyone had eaten their fill, sleep infected the ranks one by one until everyone but Odessa had fallen asleep. She stayed near the fire, her knife drawn beneath the blanket. The night sky was still and black, not the slightest shimmer in the air. No spirits came for her that night. No rotfiends slinking through the sand. Eventually, she too fell victim to slumber.

They continued east for two days. On the third day, the goats began to slow. Even with stones lining either side of the road, here and there drifts of sand covered the stone pavers and pulled against the cart's wheels. The goats persisted on dry fodder and what little water could be spared, but they were now thin and bony.

The farther east they traveled, the fewer dunes they passed. Ahead, the land leveled out, a plain of blinding white sand and sun-bleached stone beneath a sky of dingy gray. In the far distance, sharp peaks of rock rose from sands like monoliths, and far to the east eroded outcroppings and cliffs stood against the horizon. Hot wind whipped furiously at their backs and sometimes shifted to lash at their sides.

When the wind became too vicious and sand clogged their veils, the caravan found shelter in the shadow of a shelf of exposed rock. The entire caravan huddled against the shelf as the wind whipped and roared overhead in a stream of sand blown from the shelf.

Tarik found Odessa beside the low wall of bedrock, the skin around her eyes and brows raw from the abrasive gusts.

"Here," he said, extending to her and Yakun two long strips of red cotton. "I managed to get one of the merchants who tagged along to part with two lithams." His voice was faint from beneath his own litham.

Yakun took one and unwound the thin, makeshift mask from around his face.

"Thank you," Odessa said, reaching to take the cloth from Tarik.

"Please, allow me," Tarik said, holding the litham loosely between two hands. "To ensure it stays on correctly."

"Of course," Odessa said, unwrapping her crude veil. "Thank you."

He knotted the wide strip of cloth more than a foot from one end and set the litham over the top of her head so the knot was positioned at the back of her skull and the foot of loose cloth hung down between her shoulders. He wrapped the length of it around the top of her head twice, and as it came around the second time, their eyes met and lingered for a moment. He moved behind her, tucking the end of the cloth into itself. With a tug, the knot behind her head was undone and he brought that end around the bottom half of her face, pulling it snug and tucking it into the wrap around her head.

"How do I look?" she asked.

"I would prefer to see your face," he said. "But I will survive somehow."

Odessa was glad for the litham for it hid a wide, foolish grin.

They remained behind that rocky bluff for nearly an hour before the wind abated enough to travel onward.

The next day, they reached the first of the outcroppings, towering mesas eroded to thin towers of rock. The road passed between two ridges of sandstone into a field of yardangs, a field of long, rocky protuberances like overturned ships petrified in stone. They formed a sort of natural labyrinth carved at the hand of the desert wind. The road wound around them, slithering in the valleys between their high ridges.

Rounding a curve in the road, the head of the caravan halted suddenly. Far back, Odessa could see nothing but walls of sandstone on either side and the backs of caravanners and bazaks ahead of her. A sick feeling seeped into her bones as the travelers nearest her jostled about.

A shout came from the head of the caravan. "Back! Backward!" The call was repeated down the line by many voices. But it all came too late. Before the rearmost caravanner could turn their bazak around, the shouts of retreat had turned to screams.

CHAPTER 27

An arrow slammed into the side of the cart with a solid *thwack*. Odessa leapt toward the back of the cart where her bow and sword were as Yakun hauled on the lead and tried to keep the goats from bolting. Poko was in the back of the cart, burying themself deep within the heap.

Odessa stabbed the sword into the dirt and strung the bow as fast as she could. All along the ridges, tall figures in drab scale armor crouched, launching arrows into the valley below. Odessa nocked an arrow, drew back, and loosed it in an instant, sending the arrow streaking up toward the ridge. A wild, high shot that arced over a figure standing above her on the ridge.

The figure didn't even flinch. Its bow was drawn. The arrow pointed at Odessa. Before she could reach for her quiver for another arrow, the cart lurched backward, knocking her aside. As she fell, the figure's arrow slammed into the cart where she had been standing.

Odessa spun and scrambled beneath the cart. One of the goats lay collapsed on the ground, its chest rising and falling in quick, panicked breaths. Wheezing with an arrow through its neck. The other was gone, the wooden staves on its end of the yoke broken.

She peered from behind the cartwheel to see Shadows scaling the sheer walls of rock. Arrows stuck in some of their backs, but only a few fell back to the road below.

She crawled halfway out from beneath the front of the cart, sticking her head out and scanning the ridges. One Shadow was already on the ridge, sticking an archer in the stomach with a knife. The other archers were preoccupied shooting at the Shadows scaling the walls.

Odessa took her opportunity to crawl out from beneath the cart and nocked an arrow. She put it in the side of one of the archers and ran forward, sliding behind the body of a fallen bazak, its legs kicking desperately in weak jerking motions. She fired another arrow toward the ridge not blocked by the bazak's huge frame. Another archer fell.

More Shadows hauled themselves up the crest. Some fell, long arrow shafts sticking out of their chests or heads. The archers were dropping their bows and unsheathing knives curved like sabers. Odessa fired one more arrow, burying it in the leg of an archer as a Shadow descended upon it with a curved sword to its chest.

She ran through the caravan, leaping over the dead and dying and pushing past the panicked living. She had to find Yakun. She had to find Tarik.

Her breath beat against her litham as she ran. Before she took even a half dozen steps, a horn blared directly behind her. And another in front of her, more distantly.

She spun to see more figures riding creatures shaped like boars with heads that were almost canine. They were charging up the road toward her and the rear of the caravan. Between her and the charging figures was the cart and Poko. Most of the caravanners who'd been behind their cart were already dead or had fled. A few with spears hunkered down amid the corpses.

A javelin arced through the air toward Odessa as she sprinted toward the cart. Running, she loosed a few quick arrows. Most missed or glanced off armor; only one managed to stick in the muzzle of one of the loping mounts.

Another javelin streaked past her as she dashed to the side of the cart. Leaping onto the wheel, she yanked the blanket from the heap, shouting, "Poko! Poko!" She began throwing baskets and pots out of the cart, digging a hole in the heap and burrowing beneath the side panels as another javelin streaked over her head.

She found Poko in an overturned bowl and stuffed them in her bag. Poking her head out from the heap, she could see the quickest of the riders only a few thunderous strides away. As they neared, Odessa could make out horns rising from notches in the rim of a pointed helmet with a flared neck guard. And sooty gold eyes peering out from beneath those horns. Their mount was the size of a bull, and the rider was taller and broader than any person she had ever seen.

The swiftest rider's mount leaped over a dead man and swerved around a fallen bazak, the rest of the horde close behind. One of the men lunged forward from his hiding place among the carnage. He was met with a long-handled club that took his head off in a burst of red.

As the horde of nearly a dozen riders bore down upon her, Odessa rolled over the front of the cart, landing atop the dead goat and scrambling beneath it as the first rider raced past in a panting blur.

Another passed on the other side of the cart as Odessa pressed her body tight against the ground. And another passed.

Eleven in total raced by, but one passed to the front and circled the cart, the hooved creatures trotting in slow revolutions around it. Odessa's body went stiff and, cramped beneath the cart's belly, she fumbled an arrow from her quiver.

"Come out, girl," a low feminine voice said.

In front of her, only an arm's reach from the back of the cart, her sword stood upright. With clumsy fingers, she nocked the arrow and rolled onto her back so her draw arm was not in the dirt.

Hooves clattered behind her and then rounded the back of the cart. Odessa slowly drew the bowstring back, the back of her bandaged hand rubbing against the belly of the cart.

The hooves came into view, slowly crossing Odessa's field of vision. They stopped for just a moment.

Odessa let the arrow fly and it slashed open the back of the mount's ankle. With a squeal, the mount bucked and the rider cried out to calm it. Odessa rolled onto her stomach and scrambled out from underneath the cart. Stumbling to her feet, she wrenched the sword from the dirt and spun to see the rider leaping from their bucking mount.

"You little bitch," the rider hissed as they charged Odessa, a spear low at their side. Odessa's head barely came to the rider's shoulder. It wore a tunic of iron scales like those of a lizard. The long red tassel at the top of the rider's helmet hung down to their shoulder, flowing as the rider darted around the cart. With the quickness of a viper, Odessa knocked the spear aside with the flat of her sword when it came snapping toward her. The spear was longer than Odessa was tall, and it moved much too quickly for her to get in close to the rider.

Dancing around the spear's jabs, Odessa could only parry and deflect. Once it was clear that jabs would not work, the rider slashed instead and aimed for Odessa's limbs.

Odessa tossed the bow to the ground and focused solely on keeping out of the spear's range. Picking around corpses and scattered goods, Odessa was forced backward. She dodged a vicious stab, jerking her top half to the right as the spearhead passed by her ribs.

Before the rider could slash open Odessa's chest, her hand moved with dizzying speed and took hold of the shaft. The rider yanked, but Odessa's grip was like iron. The rider pulled away, trying to free the spear. Odessa let it go with a shove away from herself as she darted in close. The rider tried to pull the spear back and shove her away, but it was too slow. Odessa swung low, catching the rider in the back of the knee. The blade's curve caught the ligaments and sliced them open.

The rider stumbled backward. Odessa batted the sweeping spear away. A mailed fist crashed into her cheek as she got a hand on the rider's helmet. Odessa rammed the sword into the visor, stabbing into one of the rider's glittering gold eyes. Blood poured out of the visor and down the rider's neck.

When she tried to withdraw the sword from the rider's skull, she couldn't wrench it free. Metal ground against bone and there was terrible squelching, but it remained firm. She took the spear, retrieved her bow, and chased after the rest of the horde. She could picture so clearly Tarik and Yakun meeting the rider with the club. Their faces disintegrating in a shower of blood and bone and pulp.

The Shadows had come back down into the valley and were ripping the riders from their mounts or pummeling them with clubs or sticking them with spears. A few riders were wheeling away from the Shadows when Odessa arrived to the crush of bloodshed. Ramming the spear into the dirt, she fired the last of her arrows into the riders, unseating one and wounding two others. The wounded riders pressed flat against their mounts and made for her. She slung her bow across her shoulder, took up the spear, and ran forward, angling toward the left.

When the rider came close enough, she planted her feet and rammed the spear into the mount's chest and then spun away from the rider's club as it swung for her head. The mount toppled forward and nearly ripped the spear from her hands, but Odessa held tight, stumbling as the force of the falling beast jerked her back before she withdrew the spear.

The rider was leaping off the mount when Odessa plunged the spear beneath its armpit. She had not even pulled the spear from the collapsing rider when the second came upon her. The clatter of hooves was loud. An old terror reverberated through her bones, in time with the thunderous pounding of hooves on stone.

She turned in time to see the spear coming for her throat. She jerked the spear shaft up and deflected the spearhead. It slid along the shaft and sliced open her cheek before she could duck away.

The rider and mount passed and wheeled back around to charge her again, giving her enough time to pull the spear free from the dead rider. The left side of her face was wet and hot. Blowing sand stuck to the blood pouring from her cheek.

The mount came fast, aiming to crush her beneath its hooves. The spear-bearer steadied the spear, meaning to drive it in her chest. If she were to be trampled then Poko would be as well. If she was skewered, at least Poko might survive.

She darted to the side, leaping over the dead rider and its mount. She ripped the shield from its arm as the living rider swerved around the dead mount. She lifted the shield and knocked the spearhead away. The mount's side struck her a glancing blow and knocked over onto the dead mount.

The rider had turned sharply and the spear snapped toward her. Her shield rose but it was too slow.

The spearhead stopped short, jerking to the side and then clattering to the ground as a Shadow ripped the rider from its saddle. As the mount bucked and stomped its hooves, another Shadow came, dodging a hoof and slicing the mount's throat in one deft motion.

The Shadow had the rider on the ground and endured brutal blows from the rider's shield. The Shadow stuck its blade in the gap between helmet and armor and opened the rider's throat. The rider kept striking the Shadow even as it bled to death. Its blows growing weaker and weaker until it could lift its shield no longer.

The skull-faced Shadows did not acknowledge her at all. Once rider and mount were dead, they wiped their swords clean of blood and made their way back to what remained of the caravan.

Odessa rose, the pounding in her ears slowly receding. Panicked cries filled the air. The grunts and groans of wounded bazaks. The scent of blood and voided bowels was everywhere. So many of the caravanners lay dead around her, their blood soaked into the sand.

This was war.

This was what Odessa had agreed to.

CHAPTER 28

Odessa pushed past the caravanners clustered together at the bend in the road. Yakun was crouched with his back to her. In front of him was Tarik, propped up against a sack.

Odessa rushed to his side. He was clutching a bloody rag to his collarbone. Blood seeped through his fingers. His eyes were closed, tears welling around his eyelashes. His jaw was set as he bit back the pain.

"What happened?" Odessa asked.

"He took an arrow," Yakun said. "Punched through the top of his shoulder blade and came out beneath his collarbone." Yakun pressed a clean rag to the wound on his back. "I don't think his lung is punctured and I picked what bits of bone I could with my fingers, but he's losing a lot of blood."

Tarik had gone pale. Odessa put a hand on his arm and it was cold. The riders' arrows were larger than hers, with brutally wide broadheads. *There must be a hole as big as a plum in his shoulder.*

"What if we cauterize it?" she asked timidly. "Would that work? Would that stop the bleeding?" Before Yakun had even replied, she was tearing the bandages from her hand.

"What are you doing?" he hissed. "You can't do that here!"

"Will it stop the bleeding?"

"Maybe. But he could just as likely die of shock or infection."

Odessa took an open jug of alcohol from the ground, poured it on her bare arm, and then crouched beside Tarik. "This is going to hurt," she whispered.

He nodded weakly.

She held the jug to his lips and told him to drink, then poured alcohol into both ends of his wound. He winced and groaned. Odessa wanted to stop but she couldn't. A wound like that would surely kill him if it was left untreated. Even if treated, his chances of survival were slim.

She set the jug down and looked at Yakun. "Hold him down."

Yakun glared at her a moment then relented with an exasperated sigh. "Just be careful."

Focusing on her index and middle fingers, she brought the heat within herself to her fingertips, letting it pulse and throb. Gently, she poked her fingers into the front of his wound. He gasped and squirmed. Yakun gripped his arm and held him.

The pulse quickened. She had to concentrate to keep it within her control. Then she let the flames come out, surging from her two fingers. There was a sudden sizzle, and smoke rolled out from around her fingers. She moved them around inside his shoulder, searing everything her fingertips touched.

When she pulled her fingers out, Tarik had passed out. Yakun rolled him over and she did the same with the opposite side. She worried her fingers had not reached far enough inside to stop the worst of the bleeding, but she had to have hope.

Nearly half of the caravan had perished in the ambush. There was much debate after the area had been secured about whether the caravan should load up their dead and make a run for the river a half day away, or if they should begin the burial process so they would not be burdened with a dozen dead bodies.

The Shadows were sent far out into the desert to scout for more bands of roving devils. When they returned and relayed to Bukoris through head-shaking and miming that there were no more devils in sight, the decision was made to make camp off the road.

Yakun, still playing the part of ka-man, saw to the wounded. The myriad arrow wounds and limbs crushed by panicked bazaks were gathered and placed together beneath the awning of a tent set in the shade of a ridge.

The soulweavers set about gathering the fallen caravanners and preparing their bodies for burial. In Asha-Kalir, the traditional practice of skull removal was not taken lightly. The bodies were stripped of their clothes and scrubbed with sand. Their heads were shaved clean and then decapitated and drained of blood and ill humor. The exsanguinated heads were wrapped in shrouds of linen while the bodies were taken to be interred in the sand. The head was the cage of the soul, and it was the head that would return to the ossuaries of Asha-Kalir.

While the soulweavers decapitated their fellow caravanners, Odessa was tasked with stripping the devil corpses and butchering the slain beasts.

The armor the devils wore was brutally wonderful. Each was made from iron and hide, some in spade-shaped scale and others in rectangular lamellar, but it was all true iron, dark and resolute. Their weapons were made of iron as well. Starkly utilitarian and harsh, their clubs were just slabs of iron with pointed rivets now covered in gore; their spearheads, set on shafts of dark wood, were sharp and angular, the length of a short sword and wider than her hand. Their shields were relatively small compared to the massive bodies they were made to protect. They were circular and made of dark wood-bound iron with tassels hanging from the rim.

Stripping the devils of their armor, Odessa saw for the first time what they looked like. They did not look like the abominations she had been told of over the campfire during hunts in the Arabako.

When she took the helmet off the first devil she stripped, she was surprised to find a nearly human face. The devil's skin was dark red, nearly black. It was the color of rust, of rose ebony. The devil's mouth, twisted open in a rictus cry, held the long teeth of a predator. Human in orientation but bestial in shape and sharpness. And the two horns rising from its forehead were something similar to a goat's or bull's, curling up and gradually back until they pointed over the top of its head. The horns were black at the base and a reddish brown at their points.

All the devils she searched were female, with faces sharp and angular. There was variation in the shape of their horns, some curled and twisted while others were straight. Their skin ranged from dark red to dark blue, always on the verge of black. Most had rust-colored hair in long dreads. All of them were at least two heads taller than she was and covered in hard knots of muscle and scars long healed.

Odessa kept a cuirass, helmet, shield, and spear for herself. Any arrows she found, she slid in next to her own until her quiver was bulging. Their arrows were obscenely long and heavy with barbed, pyramidal arrowheads that could pierce through armor and bone as if they were paper.

They butchered four bazaks and one goat that day. Yakun had chased their other goat down during the onset of the ambush and had been able to hobble it into the safety of the caravan's inner guard. The loads of the four dead bazaks had to be dispersed among the remaining beasts of burden. The cart's load had to be lightened so the remaining goat could haul it.

When Odessa tried to gut one of the devil's steeds, one of the caravanners hastily stopped her. "Entehlos are no good to eat," he said. "No good at all. We leave them to the crows. Let your goddess have them. They are no good to us."

By nighttime, they had all the devils stripped and dragged off the road into a pile along with their mounts. True to the caravanner's word, they left them to rot.

A large fire was kindled beneath a nearby ridge. A whole goat roasted over the fire along with four quarter bazaks. Bazak meat was pale and soft. Almost spongey. Sizzling and popping as it seared.

They ate well. The goat was delicious. The bazak was like stringy, already-chewed chicken with an earthiness somewhat like a mushroom. With the right spices it was not terrible. Odessa helped Tarik to some bone broth and forced him to drink the concoction Yakun had made to stave off infection. After that, Tarik was back asleep, shivering despite the blankets wrapped around him.

Odessa stayed by him all night. Listening to his wheezing breath and muttered whimpers. When his whimpers turned to moans and cries, she held him. She held him through the night until she herself had fallen asleep with him.

CHAPTER 29

The wounded were loaded up in Yakun's cart, their goods having been dispersed among the backs of the remaining bazaks. Bukoris was astonished that the devils had come this far south. He had Shadows scouting the area ahead now. His own men remained by his side.

By midday they reached the banks of the Darrood. The Darrood was a wide stretch of water, the widest Odessa had ever seen, murky and slow-moving.

At the banks of the Darrood, they came to a crossroads. They took the road south for some time, following the river downstream until they came to another caravansary, this one even more ornate than the last. They did not stay long.

A boat waited for them, a wide, flat-keeled barge to carry them to Asha-Kalir. The bazaks were loaded first, and then the wounded. Odessa followed onto the barge, her stomach twisting with the gentle bob and dip of the deck.

Pressed together at the back of the ship, the caravanners and the bazaks were unfazed as the oarsmen pushed the boat from the riverbank and slipped into the center of the river's current. Their sweeping rows were loose and unhurried as the water bore them south.

Odessa pushed her way to the outer edge of the mass of man and bazak until she could breathe clean air and not someone else's sour breath. She leaned over the navel-high railing just in case the dates she had eaten for breakfast came surging back up her throat. The river was calm and forgiving, but her stomach was unsettled all the same. It was not so much the boat that unsettled it; it was the press of bodies. The jostling of men. And being face-to-face with the Shadows. Their cold masks and the cloudy white eyes staring blankly out from within them. Talara's stench worming down her throat to choke her. It was all too much to bear.

At the railing, breathing deep gulps of clean river air cleared her head and her stomach soon settled. The sky to the south was a soft gray and the air seemed clearer the farther they went downstream. The river slithered through the desert, leaving patches of harsh, yellow greenery in its wake. Towns and villages clung to its banks. Smaller boats skittered on its surface, drawing small netfuls of fish from its waters. The people on the banks seemed so small to Odessa as they passed. Bird-men and bulky bodies of red clay were always there as well. She saw more clay giants the farther south they traveled. Their sizes and shapes differed slightly, but they were always there, looming over the people as they worked.

It was in the twilight glow that Odessa first glimpsed the splendor of Asha-Kalir. In the distance, she made out glittering specks of bronze glowing in the fiery red of dusk over the desert. The city's domes and steep roofs glittered for spans on either side of the river, tiny pinpricks of light on the horizon.

As they drew closer, Odessa could make out the massive wall of pure white. In the dying light of day, it shone with a sort of ghastly majesty on the horizon.

The boat passed fields of barley with small stone buildings scattered along their periphery next to thin, spidery roads of crushed rock. The stone buildings became larger and more common as they neared the walls of the city. Other buildings interrupted the expanse of fields. Large buildings high above the banks of the river with smaller, impermanent huts along its lower banks.

As they came nearer still, Odessa's attention was drawn away from the fields and even the city walls. Her attention was on the massive clay statues flanking either side of the river near the city walls. Clad in bronze armor like the carapace of some crustacean, the giants had taken a greenish patina to contrast the red of the clay they had been born from.

It was not until the boat slipped beneath the first statue's feet that Odessa could truly fathom their size. They stood as tall as some of the tallest trees in the Night Jungle and were shaped vaguely like huge men with four arms coming from their shoulders. Each of their four hands rested on the hilt of a sickle-shaped sword hanging from a bronze belt, two on either side of their waists.

Each wore a domed helmet like the roofs in the city behind them, with a spike set at the top. The helmets flared out at the base and then swept inward near the cheeks and came to an end just past the neck, encompassing everything save for a slit for the eyes. It was the eyes that drew Odessa. They were gleaming turquoise with carved pupils that seemed to follow the boat as it glided past its feet.

The boat passed eight of the giants on its way to the city. The white walls stood even taller than the giants, and between the walls on either side of the river stretched a wide bronze gate to bar them entry. They pulled beside a dock and disembarked.

The caravan filed off the boat, and Bukoris led them through a brick-lined path surrounded by long warehouses and a sprawling shipyard. They came to a wide thoroughfare that ran directly to the huge bronze gates of Asha-Kalir. Carved into the bronze was a relief depicting a multitude of hands reaching toward a sun at the center of the gates.

Set into the wall beside the gates was a narrow door manned by two red clay soldiers. Bukoris led Odessa, the few unwounded soulweavers, and the Shadows through the narrow passage while the others went on to an inn outside the walls.

Odessa glanced back at the cart of wounded. Yakun was tending to them as they had been jostled with the cart's movement. Tarik was asleep, his face pale and slick with sweat.

They passed through the smooth stone doorway into a cramped room. Four bird-men sat on narrow stools around a table covered in small clay squares and piles of coins. A Red Clay Warrior stood by the door as they entered the room. At the sight of Bukoris, the soldiers bolted upright.

"*Shah-kahn,*" one of the bird-men said, quickly running a taloned hand over the clay tiles and sweeping them aside. "Welcome back. We have been expecting your return."

"Apparently not," Bukoris said, crossing the room with a weary imperiousness. "I wonder what type of welcome you would give a horde of devils if they came through this door. Would any of you even be on your feet before they caved in your skulls?"

He shoved open the door on the opposite end of the room and left the room in a stagnant silence. Like a cellar collected the stink of rotting vegetables, the cramped room festered with an awkward quiet as the soulweavers passed. At the sight of the Shadows filing past, the bird-men stiffened. They barely noticed as Odessa walked by, so rattled they were.

Along the thoroughfare stretching from the main gate were rows of lamps burning on high poles. Wide cones of polished tin topped each lamp, reflecting the light down toward the street. A quiet hiss came from each pole they passed and a faint, acrid odor.

High, narrow buildings of white stone loomed over the thoroughfare. Fluted columns and narrow porticos extended from many of the buildings. Elaborate capitals topped the columns of a fair few of them, flaring out like palm fronds or carved in the shape of regal animals or gruesome faces.

They followed the road until it passed beneath the arched entrance of the wall and ended at a stone staircase. They climbed gradual steps between bare stone walls until they came to a wide plaza at the top of the stairs. And in the center of the plaza was a raised platform holding a skull as tall as the main gates had been, half-sunken in sand. The skull was humanoid with a pronounced brow and its empty eye sockets seemed to stare up over the buildings and the wall behind them.

Sloping walls surrounded the plaza and directly behind the skull were walls dotted with clerestory windows along the top. It looked like a temple to Odessa.

Bukoris led them around the platform to the temple wall. Odessa couldn't take her eyes from the skull. She couldn't fathom a being that large. She wanted to ask whose skull it had been, but her present company stayed her tongue. The Shadows walking like dark clouds over the brick plaza still unnerved her. Poko was quiet in her bag, still resting from being jostled and crushed in the ambush. She was alone in a foreign land, Talara's killers her only companions.

Bukoris took them through a set of double doors beside where the center of the skull sank into the sand. The door led into a lobby of sorts, dimly lit by hissing braziers set in alcoves along the wall. The braziers bore soft blue-white flames that gave the room a sense of sickly sterility.

Several doors led from the empty lobby. The soulweavers detached from the group and took a nondescript door on the left, slipping away without a word as Bukoris led Odessa and the Shadows to the far end of the lobby and through a door on the right.

They entered a dark hallway and walked silently for quite a while in that darkness until they emerged into a long room with high, vaulted ceilings and unadorned columns. The room was lined with row upon row of clay men.

Bukoris stopped and turned to face her and the Shadows but his eyes met hers alone. "You are now the property of Khymanir, King of Bones." Were it not for the dark, she could have sworn his beak had turned to a smile. "Welcome to your new home."

CHAPTER 30

Kunza was tired. Torn between his daily discussion with the Chosen and the godlings and his nightly conspirations with Ur-Mak, he barely had time for prayer and devotion. He had convinced one of the godlings of the importance of an alliance with Asha-Kalir despite the concessions. But Azka was hearing none of it. He kept his head above such matters of state now, choosing instead to stare out over the rooftops of Noyo and ponder thoughts he never deigned to speak.

Finally finding a night to himself, he kneeled before his humble shrine and prayed. It was only a short while before he felt Talara coiling around him.

"Odessa Kusa has arrived in Asha-Kalir," Talara whispered. Kunza felt a coldness fill his core. "She is at Khymanir's disposal now."

"We should hope she dies at devils' hands then," Kunza muttered.

"Not before she is bursting at the seams with stolen life," Talara said sharply. "If she dies prematurely, the fortuity of her creation would be wasted."

"I understand," Kunza said, reluctant to agree with the girl's continued survival. But as necessary an evil as it was, it was also an interesting experiment in regard to his own work. How much divinity could the human body bear before it began to fall apart? What happened to Odessa would be a precursor to the perfected human form. A chance perversion of the divine and the human. She was a flawed, tainted specimen but with Talara's guidance they could use the knowledge they gleaned from the girl's abominable being to both sate the spreading Grey and usher humanity into the upper echelon of being. Not god but something altogether new and holy.

"I think it is time her sister joined you in Noyo."

Kunza's eyes opened slightly at Ayana's mention. "It surely cannot be time yet."

"Your doubtful nature is ill-suited to my Priest of Ashes," Talara whispered in his ear.

"It is not doubt, My Goddess," Kunza shifted, trying to settle the hairs that had risen on the back of his neck. "I was only surprised. That is all."

"Good," Talara said, no longer whispering. "For it is not time yet, but there is much for her to still learn and there may be no better teacher for her at this time than you."

"What am I to teach her exactly?"

"Teach her as you would teach your own daughter. Take her in as your own and show her what it is to be human. And what it will be." Talara's voice came close again, lapping at his skin. "Show her love and teach her war. For when the Low Gods begin to fall, she must be standing. You know what is coming. She must be ready to take the mantle."

Kunza nodded. "Yes, My Goddess."

"Ayana Kusa has taken to my teachings and heeded my words well. See to it that she also takes to yours." Talara's presence pressed against his skin reassuringly. "She will join you the day after next." With that, Talara's presence dissipated like heady smoke. It lingered like smoke pools at the ceiling. Kunza continued his prayers, and she listened to his concerns about Asha-Kalir's soft refusal of an alliance and Azka's growing incompetence. But she said no more.

Sometime between night and daybreak, in the liminal hours where all is pitch and silence, Kunza found himself on the ramparts again, walking along the wall, his mind turning slowly through familiar corridors of thought. Ruminating over the same conundrums as he had for the last year. How could he avert the same crisis that had killed the Forgotten Gods? Everything he did—would it truly be enough to keep the Grey at bay? And if Talara's plan succeeded and the Grey was stopped, what would become of him? He had already changed so much since the days before Egende was killed. What more would he have to do to meet Talara's expectations? How much further would he stray from the man he had once been? That weak, spineless coward he once was.

He missed sleep more than anything. It was hard not to resent his current form due only to the fact he could not close his eyes for a midday nap. It was stupid, but he felt it all the same. How he had taken something like sleep for granted. He hadn't known how isolating the liminal hours of full dark could be. Even with eyes that could pierce the darkness, there was nothing worth seeing. Only rats scurrying along empty streets and spirits dancing in the night sky like lost bits of gossamer cloth caught in the wind. The quiet seemed to almost seep into his core. Distant voices came sporadically from the city below, echoing through the streets. All so far away from Talara's Priest of Ashes.

When he returned to the palace, his newly appointed coterie of Shadows trailing in the darkness, he found Ketabi perched on the roof of the hall. Kunza could see the godling's luminous eyes meet his from atop the roof. On his way up the palace steps, Kunza stopped and bowed. Ketabi's head dipped in recognition and his eyes flicked away, back out toward the cityscape below.

Kunza's footfalls were loud in the empty hall, the flickering coals of the brazier set in the center of the floor warm upon his shins. He stopped in front of the god's dais, studying the dark wood carved with intricate reliefs of windswept grasses and mountains and Azka upon high. The rich purple of the cushions, so deep and intense. The high tier in the center where Azka sat was almost as tall as Kunza and more than twice as wide.

There was a flutter of broad wings and a gust whipped at the cape upon Kunza's back with the sound of paws upon marble.

"How was your walk, Kunza?" Ketabi purred.

Kunza turned and bowed deeply as the godling padded slowly toward him. "It was lovely. The night air is especially brisk tonight. Gets the blood pumping."

"I suppose it would be brisk with the little fur you have on you," Ketabi said. The bit of mirth in his tone may have been meant to put Kunza at ease but it immediately did the opposite. Ketabi strode past Kunza and took his place on the dais. "Were you admiring the dais?"

"Yes, Ketabi, I was. It is a work of art."

"Do you wish to sit upon the sovereign's seat?" Ketabi asked, folding his paws beneath him as he lay down, sinking into the plush cushion.

"No, of course not," Kunza said. His unease doubled, hanging heavy in his gut. "I am but a man. I would never dream of sitting upon the sovereign's throne."

"You wouldn't sit on it but once?"

"No, I would never," Kunza said. "I know my place."

"But do you?" Ketabi asked, his voice suddenly deepening. "Do you really know your place? Is that why you conspire with the mason as you do? What is it that you two talk about? What is so important that you two find the need to slink away nearly every night? Is it conspiracy? Is it blasphemy? Or are you two simply having an affair of the flesh?" Ketabi's lips pulled tight, a cruel facsimile of a smile. "I suppose you're probably too old for the latter, no? You humans wither so quickly."

"It is no conspiracy, Ketabi, I assure you."

"Then what is it?" Ketabi asked, his teeth still bared.

"We've been discussing Asha-Kalir. You know I have some vested interest in a continued relationship with them and I've been trying to persuade the Grand Mason to join me in pushing for the alliance we've spoken of. I'm trying to convince him to supplement wedges with Asha-Kaliran blast powders in his quarries." The half-truth came from his mouth so readily he worried it sounded rote or rehearsed.

"Yes, your proposed alliance," Ketabi said. "Your persistence is like that of a gnat. Buzzing and buzzing but somehow always evading the swatting paw and the swishing tail." Ketabi rose a bit in his cross-legged lounging. "You are loyal to my father first and foremost, yes?"

Kunza shifted uneasily. A quick lie came to his tongue, but he swallowed it. The bitter truth would be death so he would sweeten it as much as he could. But he could not lie about his faith. "My sovereign and my goddess share a place in my heart."

"Do you honestly believe your goddess can keep the Grey from Noyo?"

"Not only Noyo," Kunza said. "If I am able to carry out her will, that is."

Ketabi eyed him, his moon-shaped eyes luminescent in the dimness of the hall. "Are you a charlatan or a madman?" Ketabi asked. "I've agonized over this question since you first stepped into the palace."

"Have you come to an answer yet?"

"I believe so." Ketabi rose upon the dais. "Come with me."

Ketabi stepped from the dais and walked to the massive doors to the central palace. Kunza followed, his steps slow and reticent. He had never stepped foot through that door.

Ketabi paused before the door and looked back. "Leave your Shadows behind. There are to be no Shadows past this threshold, understood?"

Kunza nodded. He snapped his fingers and waved behind him. His Shadows would not enter the central palace, but they would be close by. He was sure of that. But would having them close by matter when Ketabi could rip him to shreds in a fraction of a second?

With a paw, Ketabi shoved one of the doors open. The heavy slab of bronze swung halfway open and Ketabi brushed past it into the wide-open atrium of the central palace. When Kunza entered, Ketabi kicked the door closed behind them.

The atrium was huge with a vaulted ceiling gilded with gold. A large fountain bubbled in the center of the room and statues stood in alcoves along the walls. More large purple cushions were arrayed around the room, set on marble plinths.

"You are the first human to enter the palace proper," Ketabi said as he walked across the atrium to another set of doors on the other side. These doors were wood, carved and overlaid with gold. "You should be honored." Ketabi pawed the door open, his paw striking a wide brass plate in the center of the door.

"I am," Kunza said quietly. His nerves were afire as he stepped through the gilded doors behind Ketabi.

They passed through another stately room and then into a long hallway adorned with colorful mosaics on its wall. Steep staircases branched off the hallway, and the occasional balcony opened from the left side of the hall, the decks suspended over the edge of the palace's base for the god and his godlings to take flight from and land upon.

Kunza's hair stood on end as he followed the godling through the empty halls. "Do you not have servants?" Kunza asked, trying to remain outwardly nonchalant.

"I had them sent away for the time being." Ketabi stopped in front of a door. "We can speak candidly here."

The door led down a steep set of stairs shrouded in pitch-black darkness. The darkness embraced him, but it was a foreign darkness. Talara felt distant as he followed the godling down the stairs.

The steps wound deep beneath the palace. At the bottom was a small chamber made entirely of limestone. A single lamp lit the room. As Kunza stepped into the room he saw a sarcophagus dominating the small space. The lamp flickered atop its marble lid. Reliefs adorned its sides, depicting defining moments in Kutali's short life.

Kunza stopped at the entrance to Kutali's crypt. "I should not be here," he quickly told Ketabi. "It is not proper."

"It's not proper that a god should die so young either," Ketabi said. He nuzzled the cold marble and sat beside his brother's temporary tomb. "I wonder, Kunza, does your heart grow accustomed to the pain of grief? Humans have such short lifespans—do you grow numb to death? Is its pain dulled over time or do you feel it all the same?"

"Talara teaches that death only brings more life," Kunza said, unsure of what the godling wanted. "But the loss of a brother . . . I don't think that is a loss that can ever be dulled. It must be the same for man as well as god."

Ketabi rested his chin upon the lid of Kutali's sarcophagus. "I have never felt a pain such as this."

Kunza stood dumbly at the mouth of the stairs, unsure of what to say.

"Do you know what killed my brother?"

"The Grey, no?"

"Yes but it would be wrong to say that it alone holds the blame," Ketabi said. "When Kutali first became ill, our father did nothing. He refused to even listen to Kutali's complaints. No, our father would rather sit and listen to the wind than to his youngest son. It wasn't until Kutali was skin and bone that our father took notice. When Kutali bled from his ears and eyes, that was when our father finally sent for healers. By the time they arrived at the palace, little Kutali was cold and catatonic." Ketabi's wings rustled and shifted. His body tensed as he sat up and stared Kunza down. "Azka could have saved Kutali. As he could have your mason's Stone Queen. He is a doddering old cat long past his prime. If allowed to continue to rule, he will drag Noyo into Grey ruin."

Kunza balked. *Conspiracy from the godling? How serendipitous.* "What is it you are suggesting?"

"I am not suggesting anything," Ketabi said. "Not yet. I only wish to broach a proposition. I will push for a definite deal with Asha-Kalir and in exchange I expect to have you and your Shadows at my full disposal. If divides fracture Noyo, the Chosen are loyal to Azka. I would need your support."

Could this be a trap? A test of loyalties? Or perhaps just bold talk. If I agree with him he could change his mind and tell his father of my treachery. But a godling would be a powerful ally. Indispensable.

"Should anything happen to our sovereign, you would undoubtedly have my support and the support of my Shadows," Kunza said.

Ketabi nodded. "Good," he said, the emotion in his voice bleeding away. "May it never happen, but should illness or the like take Azka, I am glad to have your support."

Kunza left Ketabi to his grief. Walking the halls of the central palace back to the atrium was not nearly as intimidating as it had been before. His Shadows stood on the balconies as he passed them, always alert and on edge. But one had to be so in Noyo. The city was built of rumors and conspiracy, upon a foundation of corpses.

CHAPTER 31

A few carts rolled toward Noyo's southern gates. The road stretched toward the Night Jungle, mostly empty in the early hours of dawn. Kunza had come down to the gatehouse nearly an hour before the gates opened and had to wait. He stood now outside the gates, unsure if he should go out and meet Ayana. She was only a young girl. Talara had not mentioned whether she traveled with an escort, but the goddess was not known for coddling.

What am I to do with her? He asked himself again. *I have enough to do to merely stay alive in this den of vipers.*

Around midday, he caught sight of four figures coming up the jungle road. One figure, walking between the rest, was just a bit more than half the size of the other three. The three larger figures were cloaked in black and moved like shadows across the plain. Relief eased the tension in his chest. *My Goddess, thank you for not sending her through that wretched jungle alone.*

His relief was short lived. As he approached to meet Ayana and her escorts halfway, he caught sight of something poking out from the hood of one of the figures. A white snout.

He stopped abruptly. *No. It can't be.* He took off down the road, sandals slapping loudly against the pavers, dismissing entirely both propriety and pride. Noyo had been only reluctantly receptive of his Shadows, and he was sure that was because they wore masks. To have one of his more audacious creations on display would be suicide for his reputation.

As he got closer, he saw that all three of Ayana's escorts were hunched and bore animal faces. The heads of two goats and a jackal hid beneath their hoods.

"What are you doing?" Kunza snapped when he was within a few hurried strides. His lungs burned and his words came out in a wheezing hiss. It had been a long time since he had run like that. "You can't bring our beastfolk here. Are you mad?"

Ayana stopped, and her escorts stopped in stride with her. Their animal faces stared at him blankly. "I have to bring them," she said. "They're mine."

"What do you mean they're yours?"

"They're mine," Ayana repeated. "The goddess said so."

Kunza bit back a scream. *Does she not understand what a precarious position I'm in? Does she not care?* "Fine," Kunza said curtly. They had already made it this far; there was no sense in sending them away. He glared at them. "Just pull your hoods over your faces. I could nearly see your snouts from the gates."

They only stared at him, as if he were speaking a language they'd never heard. Ayana turned to them and nodded. "Do as he says. Make sure they're over your noses. And make sure its pinned tight under your chins too."

Watching the beastfolk adjust their hoods, Kunza knew they would not go unnoticed in Noyo. The horns of the goat heads poked out beneath the hoods like tent stakes. "Ah, don't bother," he said. "Perhaps Azka will appreciate the progress we've made. Obi was a fine warrior, but his rebirth was fraught with mistakes and poor design." *Perhaps if Khymanir sees what I am capable of with beast and man he will not be as hesitant to confederation.* "Come," he said to Ayana, leading her toward Noyo. "There is much I want to show you."

The gate guards didn't stop them as they passed, but their stares followed them into Noyo. Kunza's Shadows had converged around them and escorted them through the streets. They pushed through the crowds, ignoring the stares and jeers of the rabble around them. Kunza kept a hand on Ayana's back, ushering her forward at a brisk pace until they reached the palace plaza.

Ayana stopped before the steps onto the plaza, gazing up at the massive palace above.

"It's wonderful, no?"

"It's huge," she said quietly.

"Come," he said, holding out his hand for her. "There's much to see inside. Perhaps you'll even get to see Azka today."

"I'll get to see a god up close?"

Kunza smiled. "If we're lucky, maybe."

She took his hand, and he led her up the steps to the palace doors. Her hand was small and clammy. The city was large and loud and intensely overwhelming.

Halfway up the stairs, away from the din of the city below, Ayana asked him, "How long do I have to be here?"

"What do you mean?"

"The goddess didn't say how long I'd be here. She just said to go to Noyo," Ayana said quietly.

"This is your first time from home, isn't it?"

Ayana nodded.

"Are you scared?"

She nodded again. "And I don't want to leave Mama for too long. She gets sad sometimes and if I'm not there to cheer her up she'll be even more sad."

"Your mama will be fine," Kunza said. "She's strong. And she has your grandmama, no?"

"Yes," Ayana said. "But she'll still be lonely."

They were nearly to the top of the stairs. "If you do well in your studies, perhaps we can visit her. How does that sound?"

"What studies?" Ayana asked.

Kunza stepped onto the landing. "Our goddess has much she wants to teach you. She requires much from you, Ayana. You are going to have to be strong, cunning, and tenacious. But if you can do that, she will show you things you cannot even imagine."

Their eyes met and Ayana's, glittering with cautious excitement, did not recoil from his gaze. She held it and squeezed his hand.

CHAPTER 32

Odessa found it difficult to sleep with rows of clay soldiers looming over her. Every time she began drifting off to sleep she thought she heard the scrape of a clay foot upon stone or saw movement in the corner of her barely open eye. She had spent three nights in the Red Clay Warrior barracks. *Barracks* was a very generous term the servants had used the few times they had come to bring her breakfast and dinner, though they never spoke directly to her. Only around her, as if she were a stray dog receiving table scraps. Worthy of charity but not companionship.

The Shadows, it seemed, did not eat. They stood nearly as still as the clay men, sometimes shifting or swaying so subtly one might not notice. But they were equally silent. And the silence had worn Odessa's nerves raw.

She gave up on sleep after a few hours. The barracks were always dark, so she had given up on sleeping according to the cycle of day and night. She sat up from her nest of blankets. Poko was sitting on the rim of her water bucket, their feet dangling in the water, kicking up tiny splashes.

"Hey," Odessa said wearily. "Get your feet out of there. I drink out of that."

"My feet are clean. It's fine."

"I know for a fact they're not clean because you've been walking all over this dirty floor. But even if they were clean, they're still feet and I don't want feet in my water."

"Well if you hadn't gotten yourself locked up with me still in your bag, then I wouldn't be so bored I have to splash around in your water bucket for fun!"

"You think I wanted this?"

"I think you should have left me with the old man!" Poko said.

"So you'd leave me just like that?"

"I would come to visit!"

"No you wouldn't! You know you wouldn't!"

"Yes I would! I would pop in during breakfast or something once in a while."

Odessa narrowed her eyes. "You swear it?"

"Swear what?"

"Swear that you would visit me if you were outside."

Poko scoffed. "That's stupid. I'm not gonna swear it. It's just a hypothetical."

"Then swear it."

"Why would I swear it?"

"Why won't you swear it?"

"Because I don't want to!"

"Because you know I'm right! You wouldn't visit me at all!" They glared at each other for a moment. Odessa wasn't sure if they had been joking or in an actual argument. But she was irritated all the same, so she didn't let it go. "Next time they bring breakfast or dinner or whatever it is next, you should slip out and find Yakun."

"Maybe I will," Poko said, their arms crossed.

The door opened across the barracks and they both started at the noise. Odessa turned to see Tarik peeking through the cracked door.

Odessa jumped to her feet. When he saw her, he smiled and slipped inside the warehouse. He wore a loose-fitting robe and his arm was in a sling.

"Tarik!" Odessa said, running across the barracks. "You're alive! I wasn't sure what happened to you—no one would tell me anything."

"I'm alive," he said. "Heavily medicated but alive nonetheless."

"How is your shoulder?" she asked.

"Healing," Tarik said. "They say I will probably lose some function in my arm but I got pretty lucky. They say devil arrows are usually covered in poison or shit or something equally vile."

"They don't say that!" Odessa said, but Tarik's earnest face gave her pause. "Do they?"

"They might say that," he said with a grin. "But they might not too."

"You liar!" she said.

"I'm not a liar," he said. "I'm just ignorant."

"Well at least I know you're telling the truth about that," she said.

Tarik feigned hurt. They laughed. Odessa stayed a short distance away, very aware of the fact that she had spent the last four days wallowing in her own stink. But she wanted to get closer.

"I'm sorry they put you in here," Tarik said, looking around at her accommodations. "This is no place for you."

"At least I have company," she said, gesturing to the rows of clay men.

"Ever the optimist, huh?" Tarik said. "But if you *are* getting sick of your roommates, my master is trying to get you put under her provisional control. Or at the very least get you out of here and in the actual barracks for living beings."

"There's a barracks for living things? Why am I in here then?" Odessa was indignant. Her loosening grip on sanity could have been avoided and it infuriated her.

"Bukoris doesn't like you," Tarik said plainly. "But in the meantime, while my master works on getting you out, is there anything you need? I can probably smuggle you some decent food or something."

"Yes!" Odessa said quickly. "Food. Please smuggle me food. All they give me is cold porridge and maybe four dried dates a day."

"I'll see if I can get you a fifth date," Tarik said. "Maybe even lukewarm porridge. That'd be nice, huh?"

"You're the worst," Odessa said, trying to hide her smile.

"Stay strong," Tarik said. "You'll be out of here soon. And then we can work out your arm problem. Just a little while longer."

"Thank you," Odessa said. Tarik smiled and left, leaving Odessa with a fluttering in her stomach.

Poko was sitting in Odessa's nest of blankets when she returned. "Something's off," Poko said, watching her with their arms still crossed over their chest.

"What do you mean?"

"You're acting weird," Poko said. "You're all fidgety and flush."

"No I'm not!" she said, a bit too quickly.

Poko pointed a finger at her. "You're right, you're not. But methinks that was a bit of an overreaction, no?" They stroked their chin. "Very interesting."

"You're irritating me," she said, plopping down to the floor across from them.

Poko's chin-stroking intensified. "Interesting, indeed."

Odessa groaned and let herself fall back onto the floor.

Dinner came an hour later. She could tell it was dinner by the lack of dates with her porridge. She tried again to ask the servants when she would be allowed to leave, but they said nothing. Next she asked them why they wouldn't talk to her. One servant chanced a glance at her and simply pointed at the bronze collar they wore around their neck. All the servants wore thick bronze bands engraved with flowing script.

Odessa sat back as they left, absent-mindedly picking at her porridge. Poko scrambled onto her lap and took two greedy handfuls of porridge, and Odessa did not even resist. She didn't know exactly what those collars were, but she knew well enough what collars were for. Control and domination.

* * *

When the door opened the next morning, it was Bukoris and a team of soul-weavers. Including Tarik. Tarik followed close behind a woman maybe as old as Yakun, but her beauty had refined with the years. The woman, presumably Azdava, held a strip of bronze between her hands.

"Get up," Bukoris said. Odessa scrambled to her feet as Bukoris stopped before her nest of blankets. "As property of Asha-Kalir and our eminence, Khymanir, you are bound by his word. His word is indelible. His word is ineffable. You will live by his word until our eminence sees fit. Do you understand?"

"What is this?" Odessa asked, taking a step back from the assembly before her.

"Do you understand?" Bukoris repeated. The Shadows that had been her silent companions for the last five days roused at the snap of Bukoris's taloned fingers.

Odessa stiffened. Her eyes darted to the collar in Azdava's hands and then back to Bukoris. "I understand," she said.

"Your life is Khymanir's to do with as he sees fit and proper," Bukoris continued. "Any insubordination or dissension will be dealt with swiftly and severely. Talara's pet or not, you are our eminence's property and you will be treated as such. Do you understand?"

"Yes, I understand," Odessa said sharply.

"Then you will wear the collar," Bukoris said. Azdava stepped forward.

It's not enough that I kill for you? Odessa eyed with disgust the hinged bronze crescent moon in Azdava's hands. "Fine," she said. "I'll wear your collar."

"Lift your chin," Azdava said, her voice melodious and restrained. "And try not to move." Azdava put the collar to Odessa's throat, the two ends of the crescent moon meeting behind her neck. Tarik came to Azdava's side, his eyes meeting Odessa's for a moment before he handed Azdava a hammer and a metal pin the width of his small finger. The collar bounced and dug into Odessa's neck as Azdava pounded the pin into the eyes of the collar's ends, riveting it in place snugly about her throat.

Azdava gave Tarik the hammer again. He took it, bowed, and backed away. "Now give me your arm," Azdava said to Odessa. Odessa raised her bandaged arm. "Your other arm." Odessa gave Azdava her other arm, and before Odessa could flinch, Azdava had drawn a narrow knife from the sash of her kaftan and opened a tiny cut in the hollow of Odessa's wrist.

Odessa drew back as Azdava sheathed the knife in her sash. "I require but a drop of blood," she said.

"For what?" Odessa asked, glancing down at the small drop of blood welling from the cut.

"For your collar," Azdava said, taking Odessa's wrist and smearing the blood with her thumb. Azdava pressed her thumb against the collar and began chanting an incantation under her breath. Odessa wanted to pull away but steeled herself, planting her feet and making her spine rigid as the collar began to thrum with magic. The bronze shifted, slowly tightening around her throat.

"Like strangling vine, may these words bind you in service," Azdava repeated, the collar resonating with the cadence of her chant. "Like strangling vine, may these words bind you in service."

The air around them became charged with an electric buzz that tickled Odessa's skin. When the air was laden with this buzzing energy, Azdava's chant quickened. And then it was over. The bubble burst and the energy in the air dissipated in an instant. The collar around Odessa's neck was tight and suffocating.

"There," Azdava said. "It is done."

"What is this?" Odessa asked, her hand trying to pry at the collar.

"It is insurance," Bukoris said. "If you, at any time, disobey or try to do harm to our eminence, your betters, or Asha-Kalir as a whole, that collar will start to burn and tighten until your head is off. Do you understand your position now?"

"You bastard," she hissed. The collar grew warm against her skin and pressed against her throat with just enough pressure to get her attention.

Bukoris squawked an incomprehensible phrase, making a sound Odessa could not even hope to imitate, and the pressure around her neck relaxed. "I will let that go as a learning experience. But show such insolence again and I won't stop the collar's tightening."

Odessa glared at him, still holding on to the collar.

"If you attempt to flee, the collar will tighten," Bukoris continued, ignoring her glare. "If you attempt to tamper with the collar, it will tighten. If the collar is damaged in any way, it will tighten, so take care when out hunting devils."

A sense of claustrophobia began winding around Odessa, constricting her chest and throat until she thought she might die from fright. *This was not part of the plan. Talara made no mention of me becoming a godsdamned slave. What am I supposed to do?*

Azdava and the other soulweavers went to each Shadow and fitted them with a collar in the same way Odessa had been. The Shadows did not so much as flinch as the collars shrank around their ash-pale necks.

"You and Talara's Shadows leave tomorrow," Bukoris said, leaning close to Odessa. "The devils have grown much too bold. I want them slaughtered and their heads left on pikes along the road. We will see if Talara's playthings are worth Khymanir's attention. Do well and perhaps when you return you will have a bed to sleep on. If you do exceptionally well, perhaps you can even have your own room."

Odessa's jaw clenched, but from between grinding teeth she said, "Yes, sir."

CHAPTER 33

Men and giants alike toiled beneath cracking whips and shouts from Ur-Mak's drivers. Another slab of stone was being hauled up the ramps to be hoisted upon great levers and pulleys and laid upon the rising walls.

Kunza and Ayana walked through the outskirts of the work camp, past all the weary souls going about their labor sharpening chisels or mending clothes or hurrying to and fro. Not far behind, her beastfolk followed, keeping most of the camp a fair distance away. Farther into the camp, following the narrow roads of pounded dirt, they passed a tent from which stifled sobs came, quiet and muffled. Through the tent flaps, they could make out a young boy being tended to by an older man. The man wiped blood from deep slashes across the boy's back, the product of a whip. The boy flinched each time the rag touched his torn skin, and his thin chest heaved with the force of his cries.

Ayana edged closer to Kunza's side as the sobbing receded behind them. "This is what it is to be human," Kunza said. The grand construction rose before them. A whip cracked not far ahead. "Only the gods are spared this pain and strife. We suffer and we die so that they may enjoy their long lives." He kept his voice low as they walked. "That is how it always has been, ever since humanity was created from mud. But it does not have to be like this forever. Talara sees the potential inherent in mankind."

Ayana flinched as another whip cracked near the base of the tomb.

"You must be strong," Kunza said. "You must endure the inequity of this cruel world before you can change it. Harden your resolve and let the world crash and break at your feet."

Ayana nodded. "I can endure it. My goddess believes in me."

Kunza put a hand on her shoulder. "You're destined for something far beyond what you see right now, Ayana. Do not forget that. Talara has a grand vision for you, as long as you are brave enough to walk the path she has charted for you."

Another whip cracked, this time much closer. Ayana did not flinch.

The Grand Mason's tent stood on a platform built on a slight ridge over the rest of the camp. Its canvas walls were rolled up so Ur-Mak could observe his work in every direction. His attention was buried in papers and sketches upon a heavy wood table, so he did not see Kunza and Ayana climbing the ridge until his guards moved to intercept them.

"Let them pass," Ur-Mak said quickly. "You know Kunza is a friend of mine."

Ur-Mak's guards stepped aside as Kunza and Ayana passed, keeping their eyes on the beastfolk behind them.

"Who is this?" Ur-Mak asked as Kunza and Ayana entered the shade of the tent. "A granddaughter?"

"No," Kunza said. "More of a disciple, I suppose."

"And a bright, promising disciple at that, it appears!" Ur-Mak smiled and extended a hand to Ayana. "A pleasure to meet you. I am Ur-Mak, Grand Mason of Noyo and proud son of Toth."

"I'm Ayana Kusa. From Kalaro." Ayana took his hand, her own hand swallowed entirely in his meaty palm. "It's nice to meet you."

After gently shaking her hand, Ur-Mak dismissed his masons and architects so they could speak privately. "Do you plan on introducing me to your other friends?" Ur-Mak asked, gesturing toward the beastfolk standing huddled at the far end of the tent, watching Ayana with single-minded intensity.

"Compatriots of my Shadows. They escorted Ayana from Kalaro and she has taken a liking to them, it seems."

"A girl could have worse friends, I suppose," Ur-Mak said.

"They're loyal to a fault, that much is apparent," Kunza said, stepping around the table of sketches and glancing at them. "How fares the construction?"

"We're still hobbled by inconsistent supply lines. Without Toth, Noyo has no major source of quality stone and metal."

"Have you been able to find a decent source of iron?"

"Maybe," Ur-Mak said. "I've been so occupied keeping the mausoleum upright I haven't had much time to devote to our other projects."

"We have time," Kunza said. "I still have to solidify a deal with Asha-Kalir. Although Ketabi's help is expediating the process greatly."

Ur-Mak frowned. "I'm still not sure about involving the godling."

"I know," Kunza said. "But right now, I'm afraid we don't have much of a choice. Without him, talks with Asha-Kalir would have stalled."

Ur-Mak chewed on his lip for a moment but said no more on the matter. "What plans does Talara have for little Ayana here?"

"Just education for now. Which brings me to my next matter at hand," Kunza said. "You have been in Noyo for some time. Do you have anyone among the freemen you can trust? Someone who can train Ayana in fighting?"

Ur-Mak's eyebrows rose. "This little girl, your disciple—you want her to fight?"

"Her path differs slightly from my own, but Talara wills it. She must be strong of faith and body."

Ur-Mak glanced at Ayana again. "I will see if there is anyone decent with a spear and shield who can tutor her. There aren't many freemen in Noyo whom I would say are particularly skilled fighters. I could just have some of my guard train her."

Kunza paused, unsure. "Do you think that would be wise? She's so much smaller. And she's only had a year of training in Kalaro."

"Then she won't have as many bad habits to rectify." Ur-Mak grinned, gold teeth flashing. "And she will always be smaller than what she will be fighting, no? She should learn now how it feels to fight a larger opponent."

Kunza looked to Ayana at his side. Her eyes were wide, but he could tell she was trying to be strong. The path before her was an arduous one. If she was to have any chance of surviving what was to come, she had not the luxury of being coddled.

Kunza put a hand on her thin shoulder and squeezed it reassuringly. "That is a wonderful idea," he said to Ur-Mak. "Could she begin today?"

CHAPTER 34

Odessa went to war wearing a plain brown tunic and a looted helmet on her head. The armor she had taken from the devil on the road to Asha-Kalir had proven much too large and cumbersome to wear. At the very least, she thought she could keep her head from being immediately crushed.

Marching with the Shadows through the sand-swept plains north of Asha-Kalir, the rags she'd stuffed inside the helmet to make it fit her head soaked up sweat like a sponge. Halfway through the first day's march, she had to take it off and tied it to her belt. Which was unfortunate because she liked how it looked and felt upon her head. She loved the feeling of iron. Her hand kept wandering to her belt to touch the hot metal for reassurance.

Without Poko, she felt, for the first time in a year, truly alone. She had left Poko with Yakun when she went to get her weapons. She could not help but cry when she left them with the old man. And again when Yakun hugged her and kissed her on the cheek before she left.

The Shadows moved with no wasted effort, each stride deliberate and efficient. The bird-man who led them was well-suited for the desert, long legs and splayed avian toes letting him traverse the sandy dunes with ease. It was Odessa who languished behind, leading the sparsely laden bazak. Using the devil's spear as a walking stick, she hauled the bazak forward up a dune. Its gangly legs let it easily scale the sandy slope while Odessa had to nearly crawl up.

They had taken a boat up river early in the morning and disembarked to head northwest into the rough desert, where devils most assuredly were hiding. They rested at midday when the desert's heat was at its worst. A brief respite that seemed to be for the sake of their bazak alone. Odessa ate dry flatbread and had a few sips of tepid water before she lay down in a trench she had dug in the sand and tried to sleep.

At night the Shadows and their milky, nocturnal eyes led the march. The temperatures dropped quickly as the sun retreated, and with no fire to warm her, Odessa had only the exertion of her marching to keep her warm.

As night turned to day again and Odessa trudged along trying to keep herself awake, one of their scouts returned. They carried the head of a devil.

The Shadow had happened upon the half-buried tracks of a devil scout and followed them until it had found two devils positioned along a ridge overlooking a caravan route that had been used fairly often in better days.

The bird-man left one Shadow to guard the bazak as the scout led the rest of their band to the devils' camp, hurrying to reach it before daybreak.

Dawn's rosy edges brushed at the horizon when they came upon the camp nestled in the shadow of a high dune, spread out in a dry riverbed. The Shadows slipped into the darkness and crept along the ridges above the camp, killing any guards they happened across. Odessa, the bird-man, and a party of ten Shadows waited in the riverbed below the camp. On the other side of the camp a dune had spilled between the ridges, enclosing the camp.

When the Shadows along the ridges had killed the guards, Odessa's party snuck upstream. The Shadows broke off, two splintering away from the group to kill their mounts. Devils paced around the perimeter of the camp and through the smattering of round tents. But the Shadows were one with the night. They slunk undetected and slid their blades deep into the devils' necks and chests.

Odessa and the bird-man watched from outside the camp. Odessa had an arrow nock, and her spear laid beside her.

Shadows positioned themselves near the tents, unlit torches in hand. The mounts barked and squealed. Torches burst to life and set the tents on fire. And when the devils scrambled from their tents, the Shadows would be in wait to cut them down.

A scream and a call to arms sent Odessa and the bird-man in motion. Bewildered devils poured from the burning tents. Some were cut down and some fought. Odessa began firing arrows into the devils that made their way out of the tents. She put arrows into the backs of those that fled.

When the bedlam became too chaotic for Odessa to differentiate friend from foe, she slung the bow upon her back and took up the spear.

Sand sucked at her feet as she sprinted across the outskirts of the camp. Devils, silhouetted in the reds and oranges of their burning tents, charged toward her. The head of a war-scythe flashed orange in the night as Odessa drew near enough to the camp to feel the wall of heat.

She knocked a scythe away with the shaft of her spear and jabbed forward. The devil danced backward as another rushed Odessa with a club.

Odessa drew the spear back and lurched to the side. The club tore through the air. On her back foot, Odessa launched her spear at the club-wielding devil only to have the spearhead clash against the devil's shield.

The war scythe whipped toward her again as the club wielder wheeled around to flank her. The scythe came so fast Odessa could do little but clumsily block it with a sideways jerk. The scythe rebounded off the shaft of her spear and came down toward her neck in a flash.

She moved to block the scythe with the middle of the spear shaft, but the scythe withdrew in an instant, swinging around to her other side. The club wielder approached on her side, keeping her from leaping from the scythe's imminent slash.

The scythe swiped upward, meaning to hook into her side and disembowel her on the backstroke. Odessa lunged forward, her spear launching toward the devil's leading arm. Her spearhead punched through its scale and into the meat of his bicep. The scythe's swing faltered, allowing Odessa to spin and sidestep the incoming club.

As the club drew back, Odessa feinted toward the devil's head, and as the shield rose she drove the spear into the devil's upper thigh. As the club wielder stumbled back, Odessa hooked her spearhead beneath the rim of the shield and rammed the spear up into the devil's chest.

The devil sagged as she yanked the spear free and turned her attention back to the other. It held the scythe with one hand, its wounded arm held close to its side. As Odessa ran forward, the scythe came in a wide, wheeling arc. A slash easily parried. Before the scythe could hook her spear shaft and block, Odessa rammed the spearhead into the devil's neck. A cry came out, wet and garbled, as the devil readied itself for another strike. Odessa knocked its swing away and stabbed her spear into the slit of the devil's visor, ceasing its last resistance. It twitched and shook as Odessa stepped over its dying body on her way into the camp.

Death surrounded her, screams joining the rising smoke to fill the riverbed in chaos and bedlam. The smell of blood was on the air, heavy and pervasive like the scent of morning dew after a night's rain. It set her teeth on edge and urged her feet to hasten. Her heart fluttered like a caged bird now free of its prison, spinning and twirling unencumbered. Smoke stung her eyes and scorched her throat, but she bounded through the camp, leaping over the dead and dying and skirting around the burning tents, the hide turning to ash to expose ribs of timber to the flames.

A short devil in cotton sleep clothes knelt on the ground, a motionless devil cradled in their arms. Odessa's spear pierced through the devil's back and out its chest before it had even raised its head. The devil made a choked gasping noise as Odessa wrenched the spear out and ran on, following the sounds of further violence. There was a great din where the Shadows had chased the devils into the enclosed end of the camp. Clashing metal and sharp, harsh screams. Somewhere in the camp, nearly lost amid the screams, there was coughing and crying.

Odessa ran, her blood running white hot and her arm aching with anticipation. When she reached the far end of camp, she wasn't thinking anymore. All that remained in her mind was an animalistic drive to kill and to consume. She leaped into the fray before the dune and killed without impunity. She moved like a starved animal, frenetic and wild as she thrust and stabbed and skewered.

She killed, not for Talara or family or even self-preservation. She killed for the ecstasy that her soft heart had denied her. Her hunger was a beast that needed to be let loose.

CHAPTER 35

When the sun, obscured by thick, brown-tinged clouds, rose over the dunes, what remained of the camp was still smoldering. Thin ribbons of smoke rose from circles of coal and ash. Corpses were strewn about among the charred remains of tents, and Odessa went to each of them, one by one, and carved out their hearts.

She moved in a stupefied fugue, her body working almost on its own as it trudged through ash and blood-soaked sand to kneel before another dead devil. She stripped off its armor and rammed her knife between the devil's breasts with no more compunction than if she were husking a coconut.

When she had ripped the heart from the devil's chest, she held it over her own mouth and squeezed, crushing it and letting the blood pour into her mouth. Her face and tunic were covered in blood and crusted with sand. But she didn't stop. The bird-man was watching her from the ridge above, disgust evident in his stiff posture and upturned beak. But Odessa was numb. She felt none of his judgement. She felt only vague disgust in herself.

She rose and moved onto the next devil. It was young. There had been children, young girls, among the devils. All of the devils they had killed, nearly forty in total, were women and young girls. And Odessa drank from them all. Until she could drink no more. Until her every cell vibrated with gruesome intensity. Stolen life thrummed in her blood, droning in her ears so loudly it smothered and drowned any thought she had before it reached its infancy.

When she was done, she took the blood-stained armor of a young devil and put it on, cinching the belt tight around her waist. The armor was loose and heavy on her shoulders. But the weight of the iron upon her body was reassuring. She felt as if nothing could hurt her now.

She climbed the ridge where the bird-man stood alongside the Shadows and the mounts they had taken for themselves.

"Are you finished?" the bird-man asked before Odessa crested the ridge.

Odessa said nothing. As the droning buzzed in her mind, her hunger receded. And where that hunger had been, grew a hollowness. A void now raking at her ribs. She had given in to the hunger and this was her recompense.

The band returned to their bazak and continued northwest. They rode double on the high saddles of the devils' mounts. Odessa rode behind a Shadow, the stink of Talara's rot somewhat muddled by the stink of sweat within her helmet. The litham Tarik had given her was wrapped loosely around her neck and as they rode the loping mount, she found herself touching it, twisting the fabric around her fingers whenever they slowed enough for her to take a hand from the Shadow's robes.

The stifling heat baked Odessa inside her helmet and armor but she refused to take off her iron accoutrements. No matter how much they slowed her in the sand or made her sweat and chafe. Seeing the world from behind the helmet's visor, it all seemed somewhat distant. As if there was some barrier between her and the bloody work she had been tasked with.

At midday, they rested again. The mounts panted, foam gathering at the corners of their mouths. They were given what little water could be spared and some dried chickpea fodder taken from the devils' camp.

Odessa went to lie in a shallow trench she had dug in the sand, taking off her helmet and setting it carefully in the sand beside her. When she closed her eyes, she could see fires burning on the inside of her eyelids. The pounding drone in her ears turned to screams.

She abandoned the idea of sleep. Her blood still ran hot, and her mind was clouded by the smoke of war. The stench of fire and death permeated her brain. Devil's blood stained her memories. For now, there was nothing she could do but wait for the erosion of time to rid her of the stains.

Odessa and her band of Shadows spent nearly two months in the desert, scouting out the positions of the devils' main forces and harassing their supply lines. With the devils' mounts, they were effective and brutal, able to fall upon small parties of devils, scouts, ambushers, and supply caravans.

The bulk of the devils' main force was still near the base of the highlands, not far from the Darrood. They could make out the smoke of their fires from spans away. Their scouts had estimated it was a force of at least thirty thousand devils with even more slaves at their disposal.

They updated Asha-Kalir of the devils' positions using the birds they kept in cages hanging from the flanks of the bazak. After two months, one of Asha-Kalir's birds came to rest upon the bazak's back.

They had come to camp at a nearly vacant caravansary in the northern reaches of the desert for a few days to let their devilish mounts rest. They had been forced to slaughter two in the past week for lack of water and food. Their blood had kept Odessa and the bird-man from perishing before they could reach the caravansary.

When the bird from Asha-Kalir came, Odessa was drawing water from a small pool in the center of the courtyard. The caravansary was half the size of the others Odessa had stopped at with Yakun and Poko. The rooms were smaller and dingy, with no one but the owner and his few slaves to clean them. Dust and sand had reclaimed every surface. But the clay warriors who now called the caravansary home did not seem to mind.

Odessa brought two pails of water to the stables and found the bird-man untying a small clay hexagonal prism bound in strips of flax from the bird's leg. She filled the water trough as he undid the royal-stamped wax seal around both ends of the prism.

The bird-man set the unfolded prism flat on the mudbrick half-wall of a nearby stall. His eyes scanned the small, tightly packed script quickly. Before Odessa could leave the stable, his eyes found her.

"Girl," he said. "Get your kit together. We leave for Asha-Kalir tonight."

Odessa stopped before the stable's doorway, a strange mixture of feelings welling up in the hollow place in her chest like water seeping through the cracks of dry riverbed. Both relief and dread came to fill her. She missed Poko and Tarik and even Yakun a little, despite her ill feeling toward him. But she was scared to see them again. She could imagine them seeing her, seeing who she had become, and rejecting her.

She nodded to the bird-man and left the stable, heading toward the room she shared with some Shadows.

I'm a husk of who I was, she thought as she walked. *I'm not the same. The hunger's got me. I'm not human anymore, I'm just a puppet for the hunger.*

After donning her armor and taking her weapons from her room, Odessa spent the rest of the day preparing for their departure. Before the sun had dipped below the peaks of the distant mountains, they were off toward the east, bound for the Darrood.

For two days, they headed south on the river road. They spent the next few days in a riverside village, waiting for a boat to take them downriver while they sent a bird with word of their imminent return.

A warship came from Asha-Kalir three days after they arrived in the village, a tall ship with two rows of oarsmen along either side, one above deck and one below. The prow of the ship was heavily built, with a sharp bronze ram extending just beneath the water's surface.

They loaded onto the ship and were headed downriver within the hour. By the end of the day, Odessa was passing beneath the eyes of the giants again. The gates barring the river had been hauled up, and the ship passed through the thick walls into the city. High slanted walls rose from the river in artificial banks with steep steps cut into the stone.

They passed beneath arched stone bridges until the ship pulled alongside a large pier. They disembarked and took a wide paved road until they reached the walls leading to the plaza with the god's skull. The skull, she had learned, had belonged to a giant god that died with the Serpent. Khymanir had been born from the giant god, emerging from its cracked skull in a tangle of limbs and wet flesh.

She and the devils were ushered back into the barracks before the bird-man went to report to Bukoris and Khymanir. In the barracks, where her nest had been, she found a small rope bed.

She stripped out of her armor and her blood- and sweat-stained clothes and collapsed onto the thin mattress. It was a sad thought, but she felt at home again.

CHAPTER 36

Odessa woke not knowing how much time she'd lost in slumber, teetering between deep, much-needed sleep and nightmares, to a knock at the door. Her eyelids were heavy as she pried them open to see the door cracked open.

"Odessa?" Tarik called. "Are you there?"

She jolted upright and wrapped herself in a blanket. Her mouth was dry and her voice little more than a croak at first. Her heart fluttered. She cleared her throat. "Yes, I'm here," she called, adding quickly, "but I'm not dressed."

The widening crack in the door shrank back. "Oh, I'm sorry for disturbing you," he said. She could see the embarrassment on his face. "I just wanted to relay to you that you've been allowed to leave the barracks while supervised. So if you would like to see Yakun or Poko, I could escort you there."

Anxiety sank deep into her stomach. "That's great news," she said, her voice much too flat. She looked down at her body, still covered in grime and sand and dried blood. "Could I have a bath first?"

"Of course," Tarik said. "I'll wait here until you're dressed, and then I can show you the way."

"Thank you," Odessa said earnestly but with a touch of solemnity in her voice.

"You're welcome," he said, pausing as if he wanted to say more then decided against it. He closed the door.

Odessa had no other choice but to put on the filthy blood-crusted tunic she had worn for the last month. Her only other tunic had been so thoroughly soaked in blood it had become brittle in the sun. Putting the tunic on, she could not ignore the stench of blood and sweat. She had taken a few quick baths at caravansaries along the way, but her clothes had only gone through a few perfunctory dunks in water to rinse away the worst of the filth.

Embarrassed, she cracked the door open just enough to whisper through. "Tarik?"

"Yes?" he said, coming to the cracked door.

She backed away just in case the rankness of her clothes made it through the gap in the door. "I need you to do me a favor," she said. "Can you lead me to the bath from a distance? Ten paces ahead maybe?"

Tarik was quiet for a moment. "I suppose I could. But why?"

"I need you to promise me something too. Can you do that?"

"What do you need?"

"I need you to promise me that you won't look at me. Not until I've had a bath and can get into some new clothes."

Tarik snorted with laughter.

"Can you promise me that?" Odessa said, serious.

"I promise," Tarik said. "I will not lay eyes on you until I have your permission."

Subtle relief loosened the tension in her shoulders. "Good," she said. "Turn around and let me know when you're ten paces away. Then I'll come out."

Tarik chuckled but did as he was told. He counted off his steps so she could hear him, and at ten paces she cracked the door open farther, peeked her head out to make sure he was far enough away and that he had his back turned. He was true to his word.

She followed him to the lobby and through a door into another hallway. This hallway was made of pure white stone like the lobby and led into a much larger hallway running perpendicular to the small hall. They followed the large hallway, past great windows of stained glass and reliefs of different gods in various noble poses. Tarik walked, his injured arm held awkwardly out in front of him.

"How is your arm?" she asked, raising her voice to bridge the distance between them.

Tarik turned down a narrow hallway. "I can't move it much yet but it's getting better with each day. He stopped before an arched doorway. He started to turn around then caught himself. "These are the human baths," he said. "There should be soaps, perfumes, and fresh towels for you already. While you're in there, I can fetch you some clean clothes."

"Thank you," Odessa said. "Thank you for everything. You've been too kind to me. I appreciate it."

"You saved my life. If it wasn't for you I would have bled out in the desert. It is I who should be thanking you each and every day." He shook his head and chuckled. "You know how silly this is, saying these things with my back turned?"

"I know," she said flatly. "But I'm glad you kept your promise."

"Of course," he said. "I live to serve." He took a few steps from the doorway. "I'll leave your clothes at the door."

Odessa watched him walk away before entering the bath. Another woman was inside, but she left when she saw Odessa, covered in bloody clothes. Odessa stripped out of her clothes and peeled off her threadbare bandages. She scrubbed herself, water running down her body onto the tile in rivers of dark water, ranging from rusty brown to nearly black, depending on where she scrubbed. She took the time to use a pumice stone and an abrasive paste on her arms and legs. She wondered if Tarik would notice the smoothness of her skin.

As quickly as she could, she washed her loose locks, scrubbing her scalp so hard her nails dug into her skin. The desert sand was rife with tiny bugs, and her greasy, blood-splattered hair had made for an insect's haven, she was sure. Had Tarik not offered to escort her, she would have taken the time to fully wash and redo her hair. But she did not want to make him wait any longer than necessary.

After applying an oil that smelled faintly of myrrh, she leaned out of the baths and scooped up the clothes Tarik had left for her. Along with her undergarments, sandals, and a clean length of bandage, there was a linen kaftan the color of fresh cream. The kaftan was of a different style than she was used to, the hem coming up to her shins and sleeves down to her elbows. The kaftan seemed to cascade down her shoulders and flow around her. Its soft, gentle lines smoothed the hard edges of her muscular body.

She left the baths with a hesitant joy emerging from the hollowness in her chest like a mouse trembling and sniffing the air. Tarik was sitting cross-legged in the hallway. He rose when he saw her, a broad smile on his face.

"You look wonderful," he said.

A smile touched the edges of Odessa's lips. The first smile that had graced her lips in two months. It felt foreign to her. "Thank you," she said. "I'm glad you're seeing me like this and not like the creature I looked like earlier."

"It could not have been that bad," Tarik said.

"You would not have been saying that before my bath, I assure you," she said. "Now, you said I could see Poko?"

"Yes," Tarik said. "Poko and Yakun are in Azdava's quarters. She was able to smuggle Yakun into the palace without alerting anyone of his fugitive status."

Odessa wanted to tell Tarik she did not care about Yakun or his fugitive status, but she held her tongue. Tarik led her through the narrow hallway and then down several flights of stairs until they reached a pair of heavy wooden doors.

Tarik opened the doors and led Odessa into a room filled with curling ribbons of incense smoke. Shelves lined the walls, all of them laden with scrolls and stacks of clay tablets. Plush sofas and chairs surrounded a bronze brazier crackling with flame. Sprawled across one of the chairs was Poko. When Poko saw Odessa, they leapt to their feet and darted into the air on shimmering wings.

"Poko!" Odessa said as they flew onto her shoulder and wrapped their arms around her neck. "Your wings! They're fixed!"

Poko darted into the air again, fluttering in front of her so she could clearly see their new wings, translucent slivers of paper with thin script written in shimmering gold. "Pretty nice, huh? Tarik worked day and night on them. He said he wanted to impress you so you'd like him more."

"I never said that," Tarik interjected. "And it wasn't just me anyway. It was Azdava's script and magic. I just made the wings."

"It's fantastic," Odessa said, the hollowness inside her shrinking ever so slightly. "I can't believe you can do that."

A door across the room opened and Azdava and Yakun stepped out. The shrinking hollowness inside Odessa cracked open further at the sight of Yakun.

"How are you?" Yakun asked, coming to her for a hug. He wrapped his arms around her and she stood frozen in his embrace. Her mind stalled for a moment at his touch and her skin became clammy.

Odessa freed herself from his embrace. "I've been better," she said.

"I heard you were engaged in quite a lot of combat. Were you hurt at all?"

"Some," she said. "Nothing that didn't heal."

"So you fed then, yes?" Yakun asked.

"Of course I did," Odessa said.

"Have there been any changes?" Yakun asked. "Physically or mentally?"

"No," Odessa snapped.

Yakun stroked his beard. "We'll need to thoroughly examine you."

"Not happening," Odessa said sharply. "I'm here to figure out how to get rid of this curse and that's it. So what's the plan?"

Azdava stepped forward. "It is a pleasure to meet you in better circumstances," she said. "I hope your collar has not given you much discomfort."

"It's a collar—of course it's uncomfortable," Odessa said, trying to soften her demeanor and failing. "So have you figured out how to cure me?"

Azdava seemed unfazed by her curtness. "A blood transplant seems most feasible." She glanced at Yakun, as if waiting for him to chime in, then continued. "Either we take your own blood, separate the divine and mortal, either through filtering or by simply exposing it to air and letting the godsblood burn off, and then return your own blood back to you, or we drain off all your blood and simultaneously put the blood of a person with similar attributes as yourself into your veins."

"When can we start?" Odessa asked, unfazed by the prospect of being drained of all her blood. She had seen so much bloodshed already. Her own father's blood spilling from his open throat. She herself had spilled so much. It was only natural that she should have to shed her own. There was a certain logic to it. A perverted sort of justice in it.

Azdava glanced at Yakun again. "We can begin trials immediately," she said. "Unless you have any objections," Azdava added to Yakun.

"None," Yakun said, shaking his head.

They led her to the back room. It was a sprawling room filled with tables and chairs, all of them bearing leather straps and restraints and metal chains. Corpses lay on the tables, in various stages of dissection. Tall vats dominated the back of the room with a series of tubes and cylinders connecting them. Odessa realized she did not know what, exactly, a soulweaver did. As they ushered her to a chair, she glanced at Tarik. *He is an apprentice to this?*

As she sat down on the chair facing a table covered with bronze implements and tubes, she frowned. *Who am I to judge someone's profession? After all the devils I slaughtered. At least they only deal with corpses.*

They unwrapped the clean bandages from her arm. Tarik strapped Odessa's right arm to the arm of the chair. "Just a precaution," he said quietly.

Azdava wiped the crook of Odessa's elbow with a piece of cotton soaked in pungent alcohol. She slid a needle into Odessa's vein. Her blood ran through a short tube into a glass vial. Azdava filled another vial. And another. Ten vials in total she filled before pulling the needle out and putting a dry piece of cotton over the hole in Odessa's arm.

Azdava held one of the vials up to the lamplight, gazing at the blood as it sloshed like a red tide against the glass. "It doesn't look that special, does it?" She turned back to Odessa. "But appearances serve to deceive, don't they?"

CHAPTER 37

After Odessa's blood was drawn, she and Poko were left to their own devices while the soulweavers and Yakun worked.

"Are you sure you're all well and good?" Poko asked, fluttering around her head as she lay on the sofa, watching the flickering flames in the brazier and thinking of devils.

"As well as I can be," she said.

Poko landed on her chest. "You're troubled."

"I've been troubled for a long time now."

"Yeah, but you're more troubled now," Poko said.

"Just let it go," Odessa said, almost pleading. "I missed you! Don't draw me into a fight so soon."

Poko frowned. "You know, talking about your feelings doesn't *have* to lead to a fight."

"And yet it always does," Odessa said. "So let's just avoid it altogether, yeah?"

Poko snorted derisively and took to flight again. "You're aggravating."

Poko had meant it as a joke, but it grated against her like a coarse, jagged stone raked against the back of her mind. She ground her teeth, biting back her irritation. Poko was flitting to and fro around the sofa and for a moment Odessa imagined snatching them out of the air and crushing them in her fist. For a moment she could feel Poko's broken body clenched in her hand. Delicate fractured bones poking her skin. Fairy blood oozing in her palm.

And then it was gone. The gruesome thought left her as quickly as it had intruded, but it left in its wake a frigid terror. Odessa clamped a hand over her bandaged arm and closed her eyes, not wanting to look at Poko. Guilt and fear flooded her mind, cold and dark.

"What's wrong?" Poko asked.

Odessa stayed silent, her eyes pressed shut. *Keep your bloodthirsty urges in the desert,* she told herself. *Don't you dare bring that shit here. Keep Poko out of this. Keep Poko out of this.*

Poko landed on her chest again. She jerked as their feet touched her chest. Her eyes flew open and she gripped her bandaged arm tight, in case it moved on its own, directed by its own infernal desires.

"Dessa," Poko said, sitting down cross-legged on her chest. "Talk to me, please."

Odessa's nails dug through the bandage into her skin. She swallowed dryly. "Poko," she said. The flames in the brazier lashed the air, dancing in the periphery of her vision. A tidal surge of words roared in her chest, restrained only by the tightness in her throat. She couldn't speak. There was no way to put into words everything that she felt. "Poko, I'm scared." She wanted to cry but no tears came. The maelstrom of fear, guilt, hate, and grief did not reach so far as her eyes, leaving them dry. "I'm scared of what I'm becoming. Of what I am. There's something in me, something in my tainted blood, and it scares me because I don't know what it's capable of. I have a sense, and it scares me, and I don't know if I can stop it." Her voice was shaky. "If they can't get this godsblood out of me, I don't know what I'll do. I can't become Talara's pawn. I can't let this thing inside me get the better of me. But I don't know if I'm strong enough to stop it."

"Oh, Dessa," Poko said softly. "Everything will be fine. They'll get rid of that godsblood. Azdava and Yakun, they know what they're doing. They'll cure you for sure."

Doubt dragged her down deeper into the maelstrom of emotion, an insidious current she couldn't get free from. "They have to," she said. "They have to cure me." If they failed, she would have to kill and consume again and again, an endless cycle of bloodshed. A part of her relished the thought, and that part scared her to her core. Her throat tightened, a lump stopping her words. *I don't want to kill anymore*, she wanted to say but couldn't. That part of her that grew elated when the scent of blood was in the air would not allow her to say it. It was a lie. She wanted to kill. She wanted to stab and cut and tear. To sink her arms into open chests and pull still-beating hearts out so she could sink her teeth into them and suck down scalding hot blood in deep, greedy gulps.

A muscle in her arm twitched, restless at the thought of bloodshed. Poko put a hand on her bandaged arm, and Odessa nearly jumped. But their touch was soft and calming. Poko bent down and embraced her bandaged forearm. "It'll be fine," Poko said. "Everything will be fine."

Odessa placed a hand on Poko's back, careful not to disturb their fragile wings.

Odessa and Poko stayed like that for a long while. Holding each other until the cold terror of her raging emotions settled into dark skies and choppy seas.

"Poko," Odessa said after a while. "What's your plan? Now that you have wings again?"

Poko raised their head from her arm. "What do you mean?"

"You're not grounded anymore," Odessa said, unable to look at Poko as she spoke. "You can go anywhere. There's no reason for you to stick around me and my bad blood. You should go be with your own kind. You could join up with a Fae Lord maybe. Have a good, proper life. There's no reason that you should be damned to perdition with me."

"Dessa, stop that. I'm not leaving you. We're going to get you cured and then we'll move someplace where the Grey hasn't reached and where Talara can't get to you."

Odessa forced a wan smile. "I would like that," she said a bit sadly. "I would like that more than anything."

CHAPTER 38

Yakun and Azdava continued drawing her blood each day. Odessa spent most of her time in Azdava's quarters, only returning to the barracks each night at Tarik's insistence. She heard little of how her cure was progressing. They took increasingly large doses of blood and had begun slowly introducing transfusions. Odessa felt no difference.

One night, as Tarik escorted her back up the stairs from Azdava's quarters, she asked him, "What exactly do soulweavers do?"

Tarik did not break stride, but Odessa noticed his hard swallow before he replied. "We prepare the clay for Khymanir's work."

"But how?" she asked, not wanting to push further but knowing she had to. She feared the truth but needed to know. "What are the bodies for?"

"You must know already, don't you?" he said as they climbed another flight. "Did Yakun not tell you what we do?"

"No," Odessa said. "That's why I'm asking."

Tarik stopped and sighed. "Do you really want to know?"

Odessa nodded.

Gently he took her hand and looked her in the eye. "Before I tell you, I want you to know that I don't do any of this out of want. I need you to understand that. I do this all because I have to."

"I understand," she said with a sinking feeling in her stomach.

Tarik took her by the hand and led her downstairs again. "It will be easier if I show you," he said. Down another flight of stairs, he took her down a short hallway branching off from the stairwell. He stopped at a door and pulled a ring of keys from his belt. "There should not be anyone here for another few hours," he said as he unlocked the door. His hand on the knob, he stopped and looked at her with sad, pleading eyes. "Are you sure you want to see this?"

Odessa nodded and Tarik opened the door.

The room was massive, with long rows of cages stretching out to the opposite end of the room. Cages were stacked in multiples reaching toward the vaulted ceiling and its arterial network of tubes and pipes. Stairs and walkways wrapped around all the cages like a wooden serpent looping around each tower of dull bronze bars. The cages themselves were barely larger than the nude, ragged people chained within them.

"What is this?" Odessa asked. In the dim glow of a series of lanterns hanging from the ceiling, she could make out human figures. The people locked within the cages did not even react as she took a few hesitant steps toward them, their heads hanging, sitting on the floor of their cells. Their dull, listless eyes downcast, blind to the world around them. As she drew closer she could see some were missing arms, others legs. Some farther down the row were nothing more than limbless trunks, just a torso and head. "Tarik, what is this?"

"This is Asha-Kalir. All the white marble and grand statues, it's all built upon what you see before you. The noble Red Clay Warriors, this is the heart of them. In the most literal sense." Tarik stepped forward into the aisle between towering cages. "The poor bastards you see before you are the true citizens of Asha-Kalir. They are bred here down in the dark and they live their entire lives below the city streets, never seeing the light of day. Khymanir has us lobotomize them to keep them docile. Khymanir has us twist and pervert their forms, breeding them to have longer legs and arms. Then we remove their limbs and they become components to build the Red Clay Warriors. But to make the Warriors, to make them alive, Khymanir must have the head. That's where the soul resides. After these poor wretches are hacked apart, we give them to Khymanir to do his magics. We're not soulweavers. We are butchers."

Before Odessa could say anything he was moving down the aisle. "And here, here is what makes the clay red. What makes the clay take the soul so readily." He pointed into a wider cage with large tubes and pipes snaking in from the ceiling. Inside was a man, unbelievably tall and wide. His ribs stuck out like thick planks beneath his sallow skin. Gangly legs curled beneath him, his long spine curled so he hunched forward, vertebrae poking out like a mountain ridge along his back. His arms had been removed so long ago only gnarled scars remained. Needles were stuck in both sides of his neck and in both legs. His head hung from a skinny neck, long greasy hair tangled in ratty dreadlocks. His mouth hung open, full of overly large teeth.

"This is a bleeder. Its blood is mixed with the clay so that Khymanir can shape it into the Warriors of Asha-Kalir and imbue them with a soul. We can usually drain a bleeder for almost twenty years once they hit maturity."

"Why?" Odessa asked, aghast. "Why do you do this?"

Tarik turned to her, pain in his eyes. "Because Khymanir wants it so. And if I am the one to do it, my family's well-being is assured. If I wasn't a soulweaver, one of my sisters or my mother could be hauled to the breeding floor at any time. I will never, ever let that happen. I refuse. So if I have to do these terrible, unspeakable things, then I will. No sin is too great if it keeps my family from this." He gestured to the cages stretching far down the row.

"This is . . ." Odessa spun around to slowly take in the horrors around her. "This is sadistic. This is cruel."

"Khymanir is a cruel, heartless god whose only aim is to create more puppets in the hopes that Aséshassa will find favor in him again," Tarik said. "He is an architect of misery and torment. Creatures such as he should not exist. Every moment he's still alive is an indictment of this entire world."

Odessa was still staring at the blank faces and mutilated bodies around them. "Isn't there anything we can do?" It was a stupid question that came spilling from her mouth before she could stop it.

"Not as long as Khymanir is alive," Tarik said.

They left the prison and walked up the stairs in silence. When they reached the lobby, Odessa stopped. "I can't go back in there," she said. "Not with all those clay monsters."

"You have to," Tarik said. "You're supposed to be back in the barracks by sundown. If Bukoris finds you insubordinate he'll tighten your collar in an instant."

Odessa glanced outside through a window overlooking the plaza. Twilight dappled the plaza in shades of deep blue and purple. "It's not sundown yet," she said, heading toward the lobby doors.

"Wait!" Tarik said, hurrying after her.

She sat on the ledge of the skull's platform, looking down over the walls and the city below. Tarik joined her, and they sat in silence for a while.

"I'm sorry," Odessa said. "For making you tell me. I should have asked Yakun or something."

"No, it's fine," Tarik said. "You have a right to know."

"I think doing what you're doing for the sake of your family is very brave."

"It's not," Tarik said, looking down at the plaza below his feet. "But thank you."

Without a word, Odessa took his hand in hers, entwining their fingers, and they sat in front of the skull until night came.

CHAPTER 39

Over the next few weeks, more Shadows arrived in Asha-Kalir, joining Odessa in the barracks. From what she was able to glean from Tarik and Azdava, some sort of sweeping deal had been struck between Noyo and Asha-Kalir. Huge, heavily armed caravans were making their way to Noyo in droves, taking detours far south to avoid the ever-present danger the devils in the north offered. Odessa did not like the sound of Kunza and Khymanir becoming closer, but worrying would do nothing. She had little choice but to follow Talara's instruction and kill when ordered.

Every night, Tarik and Odessa sat in front of the skull, talked, and held hands. The hollowness inside her chest always seemed to shrink and close when he was present. He understood her and she understood him. In those few weeks, she was almost happy.

Bukoris came to the barracks one morning, a retinue of bird-men in tow, and broke the placid surface of her contentment. "Servants of Talara," he announced to her and the Shadows standing in tight rows alongside the Red Clay Warriors. "You have proven yourselves to be warriors of good standing and thus worthy of Khymanir's patronage. The goddess Talara has endowed you with great cunning and martial prowess. And for that, you will be joining Khymanir's Royal Army in the extermination of the devils invading our northern borders. The devil host has made claim to the northern banks of the Darrood. This cannot and will not be tolerated. Two days from now, you will join the Khymanir's Royal Army and make your way north. Spare no devils. Slaughter them in the name of your eminence, Khymanir, and the goddess Talara." Bukoris saluted. "I will see you on the battlefield."

* * *

That night, in front of the giant skull, Odessa was quiet. "Have you heard?" she asked Tarik.

He nodded. "Yes, I heard," he said. "I wish you didn't have to go. I tried my best to convince Azdava to pull some strings on your behalf, but she says it will do no good."

Odessa squeezed his hand. "I wish I didn't have to go either, but it'll be fine. I'll be back before you know it."

"Be careful," he said. "Promise me you'll be careful." His eyes were wide and desperate.

"I promise," she said.

They stared into each other's eyes for a moment. Not a word was spoken, but a dialogue was being had nonetheless. Odessa's heart pounded and an unfamiliar sensation, warm and exciting, spread through her core.

Tarik leaned his face toward hers. For a moment there was anxiety and panic. Then his lips touched hers and all that worry melted away in the warmth seeping through her chest. She leaned into the kiss, pressed her body against his. He embraced her, and there was no fear or disgust. She wrapped her arms around him and held him tight. Their mouths moved in tandem, shy yet imploringly eager.

His hands traced the curves of her hips and then up her back, fingertips brushing her skin so lightly she shivered and her body arched into his as she pushed her lips to his.

In that moment, she was free of all the pain and grief, the hunger and hollowness. All she felt was warmth and passion. The world had bled away and left her with him, in peace and ecstasy. Everything had become simple and uncomplicated. She and Tarik were all that existed. And that was just fine.

When finally they were forced to pull apart from each other, the world around her returned with all its gravity and weight. Night had sunk into the plaza with a chill. The cold air was stark upon her flushed cheeks.

"I suppose you should be going back to the barracks," he said, not moving.

"I suppose I should," she said, returning his deep, impassioned gaze.

After an extended pause, she forced herself to rise. They held hands as they walked to the barracks. She did not want him to go but she knew he had to. They kissed once more and said good night. Odessa went to her bed, thinking of Tarik. Wanting him. Needing him. Thoughts of war and bloodshed, distant yet looming like black storm clouds on the horizon. But for now, she enjoyed what pleasant weather she had while she had it.

The next day, as Tarik escorted her from Azdava's quarters, she stopped him in the stairwell. She held onto his hand, squeezing it as she looked into his soft, enquiring eyes. "I'll be leaving tomorrow," she said. "I probably won't have time to say goodbye to you then." She stepped nearer to him, pressed her body into his. "I don't want to go. I don't want to be without you."

"I don't want you to leave either," he said, putting his arms around her. "I wish you could stay with me like this forever."

"We could run away," she said into his shoulder. "Right now, just leave and never look back."

"You know we couldn't," he whispered. "They'd kill us before we even got to the gates."

Odessa said nothing and buried her face further in his shoulder. "I know," she said finally. "Just wishing aloud."

"We're together now," he said. "That's enough for me."

It's not enough, Odessa thought. *Not even close to enough. I want all of you. Totally and entirely. Forever.* She did not put her thoughts to words. She put them to action. She kissed him, deep and intense.

Tarik led her to a small room of shelves and pots. He barred the door behind them with a heavy palm-wood cask that reeked of alcohol, then turned and took her in his arms.

Kissing her deeply, he laid her on the cold stone floor. Her fingers dug in his wavy hair as she dragged him down close to her, her mouth searching for his in the dark.

His hands slid down her body. Tiny spurs of unease tried to form around her passion, but she forced them away. But when his hand reached her breast, she stiffened. Her lips lost his for a moment. When he began to draw back she pulled him close and found his lips again. Her heart pounded a wavering rhythm. *Stop it,* she told herself as the spurs of unease prodded her throat where his kisses now landed. *It's Tarik. This is good.* But in the dark of the small store room, it was not just Tarik any longer.

When Tarik's hand slid down to her navel, Odessa's panic took hold.

She pushed him away, the warm passion within turned frigid in an instant. "I'm sorry," she whispered. "I'm sorry."

Tarik drew back. "It's fine," he said, stunned yet reassuring. "It's fine."

Their moment of passion ruined, Odessa lay on her side apologizing and Tarik lay beside her. Tentatively, his fingers brushed her arm. Her arm twitched at his touch, a subtle flinch, but she did not stop him.

He consoled her the best he could, whispering in her ear. When she grew tolerant of his gentle touches, they grew bolder until he was holding her in his arms. He held her all night, a suffocating yet comforting embrace.

Why can't anything go right? Why can't I have anything? Not even the slightest bit of happiness. I can't have it. I hate this. I hate my godsdamned body. I hate myself.

Eventually, Odessa slipped into a restless sleep, Tarik still holding her.

CHAPTER 40

In the morning, Odessa left Asha-Kalir as one in a legion of fifty thousand composed mostly of clay men and collared humans. She and one hundred Shadows took the vanguard. Most of the Shadows were on foot, but she, the bird-man, and their band of twenty Shadows rode on their stolen mounts, foreriders a few spans ahead of the main body.

Shadows scouting far ahead to the north sent word that a large contingent of devils had taken a caravansary on the banks of the Darrood. In two days, the army reached the caravansary and found it razed. The small village built around the caravansary had been burned to the ground. Nothing but the bones of buildings remained.

Odessa and the other Shadows rode through the scorched village toward the caravansary overlooking the river. Bodies hung from its walls, flayed and decapitated. Blood stained the sandstone wall in lines of brown dripping from the corpses.

Odessa could not pull her eyes from the flayed bodies hanging from the ramparts. They had passed this village on their way back to Asha-Kalir. Those people, skinned and headless, she had seen only a short few weeks ago, alive and well.

The caravansary doors were left open, exposing the destroyed remains of the courtyard. A few Shadows climbed over the walls while Odessa and the rest of the vanguard waited outside the battered gates.

"Savages," the bird-man said, sidling up beside Odessa upon his brindle mount. "If they hope to sow discontent in our collared ranks with such petty barbarism, their aims are misguided."

Odessa still stared at the bodies on the walls. Seventeen in all. Nine were bird-men and the rest human. "Why would they just burn everything?"

"That is the nature of these devils. They take what they need and burn what they do not. That is how they retain their mobility."

A Shadow emerged from the gates, waving them inside. A few Shadows stood around the small pool in the center of the plaza. The heads of the decapitated bodies were laid out on the ground before the pool, their eyes and tongues torn out.

The Shadow who led them toward the pool spoke, "Trap."

The bird-man slowed. "What sort of trap?"

"Heads have ropes beneath them. Lead underground, where dirt is disturbed." Odessa could see that the earth leading from the gates to the pool was upset, mounded and stamped down. "Water is spoiled too."

The Shadow led them behind the pool to a tiled platform at the other side of the plaza. The platform marked where the river-fed cistern that supplied the pool lay. The Shadow lifted the woven-reed lid, and out from the hole rose the overwhelming stench of decay. Butchered animal carcasses lined the bottom of the cistern. Excrement floated among the rotting corpses.

The bird-man clicked his beak in irritation. "Disarm those traps by the pool," he told the Shadow. "And scour every room, every nook and cranny for more traps. There is no limit to these devils' depravity."

Odessa watched from a distance as the Shadows set about disarming the heads. Hooks had been sunk deep into their open throats. Ropes attached to the hooks ran from the heads down through reeds buried upright in the ground beneath them. The Shadows slowly dug away the sand from around the base of each neck until they could see the reed. With a careful hand, they were able to slide a thin blade between the top of each reed and the severed heads and slowly saw at the thin ropes until they were cut.

After the ropes were cut, they excavated four barrels of blast powder buried beneath rock and rubble. The ropes had been connected to small metal clamshells rigged to spring shut when the ropes were pulled and light the barrels to spew shrapnel into the plaza.

The stables had been burned to cinders and ash and the rooms inside ransacked, but there were no more traps other than a few twisted, excrement-encrusted caltrops left in doorways and at the bottoms of stairs, hidden amid the ash and dust and splintered wood.

Once the Shadows had thoroughly scoured the caravansary, a portion of the army filed inside while the rest made camp outside the walls, fortifying amidst the wreckage of the village.

Long trenches were dug in two rows around the camp, wrapping around to the banks of the river where the three warships that had followed them came sliding along the water. Devils were not well versed in watercraft, but they were conniving. The Darrood had to be held at all costs.

Odessa made camp in the caravansary's plaza with the rest of her cavalry. All throughout the camp, inside the walls and out, huge fires were lit, sending thick plumes of smoke over the river.

The camp was quiet. Red Clay Warriors walked silently about the perimeter and atop the ramparts where they manned their cannons. The Shadows skulked about in the growing dimness of twilight. Collared humans congregated near fires outside the caravansary walls, quietly mumbling among themselves. When battle came, they would be the first to die and they knew it.

Sore from riding, as soon as Odessa curled beside her fire, she fell asleep. She found it somewhat, if not alarmingly, simple to divorce herself from thought and feeling on the warpath. She did not want to think about Poko or Tarik. She did not want to think about the possibility that she might have seen them for the last time. So she honed away such thoughts, until her mind was a keen edge suited for one thing and one thing only.

In the early morning, they left two hundred Red Clay Warriors and one hundred humans in the caravansary to keep the fires alight while the rest of the army set off into the desert in three dense formations. Odessa's vanguard followed a scout's direction, riding out far beyond the main body. A company of human archers and spearmen followed on entehlos, unsteady in their saddles as they rode.

The bulk of the devil horde had settled in the northern scrubland near the Darrood where their mounts could be fed, slowly making their way south, village to village, slaughtering and subjugating.

The vanguard raced through sandy valleys and around harsh ridges. Coming over a ridge, Odessa caught sight of the horde far in the distance. A mass of black moving east across the scrubland, as wide as the Darrood was long.

Ice gripped Odessa's heart. *We're supposed to fight them all? There must be a hundred thousand.*

Swallowing hard, Odessa put her heels in the mount's sides and spurred it down the ridge toward the horde. Standing in the saddle, she took her bow from where it lay across the pommel and drew an arrow from the quiver on the side of the saddle.

Ogé guide my arrow, she thought. *And keep me from getting an arrow in my head.*

They raced down the ridge and across a wide-open plain toward the horde. A company broke off to meet them in the middle of the plain. Odessa's company swung to run parallel to the horde.

Odessa loosed an arrow toward the outriders. And another. The human archers released a volley, their arrows streaking through the air and diving like hawks at the quickly approaching riders.

Odessa and her company wheeled away, riding hard. Arrows followed them in their flight, striking a few mounts in the sides and haunches. A human rider keeled over in their saddle, an arrow in their back.

The devil outriders made to cut them off, but Odessa's company made distance, launching more arrows to slow their pursuers.

Odessa drew back her bowstring as far as it would allow, angling the arrow high. She let the arrow fly into the outer edges of the horde.

She sent another arrow at the horde and then wheeled away, heading with the rest of the company toward the ridge. Arrows fell at their backs.

"Up the ridge!" the bird-man shouted.

They bounded up the ridge as another company detached from the horde. They reached the top of the ridge and raced down the other side as their pursuers neared the base of the ridge.

The spearmen, hidden at the bottom of the ridge, bounded past Odessa and the riders to meet the pursuers.

When the outriders crested the ridge, the spearmen fell upon them in a crash of metal and flesh. The riders wheeled around up the ridge and joined in the frenzy. Odessa leaned low in the saddle as her mount came up the ridge. A spearwoman, knocked from her entehlo, was crushed beneath the hooves of a devil's bloody mount. Odessa came upon the entehlo and thrust her spear into the chest of its rider.

The devils regained formation quickly but too late. Spears had laid low most of their mounts, and Red Clay Warriors were beating the riders down. The devils made for retreat as their second company approached the ridge. Odessa and the other archers fired upon both retreating and advancing riders.

"Retreat!" the bird-man shouted! "Retreat!"

In an instant, the vanguard was charging down the ridge away from the battle, heading east along the valley bottom. Odessa took the shield hanging from her saddle.

"Arrows!" the bird-man shouted. "Incoming!"

Odessa twisted around, one hand clutching the reins, and held her shield out in front of her, crouching behind it as arrows rained down upon them. The retreating devils had joined the advancing company in pursuit. Devils rode along the ridge to their left and behind them in the valley. More than three hundred devils in a chorus of screams and taunts.

When the valley leveled out, Odessa's company veered south, firing arrows behind them at the devils riding down the gently sloping ridges. Open plains stretched all the way to the Darrood, east in the middle distance. The black mass of the devil horde to the north had slowed.

Odessa followed behind the bird-man, but her entehlo was beginning to tire. An arrow had pierced its lamellar armor and struck its flank, slowing it. *Come on.*

Come on, she urged the beast in her mind, digging her heels in its sides more and more. *Keep going. Keep running. We're not going to die here.*

They fled due south, between dunes and ridges to their right and open desert plain to their left. Arrows continued to rain down upon them, shredding their rear. The devils and their impeccable riding skills would soon overtake them. Odessa cursed herself for taking part in a suicide mission. There was no way to employ hit-and-run tactics against an army that rode more than they walked.

Odessa's company pushed harder. A high dune rose only a few spans ahead. If they could reach the dune they might yet survive.

The devils were on their heels, fanning out to surround them, howling as they drew polearms and clubs. The bird-man screeched, high and sharp, as they approached the dune.

Odessa's heart pounded in her throat. A scream from the rear as a rider fell to a devil's strike. They were almost to the dune. Just a few more strides.

Another scream, wet and guttural. Odessa did not dare glance back. Pressed low against her saddle, she kept her eyes on the dune rising to their right.

They raced past the dune at full tilt, and the devils followed.

When the first cannon boomed it was like music to Odessa's ears. She followed the bird-man in a wide arc to the right as the division of Red Clay Warriors hidden behind the dune fired upon the devils and charged into them with polearms. The boom of cannons overwhelmed the scream of rider and mount and the clash of metal upon metal. Powder smoke filled the air as Odessa and riders swung behind the Warriors.

The devils were quickly routed. Those that had not been torn apart by grapeshot or cut down by polearms were quick to flee back to the horde. The Warriors gave chase but were quickly outrun. Odessa and her riders harried the fleeing riders with arrows before turning back to rejoin the Warriors.

Their mounts were exhausted, but Asha-Kalir had not been able to field enough entehlos to allow for everyone to switch to a fresh mount. Odessa's mount was allowed only a short respite as the Warriors assumed formation. The poor beast had foam forming at the corners of its mouth. Odessa poured water from a skin into her cupped hand and let the entehlo lap up what little water she could spare.

"The horde comes!" a scout from atop the dune's crest shouted. "Incoming! The horde comes!"

Odessa turned from her entehlo to see the black mass growing larger in the distance. Roaring across the land with the thunder of thousands of hooves.

The bird-man sat astride his entehlo still, watching the horde approach. "Bukoris was right," he said quietly. "They're proud bastards. Using their own mounts against them was enough to get them well incensed."

Odessa climbed back into her saddle, a sick feeling in her stomach. Proud or not, the devils were not as stupid as Odessa thought Bukoris may have been inclined to believe. Incensed or not, they attacked because they knew they had mobility and numbers on their side.

As the horde raced along the plain, dust rising behind it, it began to split into three large masses of troops, making to flank them on the open plains.

When the horde drew close enough, the Warriors in the front line fired their cannons, sending solid balls of stone hurtling toward them.

The three sections of the horde spread out farther as cannonballs tore into their vanguard. Arrows filled the sky, streaking down in both directions. Odessa and the other riders raised their shields but, in the back of the formation, no arrows reached them. The bird-man lowered his shield and resumed his watch. "Any time now," he said to himself.

More volleys and rounds of cannon fire, the horde a fair few spans away, the call came out, "Retreat! Retreat!"

Odessa and the other riders fanned out to either side as the center of the formation collapsed, falling back and running south. Cannons still boomed as Warriors slowly fell back. Odessa and her riders surged forward on either side of the dense retreat. Riding toward the approaching horde. A wall of mounted devils coming to crash down upon them.

The detachment of devils on the eastern flank raced to catch them as they fled southeast. Odessa and the riders surged forward, launching arrow after arrow from replenished quivers. They drove toward the charging mass in a wide arc and then wheeled away back toward either side of the retreating troops.

Warriors stood as the division rearguard, two alternating lines firing cannons and then retreating. The horde split farther in the face of cannon fire, meaning to overtake them on either side and cut them off before they could flee. But the caravansary was within reach. In the distance Odessa could make out the walls standing before the river's shimmering surface. If they rode and ran hard, they might reach it before they were overrun.

Arrows were raining down upon them. Odessa's entehlo took one to the shoulder, through its thick armor. The entehlo stumbled a bit but continued its dash. The poor beast's eyes bulged from exertion, pain, and pure terror. Odessa fired arrow after arrow at the devils flanking their eastern side, already nearly cutting off their escape.

Smoke still rose above the caravansary. The devils knew where to flee. They did not have to get inside the walls, they only had to get within the range of the wall's cannons. Odessa's shield arm jerked as an arrow buried itself in the wood with a heavy thwack. *They're too fast. We're not going to make it.*

The long, lumbering strides of the Warriors were not enough to outpace the horde behind them. But before the devils overtook their rearguard, a shout came, "Now! For Khymanir! Now!"

The more bulbous Warriors among them, squat clay men with round bellies and long legs, stopped midstride and turned, more than a hundred of them charging out in all directions. Two of them streaked behind Odessa's mount, sprinting full-speed at the devils on their flank. Arrows glanced off their sharply segmented bronze plates.

When they drew near, the devils bore down on them, and each one of the Warriors drove a fist into their bulging middles.

Explosions surrounded Odessa and the fleeing Warriors on all sides. One after another, the suicidal Warriors exploded in a shower of fire and bronze. Shrapnel tore into the devils as a plume of smoke and dust rose among their ranks.

"Left!" a voice shouted. "Left! To the caravansary!" The fleeing division charged toward the disordered devils on their flank, forming a wedge led with polearms. Cannon fire and arrows aimed at the sides of the wedge shredded the disorganized mass of devils. The polearmed point of the wedge crashed into the devils, hacking apart devil and entehlo.

The wedge pushed through the devils before they could reorganize. Odessa's entehlo leaped over the dead and dying and she spurred it on farther, kicking her legs with fervor. A short span of open plain stood between them and the caravansary.

Her entehlo breathed heavily, sucking air in shallow, pained gasps. But they couldn't slow down. The devils behind them had regained their composure. Arrows rained down upon them again, one of them sinking deep into her entehlo's back leg. It stumbled and lurched to the side with a plaintive yelp, but it kept running, limping its way forward as fast as it could.

They were almost within range of the caravansary's cannons when the devils finally overtook them. The rearguard crumbled, Warriors bludgeoned to pieces with clubs.

Odessa urged her entehlo onward, screaming in its ear. The walls were close. Just a bit farther.

The entehlo cried out as another arrow struck its hindleg and its back end collapsed. The entehlo dropped beneath her in an instant, and its forward momentum sent Odessa tumbling over the saddle. She hit the dirt in a cloud of dust, an airy wheeze knocked from her lungs as the devils rode them down.

CHAPTER 41

Bedlam surrounded Odessa on all sides. Lying dazed in front of her dead entehlo, she heard the shattering of clay men and the screams of the dying. Dust choked her nose and mouth. The desert air was thick with blood and death. Cannons fired from the caravansary walls and from the deck of the warships on the river, but their cannonballs did little at that range.

Odessa scrambled onto her hands and knees toward her dead mount. She raised her head just in time to see entehlo legs charging toward her and a club swinging at her head. She raised her shield and felt the club's force reverberate through her arm as she was knocked backward onto her rear. Her arm tingling, she scrambled to her feet and pulled her spear free from her saddle.

The club-wielding devil had rounded back upon her, and Odessa crouched low and took another blow with her shield. Wood cracked and splinters exploded from the front of the shield. Odessa plunged her spear into the side of the devil's entehlo. The beast stumbled and Odessa slashed at its rider before it could swing its club again.

A horn bellowed in the distance. From the western dunes. *They're coming,* she thought. *Just have to survive a little longer. They're coming. They'll crush them.* The trap was sprung. The two other divisions lying in wait were charging toward the caravansary, trapping the devils between Odessa's cavalry and the cannons upon the walls and onboard the warships on the river. *Just have to survive.*

A blood-chilling scream drew Odessa's attention as she ducked beneath another devil's spear thrust. Out the corner of her eye, she saw an unmounted spearman lifted off the ground by a devil a head and shoulders taller than the rest. The devil's fist was wrapped around the poor man's head, muffling his shrill screams. The man's legs kicked pitifully, and his hands scratched and clawed at the devil's iron gauntlets. Then his body jerked and shivered and went still. Blood oozed from between the devil's fingers. When he let the man's body fall, brain and scalp clung to his gauntleted fingers.

Another spear flashed toward Odessa. She knocked it away with her cracked shield and slashed at the leg of the devil's entehlo.

"You!" a deep, guttural voice like thunder and lion's roar come together shook Odessa to her core. She turned to see the giant devil pointing at her. "You are mine! No one else's!"

The giant devil approached her as other devils, having decimated most of Odessa's force, raced past them to dispel the advancing Warriors. The devil's large, curling horns rose from a winged helm with a thick red tassel hanging down over a cloak of bright crimson. It rode a large entehlo as black as obsidian with a mane of thick hair rising from beneath fine, polished iron armor. A massive halberd, nearly twice Odessa's height, hung cradled in the crook of the devil's elbow. "What are you, girl?"

Before she could think of a reply, the devil raised its hand. A cannonball struck its open palm with a terrible crash. Chunks of stone shot through the air and a cloud of dust fell from its hand. Odessa's legs felt like they had turned to a soft jelly.

"I'm human," she said, barely able to muster the words from her tightened chest. To their right, devils fought, screaming and dying as the Red Clay Warriors fell upon them. But the devil sat still in its saddle, watching her.

"No, you're not," the devil said. "Not entirely." The devil swung a leg over its saddle and dismounted. "You've got godsblood. Like us. But pure."

Odessa held her shield out in front of her, her spear poised to thrust. The devil continued its slow walk toward her, the head of its halberd scraping the corpse-strewn ground.

"This world is not kind to us half-breeds. We tainted few," the devil said. "I can sense your blood, girl. Its drumbeat is the same as mine. We are kin. You must know it as well as I."

"We're not kin. I'm no devil."

"Yet you have the blood of Ogé in your veins," the devil said. "As do I. Through my father, I bear Ogé's blood as well."

"What are you talking about?" Odessa shouted over the din of battle. Cannon fire and screams filled the air, but the devil showed no concern.

"I, Pash-Tor, son of Sak-Tor, God of Conquest and King of the Battlefield, am the grandson of our fallen god, Ogé," the devil said. "But you, you are something much purer yet more flawed. Are you an aspect of Ogé? No, there is something strange about your blood. Something too imperfect for that."

"I am nobody," Odessa said. "I am nothing. Now are you going to kill me or what?"

"I answer your question with one of my own: will you come with me to my father?"

Odessa stiffened. She thought of Tarik and Poko. Her mother and sister. And of the God of Conquest far to the north, raping and pillaging his way through entire countries. "Are you joking?" she said. "I would rather die than meet him."

Pash-Tor said nothing. He bounded forward, swinging his halberd up. Odessa jerked backward, the edge of his halberd striking the rim of her shield, making it burst in a shower of splinters.

Stumbling back, Odessa flung the shield down and took her spear in both hands. Her heart pounded and her arm thrummed in a frantic rhythm. Fear like icy water flowed through her, creating ice jams in her joints and threatening to freeze her stiff if she let it run unrestrained. She focused on the fire in her arm. Pash-Tor swung his halberd in a few sweeping twirls as he strode forward. Odessa licked her lips and narrowed her eyes, watching every movement the towering devil made. The bandages around her arm began to singe and curl as her arm grew hot. *I've killed worse,* she told herself. *I've killed gods. The bastard son of a god is nothing. I'll kill him. I'll kill him like I've killed dozens of devils.*

Flames raced along her arm, a familiar pain scorching her skin. It had been a while since she had felt its sting—it was almost pleasant, letting the fires loose.

"So you have magics too?" Pash-Tor said. His halberd snapped forward with a gust of wind. Odessa barely had time to parry it away with the shaft of her spear. "Let us see who's truly blessed then." Another swing of the halberd. Odessa ducked and scrambled. "I want to see if you are worthy of that blood in your veins!" Another swing followed by a thrust. Odessa had to leap aside to dodge its arcing withdrawal. "I'll spill that blood of yours!"

Pash-Tor's halberd spun and swung in continuous slashes and thrusts, growing faster and faster. Odessa could barely track it as it flashed in a blur of iron. She parried as best she could, but the halberd was too unpredictable.

She could feel the air whipping about the devil. It swirled around the halberd, sending it forward in furious gusts of wind. As the halberd picked up speed, she felt the wind lash at her with each strike. And with each strike, she could feel his magic against her skin, sharp and abrasive.

If I can't get close, my flames are useless. She parried a dizzyingly fast slash. Her flames burned hot, spreading up her shoulder and along the edges of the iron scales in her armor. *I'll kill this bastard godling if it's the last thing I do. I'll cut his fucking head off, I swear.* She let her rage unravel within her, filling the gaping hollowness with flame. She was sick of gods. High or Low, they were all scum. They all wanted to keep her from those she loved. And that, she would not allow.

The flames spread along the iron scales until her entire body was wreathed in dark red fire. The iron held the fire readily, letting it crawl along each scale like they had been coated in oil. Spurred by the warmth of her growing flames, she ducked past one of Pash-Tor's slashes and thrust her spear toward him. Pash-Tor knocked it away and nearly sent her stumbling.

The flames in Odessa's fist had charred the spear's shaft so that when the halberd struck it again, the shaft broke in her hand. She tossed the burnt end away and wielded the shortened spear in her left hand, letting her fiery fist be free.

Another slash of Pash-Tor's halberd with the speed of a tornado. Odessa's shortened spear couldn't deflect, and the point of the halberd slashed open her thigh. Scalding blood poured down her leg.

Pain burned with acidic intensity deep in Odessa's leg. Gritting her teeth, she focused on the fire. Urging it to burn hotter. Her rage like bellows to the flames ensconcing her entire body. Flaring alive. She drew on the fire nestled in that hollowness, widening the gap inside her soul so her flames could grow.

"Your flames will be sputtering out soon enough!" Pash-Tor shouted, strafing her while swinging his halberd in blurred arcs. A tornado of dust swirled at his feet, whipping the charred remains of the litham around Odessa's neck.

She could feel the fire building within her. The immense pressure of a firestorm thrashing upon her ribs. When Pash-Tor's halberd snapped forward, she let the pressure loose. But it did not bring flame. An immense rush of hot air burst from around her. The tornado at Pash-Tor's feet died out, dust falling back to the dirt. His halberd slowed and Odessa grabbed hold of its shaft, letting her fire eat through the ironwood. Pash-Tor jerked the halberd, meaning to slash her on the withdrawal but the charred shaft crumbled in her grip.

"What did you do, bitch?" he yelled. She threw the halberd head at Pash-Tor's face and he knocked it away with a flick of the broken shaft. But in that instant, Odessa had dashed forward, the fire around her body flaring as she darted in close.

She rammed the spear into his groin and leaped back as his gauntleted fist rushed past her. Even without his magic he was fast. And his iron armor resisted her flames. But the smell of his blood dripping to the dirt set her teeth on edge. Her skin prickled with excitement.

He stumbled back a step, clutching his groin and trying to staunch the blood pouring from around the spearhead. She picked up the spear dropped by Pash-Tor. Her flames raced along the shaft, tracing the woodgrain.

She charged Pash-Tor, sidestepped, and slashed at his knee. His leg buckled, and as he fell, he made to grab her and haul her to the ground with him. But her spear was ready. She thrust it through the visor of his helmet, letting his own weight drive it deep into his skull.

Pash-Tor's body sagged and fell at her feet.

Amidst the din of battle and the screams of dying devils, she tore Pash-Tor's armor off and dug her fingers into his chest. Dark purple skin peeled and charred. Blood and fat sizzled. She punched through his ribcage and wrenched his still-quivering heart from his chest. She ripped into it with her teeth. Striations like gold wire running through his heart sent jolts of electricity arcing through her veins and up her spine. Gulping down blood and muscle, she felt lighter than air. Her flames surged, burning white hot. And for a moment she felt the euphoria of divinity.

CHAPTER 42

Once Odessa charged back into the fray, it did not take long before the devils were crushed. Her flames were like wildfire. Her mere presence set the hair of entehlos bursting into flame. With a club in either hand, she rushed the devils' rear lines and killed without pause.

Without Pash-Tor, the devils soon splintered into smaller companies and tried to flee, but the Red Clay Warriors would not allow that. By the end of the battle, only a few thousand devils had been able to escape.

Once the battle was won and Odessa's flames had sputtered out, the Red Clay Warriors chased down the rear detachment of the horde that remained farther north. Odessa stayed behind at the caravansary, in a state between shock and elation. She helped gather their dead, which proved to be most of the Shadows and the bird-man. The skulls of their dead were taken and their bodies buried in a mass grave. The large pieces of red clay scattered about the battlefield were crushed and sprinkled about the dirt.

Odessa, tasked with disposing of the shattered clay bodies, soon saw just how they were built. Long human bones were grafted together to make up the center of each thick limb. And a human skull was set in the middle of each body, a human heart between its jaws.

It took days to clean up the wreckage left in the wake of the battle. The devils were dragged into a heap and set ablaze while Pash-Tor's impaled head was severed and sent back to Asha-Kalir in a barrel of salt.

When the main detachment of Red Clay Warriors returned, they came with nearly ten thousand slaves in tow. Some had been taken from the villages around Asha-Kalir, but some had been brought from the highlands to assist in the devils' war effort; they were all to be taken to Asha-Kalir to be sorted.

Odessa was sent with a small company of Red Clay Warriors to escort the slaves to Asha-Kalir. A strange feeling had clung to Odessa since the battle and it refused to leave her. The hollowness had grown inside her, but a part of her did not mind. It almost embraced the emptiness. And the hollowness embraced her, nearly swallowing her entirely as she walked in a sullen stupor, all the elation and euphoria drained from her body leaving only a lifeless husk.

It was not until she could see the walls of Asha-Kalir that the hollowness began to recede. A tentative excitement simmered inside her, tempered with doubt and anxiety. She was excited to see Poko and Tarik, but after her last night with Tarik she was not sure if he would want to see her. While Yakun made her feel uneasy, she was even excited to see him, to continue the cure. Without the godsblood there would be no more fighting. No more hollowness. But even that thought did not go uncontested in her mind. The part of her that embraced the hollowness rejected the idea of a cure.

When she entered the palace, her excitement had grown but so had her anxieties. Tarik was waiting for her by the barracks and took her in a warm embrace.

"You're alive!" he said. "I was so worried. I haven't slept since you left."

Odessa squeezed him and buried her face into his robes. "I missed you," she said. "I missed you every day. Every moment, I missed you so much."

"I missed you too," he said, pulling away from her and taking her hands in his. "We all have." He smiled. "Now come on, I have a surprise for you!"

Odessa smiled softly, the feeling of it strange on her lips again. She followed him through the halls to Azdava's quarters and into the laboratory where Yakun and Azdava waited for her.

"You're back!" Yakun said, taking her in a hug that lingered for too long. "I knew you would be fine. No devil is a match for you!"

"Welcome back," Azdava said with a nod. "You've come back at an opportune time as well."

"We've done it," Yakun said with a grin.

"You can cure me?" Odessa said, the part of her that rejected the cure silenced before the prospect of being normal again. She could be normal for Tarik. But as she glanced at him with a smile, he averted his gaze.

"Not exactly," Yakun said. "But we can stabilize it. We can make it controllable."

"What do you mean? I thought you've been working on a cure. I don't want it stabilized or controlled. I want it gone!"

Azdava opened her mouth but Yakun spoke before her. "I don't think you understand, my dear. What you think of as a curse is the result of years of hard work. I spent decades constructing the spell to bind godhood to man. Your father gave his life to this work. I cannot let his death be for naught. And neither can you. Why do you think your father told you to come to me? So you could fulfill your destiny. So that you can use what you have been given to better the world."

"I don't want to better the world, I want to be the way I was!"

"You would choose to be weak and powerless?" Yakun asked. "At the mercy of every tyrannical god that would wish nothing more than to have you and all that you have loved exterminated?"

"Yes!" Odessa snapped. "I can't live like this! I can't live with this hollow feeling eating me alive! I just want to live a normal life. I want to die and be with my family in Matara's embrace and I can't do that with this cursed blood in me!"

"But what about everyone here?" Tarik said quietly. "What about my family? They live under the constant threat of slavery and worse. What about them?" He took her hand and looked deep into her eyes. "If there was a way to help them, wouldn't you do it?"

"Of course," Odessa said weakly.

"This is it," Tarik said. "This is the only way mankind can ever hope to usurp gods. You are mankind's only hope. You have divinity inside you. You can be the god of humanity. You can be everything that the gods are not."

"I can't," she said. "I can't do it."

"I've heard enough," Azdava said. "I told you she should not be coddled." With a hiss and a snap of her fingers, Odessa's collar began to tighten.

"What are you doing?" Odessa gasped. "How?"

"Your collar does not belong only to Bukoris," Azdava said. "From now on, you belong to me."

The collar tightened around her throat, growing hot and singeing her skin. She tried to pry her fingers beneath the collar but it had sunk too far into her neck. Black spots gnawed at the periphery of her vision. She tried to run to the door, but she stumbled into the wall and slid to the floor.

"Azdava!" Tarik shouted, his voice muffled by the blood pounding in Odessa's ears. Just before darkness swallowed her entirely, she felt the collar loosen just enough for her to draw a shallow breath.

A needle slid into the vein in her neck, and soon the darkness came to take her again in its soft, sedative embrace.

CHAPTER 43

In the interstice of sleep and wakefulness, Odessa could hear voices. Distant and quiet. Some voices begged and pleaded while others wept. Other voices told them of sacrifice or told them to shut up.

When her eyes had finally blinked away the bleary scales of sedation, she found herself strapped to the chair again. Her right arm seared with white-hot, bone-deep pain. Her head swinging limply, she looked to find her entire arm bound in iron, from gauntlet to pauldron. Thick plates of iron carved with intricate runes, both sharp and angular, as well as flowing script, covered her arm. Bronze ran through the carvings like tiny rivers. She tried to move her arm and more pain like nails of fire lanced through it. Blood had dried at the shoulder where the pauldron met her skin, and she could see the iron was riveted into flesh and bone. She felt sick.

Yakun entered the laboratory. "How do you feel, my dear?"

"What did you do to me?" she shouted.

"This is stability. This is progress. No longer will you be bound by how much blood your stomach can hold. Much like the spellwork that first bound the godsblood to you, this gauntlet will allow you to absorb life essence as it leaves the body without having to do anything as barbarous as drinking blood. Not only more convenient but also more efficient. We've found most life essence is lost in the first moments of death."

"What the fuck are you talking about?"

"Odessa, please don't make this any harder than it has to be. You still wear the collar. You should know better by now." He sighed and sat beside her. "I had hoped this wouldn't be necessary. I had hoped you would see the importance of our work. But you're still a child in some regards."

Odessa gritted her teeth and pulled against the shackles on her wrists and ankles.

"Don't bother. They're too strong even for you. And imbued with heat-resistant magic. There's no getting out without the key."

"Why are you doing this?" Odessa asked, restraining a scream building in her throat. "Why are you doing this to me?"

"Freedom," Yakun said. "I wish only to see mankind free from the tyranny of gods. I've seen the brutality of gods. I've seen it again and again and again." Yakun leaned back in the chair beside her. "Have I ever told you about my homeland? No, I don't suppose I have." Odessa strained against the shackles as he spoke. "But perhaps it will elucidate some things. Because there truly is no reasoning with gods. There's no diplomacy to be had."

Yakun sighed, as if telling his story physically pained him. "I lived in a town in the far north. A town on a bay beneath beautiful mountains. I had a wife and a son. But in this town, we lived at the mercy of the Troll King, Yor. Every three months we would deliver unto him in his cave a few virgins we had taken from raids and the like. But one day, as I was tending to my herbs, I heard footsteps. Yor came down from the mountain a month early. Our alderman went to speak with him, to see what had roused him, but Yor crushed him beneath his foot. Yor destroyed my entire town, killing and eating whomever he pleased. And there was no reason for it. He did not have to. He did it for the simple fact that he enjoyed it. He had grown tired of us. So he killed everyone I had ever known."

Odessa pulled against the shackles once more. They rattled but held fast. "I don't care!" she shouted. "Let me out or I swear, when I get loose, I'm tearing you from crotch to throat!"

Yakun stared at her for a moment, then shook his head. "I hope you see reason soon," he said. "For your sake."

The door opened and Azdava and Tarik entered. Tarik kept his gaze to the floor. At the sight of him, all Odessa's anger drained from her body. Replaced by the hurt of betrayal. "Tarik," she said. "How could you do this? I thought—" Her voice faltered for a moment. "I-I loved you."

"I have a family to look after," he said. "And if you had just listened to me none of this would have happened. We could still be together and . . ." His words trailed off.

"How do you feel?" Azdava asked, walking in front of her. "Strong?"

"Let me go," Odessa hissed.

"You should feel quite well," Azdava continued. "You have been fed well while in sedation."

"What do you mean?"

"I was able to requisition a portion of the slaves you brought back for my own research. Little did Khymanir know that the slaves he gave me would be his own undoing." Azdava laughed.

Odessa noticed the smell of blood in the room was stronger than it had been. Then she noticed the pool of dried blood in front of the chair and the splatters of blood all over the front of her body. Her heart sank, frozen solid. "What did you do?"

"Sacrifices are required for the greater good. A young god needs sustenance."

Odessa was at a loss for words. Stunned. But after the shock, she found her rage. She pulled against the shackles again, drawing upon the fire in her iron-bound arm. Straining with all her might, she pressed her back against the chair. There was a groan as metal bent.

Azdava hissed and the collar began to tighten again, but Odessa didn't stop. She pushed harder, feeling the chair begin to give way.

"Stop it!" Tarik shouted.

With one last effort before the collar squeezed her throat, Odessa screamed and ripped the shackles from the chair. Black spots clouded her vision and deafened her ears. As she pulled her arms free, a great pressure shoved her against the chair. The chair bent beneath her as the pressure increased.

Yakun's voice boomed somewhere distant. With her head shoved downward by the force, she could make out the arc of a bronze circle set in the floor around the chair.

As the life was squeezed from her neck, she let the flames loose, forcing them from holes in the iron gauntlet. She felt the flames build and build within herself as the life ebbed from her strangled neck. Just before the darkness took her and gravity crushed her, she let it out in a burst of scorching air.

The gravity dissipated in an instant. The collar around her neck loosened. Odessa's iron hand took the collar in its fiery grip and tore it from her neck.

Tarik bolted as Odessa ripped her feet free from the shackles. Azdava made a run for the door, but Odessa was on her before she got halfway. Odessa grabbed her by the back of the neck in her iron grip and squeezed until she heard vertebrae pop. Azdava's body went limp, but her eyes were wild with terror and agony as the flames spread up her neck, burning the skin from her face, rendering the sizzling fat of her tongue, and melting her eyes in their sockets. A warm feeling sank into Odessa's arm as Azdava's life faded.

When Odessa dropped Azdava's dead body, Yakun and Tarik were gone. She left the laboratory in a hurry but stopped short when she heard a muted cry. On a shelf, nestled between scrolls, was a jar with a fairy inside.

Odessa extinguished her arm and ripped the lid from the jar. "What happened?"

Poko stared at her arm. "What happened to you?"

Odessa shook the fairy. "Why were you in a jar?"

"They put me in there! I finally put together what they were doing and they stuffed me in a jar with a single airhole in the top!"

Odessa let the fairy loose and they flew around her head. "I will find them and I'm going to kill them."

Poko started to speak but Odessa had already taken off out the door and up the stairs. Poko followed.

When Odessa reached the top of the stairs she heard a commotion and the sound of clay feet pounding the tile.

"We should go," Poko said, fluttering by her ear. "We should go now."

"But—" Odessa started.

Four Red Clay Warriors entered the hallway and charged at Odessa. "But nothing!" Poko said and darted down the hall.

Odessa followed the fairy, soon catching up to them and their tiny wings. Odessa snatched Poko from the air and leaped into the stained-glass window at the end of the hall.

In a shower of multi-colored glass, they fell into the plaza below. Odessa clambered to her feet and ran as fast as they could take her. The streets were quiet in the dead of night. The only noise as she ran came from the fire spreading through the palace's lower quarters.

Odessa found the stables, saddled up an entehlo, and fled for the city gates. She expected a fight at the gates but to her surprise found them open.

Four Shadows stood, holding the gate ajar. Odessa came to a halt, waiting for the Shadows to attack, but they did not. A Shadow opened the gate wider for her. As she tentatively made her way through the gates, another Shadow pointed to her hand and then to its own.

The deal was still on. Odessa turned her back to the Shadows and dug her heels into the entehlo, an icy shiver running down her spine as she rode off into the desert.

CHAPTER 44

Kunza stood outside the hall's doors holding Ayana's hand. All of Azka's Chosen were already inside and Azka and his godlings had most certainly taken their seats upon the dais. But Kunza waited.

The explosions rocked the palace like an earthquake. Kunza squeezed Ayana's hand as she trembled, pulling slightly away from the doorway. Kunza waited a moment longer, listening to the pained groans and confused cries.

He opened the door, shoving bits of rubble aside as he stepped into the hall. Dust and smoke hung in the air. The Chosen littered the hall, torn to shreds by shrapnel. The blast powder from Asha-Kalir laid beneath their cushions had sent bits of sanctified iron rocketing through their bodies.

As Kunza walked along the brazier, past the slowly crawling Chosen, his Shadows climbed into the hall, iron swords in hand.

Only Ketabi was absent. Azka and his other godling lay in the splintered wreckage of their dais. Down floated in the air among the dust and smoke, settling upon their bloody coats. The dais had been packed with enough iron for a small army.

Azka breathed, weak and raspy. Too weak to move as Kunza and Ayana approached. Behind them, Shadows began cutting the throats of the Chosen. Azka's eyes followed Kunza as he drew the iron blade from his robes.

Azka tried to rise as Kunza stepped onto the splinters of the dais. His massive paw swept toward Kunza, but he easily sidestepped it and came beside the god's chest. He sunk the blade in deep, godsblood pouring out over his hands. But Talara's blessing protected him.

Azka cried out and shook as Kunza opened his chest. He ushered Ayana to step forward. Hesitantly, she did.

Kunza cupped his hands beneath the hole in Azka's chest, letting the blood fill them up. He turned, his hands dripping shimmering crimson, and poured the blood over Ayana's head. Anointing her in godsblood.

She drank from his cupped hands, letting the blood seep into her body.

And by Talara's grace, she was made whole.

ABOUT THE AUTHOR

Jeremy Knop is the author of All That Is Holy, a series that began on Royal Road as an experiment with serial fiction. He spent many years honing his craft, but it wasn't until after a yearlong battle with cancer that he truly pursued publication. Knop lives on a small farm in Michigan with his beautiful wife, Ashley, and their two dogs. Visit his website at www.jeremyknop.com.

Podium

DISCOVER STORIES UNBOUND

PodiumAudio.com

Milton Keynes UK
Ingram Content Group UK Ltd.
UKHW030513041124
2549UKWH00002B/10